GEM WARFARE

LEXI GRAVES MYSTERIES

Camilla Chafer

Copyright: Camilla Chafer, 2024

All rights reserved. The right of Camilla Chafer to be identified as author of this Work has been asserted by her in accordance with sections 77 and 78 of the Copyright, Designs and Patents Act 1988.

First published in 2024.

No part of this publication may be reproduced, stored in retrieval system, copied in any form or by any means, electronic, mechanical, photocopying, recording or otherwise transmitted without written permission from the publisher. You must not circulate this book in any format.

This book is licensed for your personal enjoyment only.

ISBN-13: 9798281255493

Visit the author online at www.camillachafer.com

ALSO BY CAMILLA CHAFER

Lexi Graves Mysteries:
Armed and Fabulous
Who Glares Wins
Command Indecision
Shock and Awesome
Weapons of Mass Distraction
Laugh or Death
Kissing in Action
Trigger Snappy
A Few Good Women
Ready, Aim, Under Fire
Rules of Engagement
Very Special Forces
In the Line of Ire
Mission: Possible
Pied Sniper
Charmed Forces
Gem Warfare
Operation: Sapphire

Deadlines Mystery Trilogy:
Deadlines
Dead to the World
Dead Ringers

Calendar Murder Mysteries:
Murder in the Library
Poison Rose Murder
Murder by the Book
Murder at Blackberry Inn
Curated Murder
Dressed for Murder

CHAPTER ONE

I sat in the hairdresser's chair while she held a mirror behind my head and asked if I liked the style. My hair was two inches shorter with three shades of caramel highlights. I did like it but more importantly, seeing the hairdresser's scissors were only inches from my jugular vein and her expression mildly threatening, saying no wasn't an option. It was a good job and I approved of the cut and color but because I was so disconcerted by her demeanor, I would have told her I liked it even if she'd given me a mullet with neon balayage.

"I love it," I said, giving my head a good shake.

"I wish you'd let me take you back to blond," she said with a sigh. "You looked so cute in the photos you showed me."

"Too much maintenance," I replied, although not completely decisively. Lily was rising from the chair next to me, shaking out her recently tamed mane of natural blond curls. With the light streaming through the salon's plate glass windows, she looked faintly angelic. Then I glanced again at her t-shirt printed with a single word: *No*. I knew exactly how she felt.

I, Lexi Graves, private investigator, was getting a lot of experience at saying no.

Only this morning, I'd said no to three cases that came in. One involved diving for treasure off the coast and I was not equipped for that. Plus, the prospective client didn't have any evidence there *was* a treasure beyond a really enthusiastic hunch and a stack of maps. Then I'd said no to my mother's suggestion that I take up basket weaving with her. I had no need for any baskets and, if I did, I knew where the mall was. I didn't need to make my own stuff. Finally, I'd said no to the blond my hairdresser so badly wanted to reintroduce to my head. When it came to saying no, I was nailing it.

"Do you love it?" asked Lily, circling a finger in the air around my hair.

"Yes," I said. Damn! There went my "Say no" streak.

We paid, declined to buy the overpriced salon products, and headed out the doors, away from the overly bright fluorescent lights, thumping dance music, and black-clad stylists. Lily hooked her arm into mine. "I feel like a new woman," she said. "Or, at least, one that doesn't have any apple puree in her hair."

"The joys of motherhood."

"You'll know how much of a joy it is soon," she said, taking a pointed look at my rounded belly.

"That's just my breakfast," I said. "Nothing else is happening down there."

"I'll be the first to know, right?"

"I feel like my husband should be first to know."

"Why? What does he have to do with it?" she asked indignantly.

"He's crucial to the process. If it happens..."

"When," cut in Lily.

"If, and *when* I find myself pregnant, I'll tell Solomon first and you second, okay? But for now, no dice. Let's hang out here," I said, pointing to the café three lots away from the hair salon. Several bistro tables had been set up behind a cordon on the sidewalk, each panel punctuated with a large faux palm in a green stone vase. The nearest table had a perfect view of the salon.

We plunked into the seats and picked up the menus. I took turns glancing at the menu and then at the salon.

"I love it when you get a job with perks. I smell glorious," said Lily, taking a whiff of the ends of her hair. "Can you investigate a manicurist, a spa, and maybe somewhere hot for a vacation?"

I held back a laugh. "I'll do my best."

My client had rushed into the Solomon Detective Agency only a few days before, almost in tears, certain that someone on her staff was stealing. Her data was clear. Expensive products were going missing and the takings didn't tally with the appointments. Sometimes the till had been out by several hundred dollars. The problem was, she couldn't imagine anyone on her staff stealing from her. Yet someone had to be.

None of the guys on our staff would blend into the hair salon - they all had short hair, curated from several decades of law enforcement and adjacent careers, with the exception of our resident tech geek, Lucas. His blond hair was a messy surfer style, a look I'd come to realize was as much by design as it was owing to a lack of brushing. So, I'd taken the case, knowing my feminine looks ensured I could enter where they couldn't. Lily came along for an extra set of eyes, and a treat, since the salon owner had thrown in two cuts with all the extras as a way to get us in the door to observe her employees. Unfortunately, that had thrown a moral problem my way. Both Lily's and my hair stylist had done such terrific jobs, I didn't want either of them to be guilty. I wanted to keep going back.

That left six other stylists, the two reception desk ladies, four assistants who undertook the hair washing, sweeping, and general gophering, plus, a cleaning lady who came in after hours. Yet my client said none of them had raised any red flags during their employment. So where were her missing money and products?

"Did you get any feeling while we were in there?" asked Lily as she gazed at the menu.

"A numb left foot."

"And that led you to think..." Lily prompted.

"That I should do more exercise," I said. "And maybe buy a new pair of shoes."

Lily's face fell. "I hoped it was intuition and your numb foot would lead you to a loose floorboard where the cash and contraband shampoo would be stashed."

"It would have to be a very large floorboard to store two thousand bucks worth of shampoo, conditioner, hairspray and the rest. Plus, the floor is tile," I added. I'd spent considerable time looking around the salon after hours, trying to imagine where someone might have squirreled away the contraband. Yet there seemed to be no hiding spots. The walls held mirrors with sliding shelves that contained the stylists' gear. There was a tiny cloakroom with open square shelving for purses and bags. And a small restroom was available for clients' use.

My client had mentioned a small break room and separate restroom for the staff but they didn't conceal any hidey-holes either. The small, square room had little more than a unit of cabinets on one side, making a kitchen with a microwave and sink, while the other side seemed to be open lockers for hanging coats and stashing bags. As a client, I'd barely gotten more than a glimpse of the break room when the door had been left ajar. There was no way customers were getting in there.

We ordered slices of cake and overpriced fresh juice blends, keeping our gaze on the salon as we waited.

"I get stealing the money. Money can be spent anywhere," said Lily, after the waitress told us she'd be back in a couple minutes. "But I don't get the product thefts."

"Whoever it is must be selling them," I said, "but I've checked the online auction sites as well as the preloved apps and I can't find any of the products there. They could be selling them by word of mouth or at a market or even shipping them out of state. Did you know the smallest bottle of shampoo is thirty bucks alone?"

"Worth it. Smell my hair," said Lily.

"I won't. I'm too busy smelling my own." I inhaled the gentle floral notes. I smelled delicious.

As we waited, two clients left the salon, and three more entered.

"Do we have to watch them for the rest of the

day?" asked Lily. "If so, we're going to need more cake."

"Watching is all I have left. I've conducted background checks on all the employees and nothing stands out. They've all worked there over a year. None of them have had a sudden influx of unexplainable income or made any suspiciously large purchases or begun leading extravagant lifestyles. All I can do is watch."

"You sound like a perv."

"Or a PI."

"I'm glad we ordered vegetables," said Lily. "I feel healthier already."

"It's carrot cake," I said, craning my head to see another waitress approach ours. Snatches of their conversation drifted towards me and I frowned.

"What's the difference?" asked Lily, distracting me.

"Several cups of sugar and a half inch of frosting," I said, smiling at the generous portion of cake when the waitress quickly returned and set down our plates and tall glasses.

"Real, grated carrot," said Lily, pointing to the menu. "Grown in a field. In dirt!"

"Where else are you supposed to grow a carrot?" I wondered.

Lily shrugged. "I own a bar. I'm not a farmer. It's a carrot. Vegetables are good for us, and with these fruit juices, we're nailing healthy. Mine has kale in it. That's two vegetables in one healthy snack."

"Would you feed this to Poppy?" I asked, breaking off a chunk of cake as soon as the waitress departed.

"I wouldn't need to. Her face would be in it

before I could even offer her a tiny, little fork."

While we ate our treats, no one else entered the salon. Gradually, it emptied out and my client appeared, turning the sign on the front door to "Closed."

"The salon's closing," I said.

We waited for the employees to filter out, singly or in pairs, saying their goodbyes as they headed off to their lives outside work. I knew what they all did from book clubs to clubbing, and exactly what times. If I weren't me, I'd find my knowledge of strangers creepy. Thankfully, they would never know.

"What happens now? Why aren't their bags being searched?"

"The owner doesn't want anyone to feel accused if there's possibly another reason to explain the thefts. She feels it will damage the trust in the salon." I paused as the salon become dark, and Marie, my client, stepped out and turned the key in the locks. She gave the door a push, confirming her locks were working, then headed to her car.

"It's hard to keep employees if they think you think they're a thief," said Lily. "But we can't sit here all night. I have to get to work. What're you going to do?"

"Sit here all night." I sighed as I forked another piece of carrot cake into my mouth. Surveillance wasn't at the top of my list of enjoyable ways to spend my evenings but an irregular job sometimes called for irregular hours. I'd undertaken plenty of hours of observation and I had a system in place. Make sure I used the restroom promptly before ensconcing myself in my car, ensure the camera was fully charged and there was space on the memory card, and, most importantly, make sure I had plenty of snacks. Lately, I'd added playing an audiobook to my roster; anything to keep the boredom at bay while I surveyed my target.

"Make sure you check in with me. I want to know if anything happens," said Lily, "If it's my stylist, I'll be devastated. My curls have never looked better." She pulled one and it corkscrewed back into place.

"I feel the same about mine. She's a genius with scissors."

Lily insisted on paying for the cake since I'd scored her the free hair appointment; then she walked me to my car before leaving for her shift at the bar she owned. I hopped in and drove the whole block down the street, parking in one of the newly empty spaces opposite the salon.

By the time Solomon rang a half hour later, I was already tired of staring through the empty windows.

"What's the score?" he asked.

"Nil to me," I said. "I have no idea who could be committing these thefts."

"Someone will turn up. Do you want company?"

"No, I'm good. Nothing's happening. I'll stay until midnight and if still nothing happens, I'll come home. I'm thinking our next step should be a couple of discreet cameras in the salon."

"Good plan. If I'm not home when you get there, I'm still out on the mall job with Delgado. We're working out the weak spots in their night security. Don't wait up."

We disconnected and I shuffled in the seat, trying to get comfortable. An hour later, and a couple of chapters into a funny audiobook, I noticed movement. A man in jeans and a t-shirt, a messenger bag slung over his shoulder, dawdled to a stop. I reached for my camera as the man covered his eyes and leaned in to peer through the windows. I snapped a couple of shots, my shoulders dropping as the man turned and continued walking.

A tap on the passenger door made me jump. On the sidewalk, Maddox grinned and signaled to unlock the door. I leaned over and popped the handle before he hopped in.

"On a job?" he asked. "What's going on?"

"Yes, and nothing."

"Fill me in."

I gave him the lowdown, indicating the salon. "There's only one entrance," I said, "So if someone's coming in after hours, it's through there."

"Are you sure about that?"

"I'm sure. I walked around the building yesterday. There's a rear door but the city is making repairs to the drains and it's currently inaccessible."

"Ooh, a mystery. Can't wait to hear how this one goes down. I'm hoping it'll involve a helicopter, a ring of fire, and maybe a giraffe."

I could only gape at his suggestions. Maddox shrugged. "It doesn't seem impossible for you," he said with a shrug.

"I'm not sure where you think I'd get a giraffe from."

"I'm not sure why you seem to think getting a helicopter is a more viable option. You concern me sometimes."

"Only sometimes?"

"Only when I'm awake. Sleep is bliss." Maddox considered that, then added, "Until you turn up anyway."

"Stop dreaming about me."

"They're more like nightmares."

"You're incorrigible."

Maddox reached for his phone. "I need to look up that word."

"You're distracting me." I returned my attention to the salon. Nothing was happening so in reality, he was distracting me from a whole load of zilch. "Why are you here anyway?" I asked.

"I was going to grab something to eat on my way home and I saw you and thought you'd be more fun than fried chicken."

"Thanks. I'll print that on my business cards."

"You should. It'll *drumstick* up some customer. Ha ha."

"Your chicken jokes need work."

"It's true. I can't *clucking* argue with that."

"Do you have *any* interesting cases?" I asked, desperately hopeful. Anything to stop the puns.

"One that is a longstanding headache. I might need to go to Europe soon to pursue a lead on a jewel heist. Several, in fact."

"So sorry to hear that. How awful for you. Europe. Sexy jewel heists. All on the FBI's dime." I shook my head in mock sadness, and made a mental note to ask Solomon if he ever planned to take the agency international. A Paris office would be terrific. Maybe Milan.

Maddox merely grinned. "There's no way the MPD would have ever sent me to Europe, and the case is way beyond their purview, so I'm very happy with the way my career is going. Unfortunately, catching my thief is the headache part. She's slipperier than an eel."

"She?"

"Plenty of female criminals around," he said. "You constantly surprise me by not being one. Anyway, I've lost her for now but she'll pop up again. Maybe when…"

"Hold on," I said, catching movement in the salon. Not by the doors where I expected, but from the ceiling. Someone was entering the salon from a direction I'd never considered.

I pointed and Maddox leaned in. "Would you look at that," I said, as we watched the figure wriggle, dangle in the air, then drop to a crouch on the floor. "Yours might be in the wind but I think we can catch this thief."

CHAPTER TWO

"Guess I'll leave you to it," said Maddox, reaching for the door handle.

"Where are you going?"

"I don't want to crash your party."

"You're invited to the party since you crashed the pre-party."

"Shall we divide and conquer?" he asked, grinning, and making me wonder if he'd just engineered the invite by feigning disinterest. It didn't matter; I needed the help.

"I'd suggest I take the front and you take the back but I'm sure they can't escape that way. They must have been entering and exiting through the ceiling the whole time," I said, struggling to think of exactly how. I couldn't see a ladder and the figure had dropped a little way from any of the furnishings. I couldn't see how he or she could climb back up.

Since I'd learned a few things during my time as a PI, I did the sensible thing and called Solomon before I walked into who-knows-what kind of mess.

"How's the stakeout?" he asked.

"Paying off. I just watched someone drop through the ceiling into the salon."

"Creative."

"I have Maddox here but we might need backup."

"I'm a half hour out. I can call Fletcher and Flaherty and see if they're closer but I think you'll be good with Maddox." Fletcher and Flaherty were my fellow PIs and usually worked as a duo. With backgrounds in CIA and the police force, Solomon had found them perfect fits when he was setting up the agency. I'd initially found them stony and skeptical, but now I knew them to be big-hearted men who always strove to do the right thing. Unless it involved donuts, in which case they would trample over everyone they loved to get the flavor they wanted.

"I'll try to keep her under control," said Maddox, loudly enough for Solomon to hear. Solomon snorted a laugh and I thought I heard Delgado laughing too. Then Solomon hung up. "He doesn't believe me," said Maddox. "I don't know why I said it. I didn't believe it either."

"He's too far to be of immediate help. I'm going to call Jord. Burglaries are his thing."

"I'm sure he'll appreciate arresting a criminal red-handed."

"Sis'," said Jord, answering. "Lily enjoyed your surveillance afternoon."

"Glad to hear it."

"Shame you didn't catch the perp."

"Not so fast. I have my eye on the suspect and I'd appreciate your help. Do you want an easy arrest?"

"Sure! Wait... what did they do specifically?"

"So far, burglarizing a salon on Plover Street." I paused, watching the figure pass through the shadows towards the back of the salon where my client kept her boxes of backstock. "Can you hurry?"

"Sure. Sit tight and I'll be there in fifteen."

I watched as the figure returned, lifted a bag into the air, and waved their arms around. The bag drifted upwards and disappeared into the ceiling.

"How did they do that?" I asked. "It looked like it floated and disappeared."

"And so is our perp," said Maddox, pointing.

We watched as the figure stretched and seemed to float upwards only to disappear. "No!" I wailed as my opportunity to catch the thief seemed to vanish with them. Jord was on his way. Solomon and Delgado might be too. What was I supposed to give them? I'd promised a thief and all I had now was fresh air.

Then I stopped, forcing myself to think.

If the thief could go up, so could I.

"I don't like that look on your face," said Maddox.

"Yes, you do," I countered.

"Okay, yes, I do, but it scares me too. I'll need to speak to my therapist about that."

"I'm going in."

"I'm right behind you. Literally. I don't have a bullet proof vest with me and we don't know what we're walking into."

I gaped at him. "You would use me as a human shield?"

"Absolutely."

"I don't think anyone brings a weapon to steal shampoo."

"I guess not. One could call it a *squeaky-clean* crime."

I shook my head and sighed.

"I'm going in," I said, reaching for the flashlight I'd stashed in the glove box.

"Is this breaking and entering?"

"No. My client gave me a spare set of keys and signed a form. It's all totally legal," I said, already halfway out of the car. Maddox wasted no time in jogging after me as we crossed the road, dodging a bus that trundled past.

I unlocked the door, pushing it open as quietly as I could, and entered the code on the keypad to disarm the door alarm. I reached for the lights and paused. I didn't want to alert anyone to our presence but then… I couldn't hear anyone. No rustling or shuffling, or breathing, nothing that would suggest someone was hiding.

No, the salon was empty.

I could feel the emptiness.

Then Maddox poked my shoulder and I felt his warmth close to me.

"I'm going to check the stockroom," I whispered as we took a cautious look around. Jogging across the salon, glad I'd worn soft-soled sneakers, I reached for the stockroom door and pushed it open. Using the flashlight's beam, I scanned the several open boxes. It was impossible to tell what had been stolen and what had been legitimately used so I pulled the door closed behind me, returning to Maddox.

"There," he said, softly, pointing to a square panel in the middle of the small waiting area.

I squinted up. The panel didn't look any different from the others.

He pointed his phone's flashlight to the floor. "See that?" he said. "The perp didn't notice in the dark but they dislodged a smattering of dust. The panel isn't quite in the frame either. It's lifted a little in the corner. Sloppy."

"I see," I said. "But how did they get up there? I couldn't even put one foot on the reception desk and launch myself up. Neither could you and you're taller than me. But there's a ladder in the stockroom. We could get that."

"I'll help."

We crept across the salon, careful not to knock over any chairs or equipment carts, or the boxes in the stockroom, as we lifted the ladder and moved it into position under the tilted panel. Maddox withdrew his weapon, holding it ready at the ceiling. "Hand me the flashlight and I'll go up," he said.

"You can't! It's not your case."

"I can. I have the gun. Did you bring a gun?"

"No. It would have looked out of place in the salon and I didn't have time to go home and get mine. I figured I'd be okay since it's a non-violent crime."

"We don't know who's up there. Hand me the flashlight and I'll go up. I'll make sure it's clear and then you come up, okay?"

"What about using me as a human shield?"

"As if I actually would!" Then very softly, I thought I heard him say 'today.'

I weighed the options. As much as I wanted to argue, Maddox had a point. I had no idea what we could be getting into. Plus, hoisting myself the rest of the gap between the ladder and the ceiling while holding a gun, a flashlight, and attempting to aim, would be no small feat. The simple fact was Maddox had more experience. And the gun.

"Okay," I agreed, handing him the flashlight.

"This is definitely more fun than watching TV with my takeout," he whispered. "We should hang out more often."

Since he was potentially facing danger, I decided not to point out we hadn't planned on hanging out. Instead, he'd simply appeared but it would be churlish not to admit his backup was coming in handy.

"Hang tight," he said before climbing the ladder quickly and quietly. Pausing at the ceiling, he rested the gun and flashlight on the ladder's top flat shelf and tested the panel. It moved easily.

Maddox gave me a thumbs up, scooped up the gun and flashlight and carefully pushed on the panel. He slid it to one side and poked his head and hands inside, the beam from the flashlight barely visible from my position below. "Seems empty," he whispered, his voice almost too soft to catch, then he pushed himself up and disappeared into the void. Gentle creaks echoed down to me and I waited, ready to rush the ladder if needed. Then Maddox's face appeared in the opening and he beckoned me up. I climbed quickly and he helped me through the opening.

"Is that a winch?" I whispered, pointing to a piece of machinery no bigger than an electric cake mixer. We knelt by the side of the opening, almost enveloped in darkness.

"Yep."

"So the perp hooks themself onto it and lowers and raises it as they please."

Maddox nodded. "They don't have to break a single lock."

I frowned, remembering something. "I think there're two people. Remember how the bag seemed to float and disappear? Someone had to operate the winch and unhook it from above."

"Makes sense." Maddox passed me the flashlight and I used it to look around, terrified I was going to illuminate an unknown face close to me even though I had that same feeling of aloneness as before. "Be careful. These makeshift floorboards are all loose."

"Where are we? The apartment above?"

"I'm not sure. The floorspace is just about big enough to be a studio apartment but it's not high enough. It doesn't look like anyone lives here legally. No furniture or anything to suggest someone even camps here."

I tried to stand, then bumped against something. I sank again, rubbing the top of my head where I'd knocked it against the ceiling. "I think we must be in some kind of crawl space. Or attic space? Maybe for storing things? But it looks like the salon doesn't have access to it or doesn't need it since there's a small storage room below."

"It goes further than the footprint of the salon," Maddox said pointing. "There's an opening in the wall over there."

"And there," I said, pointing to the other side. "I bet it goes the whole way across all the businesses in this strip. Hey, I overheard the waitress in the café a few doors down saying things were going missing there too. Do you think there could be access to all the businesses?"

"There's only one way to find out." Maddox took off in a bear crawl to the nearest hole in the wall, squeezing through, only the small beam from his phone's flashlight illuminating the way. I followed him, scanning the room with the big flashlight.

Goods lined the walls. Products from the salon were stacked haphazardly. Shampoos, conditioners, mousses, hairsprays and more. Beyond that was a stack of cans and jars. I crawled closer, picking up a jar to check the label, recognizing it as the fancy Italian deli next to the salon. Artichokes in oil, sundried tomatoes, capers, olives, packets of lemon risotto and several panettones. There were enough luxury foodstuffs to stuff several hampers.

"There has to be hundreds of dollars of goods here from the deli," I whispered after I squeezed into the next room and found Maddox crouched nearby.

"Same here." Maddox held up a leather dog leash and a laser cut collar, illuminated by his cellphone light.

"There's a luxury pet store at the end of the block," I said softly.

"I count twenty collars and leashes like this. The tag says a hundred and twenty dollars! There're also pet beds, bowls, and all sorts of things."

"They must have found a way into all the shops below," I said decisively.

"What else is in this strip? We've got items from the salon, deli and pet store."

"There's also a manicurist, a shoe shop, a high-end liquor store, and a dental surgery."

"I don't see any nail products or shoes but there're a couple of crates of wine in the next space."

"What could they steal from a dental surgery?" I wondered. "I don't see them breaking in for a self-service hygienic cleaning."

There was a long pause, then Maddox said, "Drugs."

"This just got a lot more serious."

"Shhh." Maddox's cellphone went dark. I slid the off switch for the flashlight, plunging us into darkness.

I stopped, stilled, and listened, trying to find what had alerted Maddox. After an impossibly long time in the dark, I heard it. Scuffling and an "Oof!" with a small electronic whir. Whoever it was seemed to be climbing out of another store and returning to their secret storage place.

"We should go back and wait for Jord," I whispered. "I don't think we should alert them that we've found their stash."

"I agree. Let's head back the way we came. Go first. I'll be right behind you."

I was already moving, feeling my way in the dark with my hands for the hole between spaces before Maddox said anything. I squeezed through the hole and just as I was wriggling my hips through, a hand on my butt gave me a push. I popped through, like a stuck cork emerging from a bottle neck and landed on my palms, wincing but biting my lip so I didn't make any noise.

"Sorry," said Maddox, squeezing past me. He grabbed my arm and pulled me into the corner furthest from our entry. "They're coming. There's no time to climb down," he said, popping the panel back into place before re-joining me in the corner. "Crouch down and stay quiet. Hopefully, they won't come this far."

Soft whispers carried through the crawl space as we crouched, the words still indistinguishable, but I was sure I could make out two voices. Male and female.

"This is cozy," whispered Maddox. "Just like the

old days." His arm pressed against mine, so I elbowed him lightly, gratified to hear a small huff of surprise.

I didn't need reminding of the day I'd stumbled upon a terrible crime and then promptly had to hide from murderous goons. At least this pair of thieves seemed to be into luxury crime. Hopefully, that meant they didn't want to get their hands too dirty.

The voices were coming closer, the footsteps, although still soft, also became clearer. "We have enough," I heard one say. The woman, her voice young. "We can sell all of this and have enough."

"I've got a deal set up," said another. The man this time, although I couldn't be absolutely sure. The voice was too soft, and too far away.

In my pocket, my phone vibrated but I didn't dare pull it out. The bright screen would shine like a beacon in the dark. Seconds later, another vibration. Maddox's phone. I hoped that meant help was close by.

I also hoped the two people in the crawl space would turn back and go the other way, giving us enough time to shimmy through the hatch into the salon below.

But instead, the voices seemed to be coming closer.

"We're going to get caught!" The woman again, louder now.

"No, we won't. They're all too dumb anyway. Plus, don't you want the money, babe? We can buy a van and go anywhere. We'll be free spirits. We can go wherever the wind takes us." The man's voice was distinct.

"I don't know that I want to live in a van."

"It was our dream."

"It's *your* dream."

"Whatever, babe. Go add this to the other stuff."

"What is this?"

"From the dentist's surgery. They have crappy locks on the drugs cabinet," said the male with a laugh, his voice so clear I was certain they could only be yards away, just the other side of the hole.

"You stole drugs?"

"Yeah."

"Why? Why would you do that?"

"I took a look a couple of nights ago. I Googled the names on the bottles. That shit is worth good money!"

"You said we'd only take a few things to mess with them. Not drugs!"

"Well, I'm not going to get anything for a box of surgical gloves, am I?"

A grunt and a sigh. "It's not fun anymore."

No answer.

"I want to go home." Softly now, defeated. "We only said we'd do it to mess with Liv for screwing with us. It's not funny anymore."

"Yeah, but look at everything we nabbed. I've got buyers for everything and with the drugs, we'll be rich. None of them have even noticed anything's missing. Stuck up idiots. They don't need the money. We do."

"I don't want any part in the drugs. That's not what I wanted to do, Landon. I don't like it."

"Shut up your whining already. I'm going to get stuff from the pet store and then we can be done tonight. I saw Liv get a delivery yesterday."

My phone buzzed again, quickly followed by Maddox's.

"I'm not..."

"Shush..."

"What..." Both voices came at once.

"Did you hear that?"

Silence slipped around us and I slid my hand over my pocket where the phone was, hoping to dampen any more noise. It was only the quiet in the small space that made the vibration's buzz audible. I felt Maddox do the same, then his other hand closed around mine, a small comfort amidst the tension. Then he sniffed my hair.

I pulled my heels a little closer, ready to pitch myself forwards as soon as the thieves retreated.

The voice remained far too close. "I don't hear anything," said the woman.

A soft thump sounded a short distance away and I struggled to be sure where in the dark. Possibly in the next room.

"Sorry, I knocked that over. There's so much stuff in here."

"Be more careful and watch where you put your feet," snapped the one she'd called Landon.

"I am!" A rustle and I felt the presence of another being in the room. One of them had squeezed into the small room where we hid.

"We'll move it all tomorrow. Just a few more things tonight to fill the orders I got and we're done."

A huff and a sigh. "Fine. I'm coming through."

Another soft thump and something rolled against my arm. I bit my lip so I didn't cry out but when the thing didn't move, I forced myself to feel with my fingers. A canister. Not a mouse. I held in the sigh of relief.

"I think I knocked something over again," she

said.

"You're clumsier than an elephant."

"That's rude!"

"Not my fault. Here, help me with this."

A bigger thump this time followed by several more. "What are you doing?" asked the man angrily. A light flashed on, illuminating the ceiling hatch and a stack of products now tumbling between the rafters where the makeshift floor panels didn't quite meet. "Grab them."

"I can't see."

"I'm using the flipping light! Are you blind?"

"I'm not… off!" A hand landed on my sneaker, stilled and squeezed. "Where did you get sneakers from?"

My hand closed around the canister, feeling for the nozzle.

"What kind of question is that? You know where I got them from."

"No, I mean…" A scramble, then a light flashed in my eyes. I squeezed them shut, suddenly blinded. "Oh, my god!" screamed the girl. "There're people! There's…" The grip loosened on my foot.

Maddox and I launched forwards, but I wasn't sure if we were aiming for the hatch or the people. We all seemed to be caught up together, the flashlight shining all over until it blinked out into darkness.

All attempts at quiet were lost. A man shouted and I heard an "Oof!" and a loud thud. I grabbed an ankle, clad in leggings. Definitely a woman's leg. She kicked and flailed and a can bounced off my forehead. Then, more products were falling and a bottle hit me in the chest. I scrambled for something, found a canister, pressed the nozzle and fired. The woman squealed and fell against me. She kicked and clawed at the ground, dislodging the hatch. I wrestled, trying to turn her away from the hatch, uncertain if I could drop through even if I got clear access. I couldn't leave Maddox behind to the mercy of the thieves!

The woman grabbed my arms, we grappled, and then I tripped, losing my footing. We hit the floor, crumpling between the rafters.

A terrible crack sounded below us.

Then we were falling.

CHAPTER THREE

Cans, tubes and shards of the ceiling hurtled past as the floor rushed up to greet me and the woman flailed beneath me, her eyes wide with fear. A scream accompanied us as we landed with a crunch and a squish.

Foam squirted from beneath us, billowing in a cloud of marshmallowey fluff.

A moment later, Maddox crashed through the ceiling, hanging onto a leg.

Lights flicked on, illuminating Jord and several uniformed police officers pointing their weapons at us. Beyond, standing just outside the salon was Solomon, his arms crossed, his face expressionless.

I pushed off the woman, flipping myself onto my back and landed like a starfish, another puff of foam shooting from under my shoulder. A small jar dropped through the ceiling and smashed open, leaking sundried tomatoes.

"Hey," I said, lifting a hand to limply wave.

"I wondered when you'd drop in," said Jord, a

small smile playing on his lips.

"Ha ha."

"My eyes!" cried the woman next to me. She curled up into a ball and the tubes under her squirted gel in every direction.

"Found a thief," I said, limply flapping a finger towards her.

"Yep, got that," said Jord. A can of olives rolled towards him and he stopped it with his toe. "I don't think I've arrested anyone for stealing olives before."

"Wait until you see everything else," I said as several packets of imported pasta dropped to land at Jord's feet.

"Let go!" shrieked the leg. Its pair kicked at Maddox. Maddox renewed his grip and glanced down. The legs' pants began to slip until they were hanging around the knees, revealing Superman boxers.

Guns swung from us to them.

Maddox, clinging onto the man's lower body, gave a hard tug. The ceiling cracked and whoomph! The two men fell through, landing in a heap on the floor.

"This can't be the real caped crusader," said Jord. "Someone cuff him before he flies outta here. I'll take the sidekick."

I wiggled my fingers and toes, then my limbs. Nothing seemed to be broken so I sat up, wincing. My pants were soaked with sticky substances and foam clung to my face. I brushed it off, saying, "That's sexist. How do you know she's not the boss and he's not the sidekick?" I pointed between them.

"The crying is a clue," said Jord. He reached for his radio and requested an ambulance before stooping to check the woman. She wriggled upright, holding her wrist, and crying louder.

I looked around for Solomon, finding him poised at the door, ready to run inside the moment Jord gave the okay. I caught his eye and grinned. He raised a single hand in return and turned his gaze to the ceiling. I followed his gaze, grimacing at the large holes we'd crashed through. Yet as we watched, all kinds of goods began to tumble down, giving us a few seconds of a very weird game of dodge.

Climbing gingerly to my feet, I rolled my shoulders, made a few more checks that I really was miraculously uninjured, and skidded through the leaking gels and foam to Solomon. "I think I solved my case and I need a shower," I said.

"You smell like the salon," he said, picking up a thickly coated clump of hair languishing over my shoulder. "And slightly tomatoey. You look like you've gone through a car wash." He wrapped an arm around me, pulled me against him and hugged me hard. I rested my head against his chest, only mildly sorry that I was probably ruining his cotton sweater.

"I'm okay," said Maddox, getting to his feet, one fist pumping the air like he'd won something.

Superman was wriggling and kicking, simultaneously trying to pull up his pants and escape the police. After a couple of minutes of skidding around, they dived on him, wrestling him into handcuffs before sitting him upright. He looked around, scowling.

"Meet the thieves of the block," I said. "There's more contraband up there and if you check his pockets, I'm pretty sure you'll find drugs from the dental surgery."

Jord passed off the sobbing woman to an officer

and searched Superman. He held up several small vials, counting them into an evidence baggie that was handed to him. "Well, you two, it looks like we're going downtown," he said, grinning.

"I'd rather go home," I said.

"And I'd rather not do any paperwork on this," added Maddox.

"Not you two," said Jord, shaking his head. "Just as soon as we get these two checked over, they're getting booked. As for you two, stick around. I want you to get checked out too. That was quite a fall you took, especially you," he added, giving me a pointed look.

"I'm fine. Just sticky."

Maddox looked at me and laughed, then he plucked a sliver of plaster from his hair and brushed out a plume of dust.

"Do I want to know?" asked Solomon.

I looked around at the oozing mess on the floor, the sobbing woman, and the handcuffed man whose pants were currently being pulled into a more gentlemanly position, and shrugged. "I think you can get the gist," I said.

An ambulance pulled up, cutting out its wailing siren but leaving the lights flashing. As we stepped outside, the usually sparse evening crowd growing, a man holding up a phone gave us the thumbs up. "I got all that on camera," he exclaimed. "That was awesome! It's going to go viral for sure!"

I deflated and Solomon guided me to the ambulance. A few minutes later, our vitals checked and with a confirmation of no broken bones, both Maddox and I were cleared to go. We hung around to give statements to Jord, then Maddox took off with a cheerful wave, announcing his intent to pick up his takeout at last.

"He's remarkably happy," said Solomon, glancing from Maddox's retreating back to the disastrous salon.

"I don't know if it's his superpower or a fatal flaw," I said, seeing a white Mercedes sail past Maddox and park. "My client just arrived."

She pushed her way through the crowd, gaped at the destruction inside the salon and gaped again as the two perpetrators were loaded into police cars. Then she saw me and made a beeline in our direction.

"Hi, Marie," I said.

"What happened?" she asked. "I thought you were going to conduct surveillance?"

"I did, and your thieves have been arrested."

"What happened to my salon? Why are there cans and jars and things all over? What happened to the ceiling?" Her voice rose with every question.

"You weren't the only one being robbed. It looks like they were stealing from the whole strip. Did you know there's a crawl space above the salon? It spans all the shops. They found hatches to drop into the shops and set up a winch to lower and raise them and everything they stole, out again."

"You have got to be kidding me," she said, turning to gape again.

"We fell through the ceiling," I added. "Sorry about that."

"I can see that. I've never been more thankful for my business insurance."

"You should see if your repairers can open up the ceiling. The rafters look in good condition and you'll get a lot of extra ceiling height," said Solomon.

"That would look great," I agreed. "Very chic too."

"I suppose I could ask the eventual contractors if that's possible. I don't like the idea of anyone being able to access the salon like that again." Marie gazed at the salon in disbelief. "I think the shops were all one big home improvement store at one time. They must have left the winch mechanisms behind when the store was turned into smaller shops. My gosh, is that what's been happening all along?"

"It appears so but once the police get into the crawl space and find all the stolen goods, they'll have a better picture."

"Do you know who they are?"

"No, but I think one or both of them worked for one of the other shops. For someone called Liv."

"Liv owns the pet store. I feel so ashamed that I thought one of my employees might be stealing from me." Marie's lower lip quivered.

"You did say you couldn't imagine it was any of them," I reminded her, "and now there's proof. I just wish I didn't have to leave you with all this mess."

"You really fell through the ceiling?" she asked, looking me over from head to toe. The last time she'd seen me was when I left the salon, gorgeously coiffed. Now I looked like a sewer rat.

"Four people to be precise," I said, "but I'll put it all in a report for you and send it to you in the next day or two."

"I look forward to reading it."

"This is Detective Graves," I said as Jord walked over. "He's in charge."

I left Marie with my brother and Solomon walked me to my car. "I can follow you home or we can take my car and I'll send someone to pick up yours," he said.

"Follow me home. I can drive." Foam dripped off me and I attempted to wipe the last remaining plumes from my shoulder. I had a picnic blanket in the car that I threw over the driver's seat, then I hopped in and headed home, entirely unsure whether I'd had a weirder evening recently. Then another thought hit me: Lily would be so disappointed to have missed this.

I grimaced. She'd have to watch the rerun on the bystander's video.

At home, I stripped off my clothes and stuffed them and the picnic blanket in the washing machine. After attempting to wipe away the puddle on the floor, I hopped in the shower. By the time I dressed, sadly putting aside my fairy-winged kittens-in-crowns pajamas, in favor of yoga pants and a t-shirt, I was squeaky clean, dry and still smelled like a salon. Plus, the cut I'd been given was so good, it stood the rewash and home-dry test.

I was in a good mood when I joined Solomon in the kitchen where he was making sandwiches. He pushed a bowl of salty chips towards me and a glass of wine.

"Any news?" I asked.

"None. I assume Jord is busy interviewing the thieves. Your parents don't seem to have caught wind of this yet."

"Good." I thought about the guy filming on his phone. It was only a matter of time before that got out. "Mom can't complain. I was barely in any danger."

"Are you sure?"

"They didn't have any weapons."

"You crashed through a ceiling."

"Accidentally."

"You could have been seriously hurt."

"The thief broke my fall."

Solomon laid down the knife, walked around the island and pulled me into a hug. "Why do the weirdest things happen to you?" he asked, his breath ruffling strands of my hair.

"Hard to say but I *did* solve the case. After I've delivered the report, can I take the day off?" I asked.

"Of course. What're you going to do?"

"Absolutely nothing."

"Take the whole week if that's the case. It'll stop me wondering what the heck you're doing if I know you're actively doing nothing."

"Maybe we can get back on that baby making thing?"

Solomon pulled away and smiled down at me. "I wasn't aware we'd stopped."

"We could not stop tonight too? Tonight could be our lucky night. Maybe I'll buy a lottery ticket too." It hadn't been our lucky night since we'd started trying but apparently, these things took time. I wasn't sure how much time but I was committed to the cause. Practice, after all, made perfect.

Then my phone buzzed in my jeans' pocket. I fished it out, entirely intending to ignore it when I saw it was my mom. As soon as the call ended, a text message flashed up: *911!*

"It's my mom."

"Ignore it."

"She texted 911."

"Take it."

"I'll be as quick as I can."

"Then I'll be as slow as I can," said Solomon, a gradual smile spreading across his lips.

Oh boy.

"What's up, Mom?" I asked, the phone next to my ear as I pressed one hand to Solomon's chest, weakly holding him at bay. I could imagine the onslaught about to come: *I should be more careful! What was I thinking! Was I hurt?*

Instead, Mom said, "I need you back at the house."

"Why? What's happened? Is it Dad?"

"No, he's had the best evening. His team made second place in his golf tournament. I'm not sure what I'll do now he'll be home more often and not practicing his swings. Or, even worse, at home, practicing his swings. I might have a case for you."

"Really?" Skepticism leaked from my tone. I did not want a lost cat case, or a lost headphones case, or even a lost spouse, although the latter would be the most interesting. Unfortunately for me, it would probably be as simple as a neighbor grousing that his wife couldn't be found when all she was probably doing was taking a few hours to herself. The chances of my mom stumbling across an actual crime was... medium likely. Also, there was the potential that *she* had committed the unknown crime. "Did you do something?" I asked, suspicion lacing my words.

"Don't take that tone with me, young lady!"

"Sorry... Did you?" I couldn't help myself.

"No!"

"Is anyone injured?"

"Well... not exactly."

I narrowed my eyes. "What does that mean?"

"If you came over, you'd see!"

I frowned. "Are you sure you shouldn't call the police?"

"Someone probably already did, but this has you written all over it."

"What do you mean 'someone probably already did'? They either did or didn't."

"Well, I don't know but I'm standing outside and there's a lot of commotion going on inside. Well, outside but *inside there*," she hissed.

"Where are you?" I asked, my frown deepening. "What's happening at your house?"

"I told you already!" huffed Mom in exasperation. "I'm at the end house. The one with all the construction work. Oh, my! Come quick!"

"No, you didn't tell... Mom? Hello? Mom? She hung up!" I squeaked, staring at the blank phone screen.

"I got the gist of the conversation."

"I'm glad one of us did." I paused, irritated and puzzled. "We should probably go," I said, the decision reluctantly made. "But if it's a fool's errand, I'm going to tell my mom how irritated I am."

"A fair exchange." Solomon reached for his keys. "Let's go."

Since my mother hadn't made it appear like a life or death situation, we took our time driving to my parents' place, eating the sandwiches on the way, and although the evening commuter traffic had long since died down, construction work on the roads burdened us with crawling slowly through a half mile section before we could break free.

By the time we turned onto my parents' street, it was twilight. I'd consulted my phone repeatedly, both puzzled and relieved that Mom hadn't called again, and somewhat furious that she hadn't picked up any of my three calls. Nor had my dad until he'd finally texted: *No point asking me. I'm the last person to ever know what goes on in my own house. Love, Dad.*

Before Solomon slowed the car to pull in, I pointed ahead where a blue and white cruiser was parked next to the corner house, its lights emitting a steady flash.

"We'll leave the car at your parents' and jog over," said Solomon. "I don't want the car to get stuck with no way out if more emergency vehicles arrive. Clearly, something happened over there."

"Okay," I gulped, my heart thudding, more concerned than ever at what my mother had become involved in.

As we jogged over, curtains twitched in the neighboring houses, yet only a couple of households had moved to their porches to unashamedly watch.

We slowed to a walk when we reached the house and followed the sounds of voices around the side. My mom stood with a couple about my age, nodding as the younger woman waved towards the partially fallen fencing, and said something we were too far away to hear.

"Mom!" I called out as we approached and my mother whipped around.

"There you are!" said Mom, beckoning us, then, "This is my daughter, the investigator. Not the one that went to Harvard. That's my older daughter, Serena. This is the younger one. She did go to college though and now she fights crime as a private citizen. The rest of the family fight crime legally on the police force."

"Thanks for the introduction," I said, holding in the internal sigh that threatened to break forth every time my overachieving older sister was mentioned. "I'm Lexi. This is my husband, John Solomon. We're both PIs."

"Thanks for coming," said the younger woman. She wrung her hands, alternating between looking at us and back toward the yard. "Your mom said you'd be able to help and I just don't know what to do."

"Do you live here?" I asked, pulling her attention back. The "For Sale" sign had disappeared a couple months back but I hadn't kept tabs on who had bought it. My mom had mentioned construction work had started but I couldn't remember when that was.

"Oh, yes, we do. I'm sorry. Where are my manners? I'm Carrie Dugan and this is my husband, Pete Dugan. We own the house." She nodded towards the house that occupied the end lot.

Solomon had stepped away momentarily, monitoring the yard and when he returned, he asked, "Did you call the police?"

"Yes, it seemed the right thing to do," said Carrie. "We showed them the yard and they've been in there ever since."

"I'm not sure how we can help in a way the police can't but perhaps you can tell us why you called them and we can figure something out," I suggested, glancing around for sight of the police officers.

Carrie eyed my mom, who nodded encouragingly, and grimaced. "We were just doing a little light evening work. It's too late to use any power tools at this time, but Pete wanted to get started with the landscaping so that our little girl can play in the backyard. She's at my mom's tonight so Pete was just excavating—"

"By hand," chipped in Pete. "That is, with a shovel. I wanted to get the foundation dug out for a small retaining wall around the patio area since the lawn slopes a little on our plot."

"Exactly," agreed Carrie, nodding along. "So Pete was digging and well…" she trailed off, looking at her husband.

He took a deep breath, paling. "That's when I found the body," he said.

CHAPTER FOUR

"A body?" I repeated, wondering if I'd heard him correctly.

"Not a fresh one," said Pete as his wife elbowed him. His already flushed cheeks reddened further. "I don't mean to be disrespectful. I meant it's obviously been there a while. It's a skeleton. I thought it was a prank at first. I actually laughed! I thought they got me good! I thought maybe the construction crew were playing a joke on me because I mentioned I wanted to get this done while they finished working on the interiors, but then I looked closer and well, it looked real."

"Because it *is* real," said Carrie.

"How can you be sure?" asked Solomon.

"They're sure," said Mom, shushing him. "Tell them."

"I dug up more of it," said Pete. "I thought since the guys went to the effort of this big prank, I might as well dig it up anyway and see what other business the crew had in store for me. But the earth was more compacted than if it had been freshly dug, which was weird and when I started to reveal more of it, that's when I got the horrible feeling it was no joke. I called Carrie out to check."

"I got the fright of my life," said Carrie. "I knew right away it was a human skeleton. I'm a doctor. I've seen enough of them in medical school to know a real one when I see it, even if it *is* caked in dirt."

"I just happened to be walking past when I heard a yelp. Since the fence was down, I figured I'd make sure no one was hurt," said Mom.

"We were concentrating so hard on the body that we didn't even hear Mrs. Graves come into the yard. We got a second fright when she spoke and then it was just such a relief that we were all stood there, agreeing we weren't seeing things and were, in fact, seeing the same thing," said Carrie. "Pete got on his phone to call the police, and Mrs. Graves said we should call you too. She said if anyone could figure out why there's a body in our yard, it would be you."

"That's nice of you, Mom," I said. "But you *do* remember your oldest son is a homicide detective?"

"Homicide!" Carrie clapped a hand to her chest, her eyes widening.

I pulled a face, realizing my faux pas. "I'm sorry, I didn't mean to say that's what it is. Only that human remains in your yard is suspicious so it's likely there will be an investigation into the death and improper burial. My brother is the type of detective who would ascertain if there were any wrongdoing, and how the body came to be buried in your yard."

"But he would be on the side of the police. If you hire Lexi, she'll be on your side," said Mom.

I flashed her a look. On the one hand, it was nice

she was trying to drum up business. On the other, the Dugans looked even more worried. Plus, I wasn't sure what Mom was trying to say about my detective brothers. Or my ex-detective dad.

"There's no way we could have done this," said Pete. "We only bought the house three months ago!"

"I'm sure the body has been in the ground much longer than that," said Carrie. "I'm not an expert on decomposition but I'm positive that the body was put there long before we gained ownership, and we can guarantee no one had any opportunity to place it here since we bought the house."

"How can you guarantee that?" asked Solomon.

"We put up security cameras as soon as we could. We couldn't move in immediately because of the work that needed to be done. Then a friend of ours scared us with a story about squatters moving into their friend's newly bought home and the expensive legal fight to get them out so we wanted to put up cameras for some peace of mind. We put one at the front of the house and one at the back," said Pete. "The only time we get an alert, it's a cat."

"It's pretty annoying," added Carrie, with an eye roll that seemed to momentarily distract her from her worries. "But I'd be more worried if we hadn't installed the cameras. It's costing us more than we anticipated for the renovation and a legal fight would be more than we could afford."

"The point is we would absolutely have been alerted by the system if someone decided to bury a body while they thought the house was unoccupied. The system records everything and we can access the recordings any time."

"I'm convinced its burial pre-dates us moving

here," said Carrie. She rubbed her arms and glanced toward the yard, worry written across her face.

"Damn right it does," scoffed Pete. He darted a glance towards the backyard, his jaw stiff.

"Security was a smart choice," said Solomon. "Make sure to offer the police access to the system when they ask so they can rule you out of any inquiries."

"There's going to be an investigation, isn't there?" asked Carrie. She folded her arms across her chest, almost hugging herself.

I nodded. "Almost certainly. The police will want to know how the deceased came to be that way, and how they got into your backyard."

"What are the neighbors going to think of us?" Carrie asked as she looked around. "I know it's selfish to think that way but we just moved here. They must all have seen the police car by now."

"They'll be feeling awful sorry for you," said Mom, reaching to pat her arm. "No one will think badly of you and hardly anyone will think you did it."

Carrie let out an upset squeak and clasped her hand over her mouth.

I flashed a look at my mom. She shrugged and raised hands in surrender, mouthing, "What did I say?"

Flashing lights appeared in the periphery of my vision before two dark, unmarked, sedans rolled to a stop. I turned away, ignoring the slamming of the doors until the police officers emerged from the backyard burial site and moved to greet them.

I twisted to see who had arrived. A familiar face made me smile.

"Hi, Garrett!" I called, waving to my brother as I

seized the opportunity to be not only noticed but acknowledged by the most senior ranking officer on scene. It wasn't often I got to work with two of my brothers in one day, a fact that didn't seem to have reached my mom yet. Long may that continue.

"Not a surprise to see you here," said Garrett, his face an expressionless mask. "I hear it's been an evening of mayhem." Then he spotted my mom and swallowed a groan. "Or you," he added. "Stay here, all of you. I mean it." He barely broke stride as he spoke, waving a stern finger, and then he was past us, disappearing through the hole in the fence into the yard. As I began to follow him, one of the officers blocked my way. Then Solomon, my mom and the Dugans joined me. I thought about getting them to rush to one side and distract the officer while I made it through but it didn't seem fair with five against one. Plus, Garrett would shout at me.

Stepping to one side of the officer, who seemed content with allowing us to watch so long as we didn't edge past, I regarded the scene of devastation that had once been a yard. Piles of dirt were heaped around the corner lot, shrubbery had been cut back, but the flower beds were long overgrown, shapeless, and weedy. The area spanning the length of the back of the house had been cleared but not leveled and a pallet of stone pavers had been deposited close to the fence disruption. A shovel lay abandoned on the ground where the yard level abruptly rose up.

Garrett came to a stop by a pile of dirt, knelt and surveyed the scene. He pulled on gloves and reached for something, taking a long look at whatever he found.

"Should we hire you to represent us?" asked Pete,

watching Garrett examine the ground.

"We're not lawyers," replied Solomon. "We can't represent you in any legal matters, but we can help you find out what happened and also make sure any evidence exonerating you is looked at. Fortunately, we have a good relationship with Lieutenant Graves." Solomon nodded in Garrett's direction.

"He's my son," said Mom.

"A son for a police lieutenant and a daughter for a PI. That's impressive," said Pete.

"And another son who is also a detective, and another who just joined the FBI, and my other daughter is at the top of her field. She owns her own business now."

"That's a lot of children," said Carrie, quickly adding, "I mean, those are amazing achievements."

"I don't recommend more than two," said Mom with a decisive nod. "One child for each hand."

"If I count your two hands, and Dad's two hands, that leaves one of us over. Which of us would you give up?" I asked, my attention briefly distracted from Garrett's poking in the dirt.

"It depends on the day," said Mom but before I could ask about *today* she nudged me. "Garrett's coming over."

"I'd like a word with the homeowners," he said, addressing all of us and then the couple. "You're Mr. and Mrs. Dugan? You called in the discovery? Can you step over here for a moment?"

"Those poor people," said Mom when the trio had moved away, just out of earshot. Then she smacked my arm.

"Ow! What was that for?" I rubbed my arm.

"I thought you'd be more helpful. You didn't

even examine the body!"

"We can't do that. The police are here!"

"We'd be contaminating the scene," added Solomon. "That would be unwise to do."

"Oh, well, all right then, but I thought you'd be more reassuring," huffed Mom.

"I can't say how reassuring I would be examining a skeleton. I don't know how to examine one for starters! I think we're making it obvious we don't think the Dugans are murderers," I said. "They seem relieved by that. Plus, we all know Garrett. He's hardly going to railroad them into confessing a murder they didn't commit. He'll want to get to the truth."

"We do have to consider they might have something to do with it," said Solomon. He shrugged as Mom and I both turned, open-mouthed. "I agree it's unlikely but the Dugans will need to be ruled out. I've seen very convincing suspects before who have sworn on their mother's grave it wasn't them and later proved it was."

"But they didn't buy the house until years after the death according to Carrie," I pointed out.

"That may be so but it doesn't mean they don't have an existing connection to the house or the body," said Solomon.

"Let's say they *did* do it," I said, softening my voice so no one around us could possibly hear. "Why wouldn't they just stuff the body under the new foundation and never let it be found? Why call it in?"

"We have to stop calling it... *it*," said Mom.

"We don't know if it's a man or a woman. So it's an it," I said. "Although we could call it Roger, if you like?"

"Why Roger?"

"Why not Roger?" I countered.

Solomon cleared his throat, pulling attention back to him. "They might want to get rid of it. Not everyone wants to live in a home where they know a corpse is buried. Even murderers get the heebie-jeebies. Plus, let's say it..."

"*Roger*," said Mom.

"Let's say *it* was hidden under the foundation. They can't be certain one day something doesn't happen that ends up in the body being revealed and then it's easily proven that they did the renovations and had the means to put it there or knew about it. Now a surprise discovery during the renovations could be blamed on countless other people, especially with the house lying empty for a period."

"He has a point," I said. "Although they did volunteer the security footage to prove it didn't happen under their ownership."

"Could have been tampered with," said Solomon, "But at present, I assume not. They're candidness works in their favor."

"I still can't work out that even if they did do it, why come back here at all? Surely most murderers like to put some distance between them and their victims," I said, pondering out loud.

"These are my *neighbors*," said Mom, not even trying to hide her disgust at the discussion.

"They live at the end of the block," I said.

"It doesn't matter. A neighbor is a neighbor. We don't have murderers as neighbors. I would know!"

"Well, you definitely had a dead body as a neighbor and you didn't know anything about that," I pointed out. Mom narrowed her eyes at me and I contemplated stepping behind Solomon, out of her glare. Not that I was scared of my mom but... well, yes, she was scary.

"Looks like Garrett is wrapping up with the Dugans," said Solomon. "Let's split tasks. You find out what he knows, and I'll quiz the Dugans."

"And then you'll take the case?" asked Mom.

"They haven't asked us yet," I said, while nodding my agreement to Solomon's suggestion.

When the Dugans returned to our small group, their worries still evident across their faces and the way they clenched their hands, I took the moment of distraction to slip away and walk over to Garrett where he stood, his phone pressed to his ear. I made sure he saw me, then waited for him to finish the call.

"I'm told Mom called you," he said, glancing at her. "I don't see why. There's nothing here MPD can't handle."

"I don't doubt it. Have you had a case like this before?" I asked.

"Here and there, although residential neighborhood cases are rare. I think I recall handling two cold cases in the past year and before you ask, there are no similarities so far. One was under a flowerbed for twenty years and the husband definitely did it. The other victim had been killed by his housemate and when the housemate died years later, and the drywall was being ripped out prior to the sale, there he was, just hanging out in the wall cavity. Another clear-cut case. You probably read about them in the newspaper."

"The first one sounds familiar. Was there a trial?"

"Yeah, it went on for a while too. They ended up tearing the house down. No one wanted to buy it and with the homeowner in jail for the rest of his life, no one was maintaining it. I think the bank foreclosed on it eventually, and sold the land to developers who replaced it with condos."

"It is kind of creepy," I said.

"Yeah, but not altogether rare. Anyway, you might as well take off. I've got this covered. I'm waiting on the medical examiner to get here. I think the body will be declared dead," Garrett added with a chuckle.

"Very funny. I think I'm going to stick around. The Dugans might want to hire us to help them navigate all this."

"They'll be wasting their money. Hope you tell them that."

"We'll discuss the merits of the case with them before we take it, if it comes to that."

"And Mom?" asked Garrett.

"Can you talk to her?"

"Nope. She didn't call me."

I sighed. "What can you tell me? Is there anything you can say about the body, or the location, that stands out?"

"Nothing about the location. Just a regular house. I think I've known every owner since we were kids. There's been three? Maybe? I don't recall anything weird about any of them but who knows? I'll need to think about that and ask the neighbors if anyone remembers any of them or one of them seemingly disappearing. The backyard isn't exactly an odd location for concealing a body. It's convenient and the location isn't readily visible to other homes. The deceased might have a connection to one of the prior owners so once I get an identity, I'll be looking into that first."

"And the body?"

"I'd like the ME to confirm, but it's most likely a man in his fifties when he died, and it looks like he's been there for years."

"As in a few years? Or decades?"

"Hard to say. I'll need a better look at his clothing and the coroner will run tests, but it's definitely not clothing we would consider fashionable now."

"So he still looked… male?" I asked, trying to find words that had the intent of "partially intact body" but wasn't quite as gross to say. "Or you could tell from the skeleton size and appearance? That's impressive."

"I'm not *that* good at skeletal anatomy and this one has definitely been in the ground long enough to lose its features. No, as it happens, I pulled a wallet from the deceased's jacket pocket, which was a nice surprise."

"A wallet? Really? What was inside?"

"Driver's license, a photo, and a few other things. Some of the paper is very degraded but the license and photo were in a reasonable state."

"So you know who it… who *he*… is?"

"I know who the license belongs to. Whether that's the deceased is another matter."

"Can I see?"

Garrett's eyebrows knitted together and he gave me a look that suggested my question was utterly absurd. "No," he snorted.

"Please."

"No. I'm not showing my key evidence to random bystanders."

"I'm not random or a bystander. I'm your sister!"

"Guess I'll show Mom then too since she's my

mom." Garrett chuckled.

I gave him the sisterly death look. "I'm a PI too."

"You already said you haven't been engaged on the case. However, I have been, by virtue of the Montgomery Police Department."

"You know Traci asked me to babysit next week? She said you two are going to dinner and a concert."

"Yeah. And?"

"I might be busy that night." I stared him down, daring him to defy me further.

Garrett's face fell. "You wouldn't dare."

"Really, really, super busy," I said, turning my gaze to check my nails. They looked surprisingly nice given the evening's events.

"Are you really trying this?"

"And I probably misplaced the craft kit I was going to bring around for the kids." I shrugged nonchalantly.

Garrett narrowed his eyes. "I can show you *something*," he said.

I returned my attention to him and held back the grin. "Okay!"

Garrett reached into his pocket and pulled out a couple of plastic baggies. He shuffled the packets in his hand and held one out to me. I took it, peering at the contents in the darkening night. The photo was rumpled around the edges and peeling in the lower left corner but the image was clear enough despite some fading. Two men standing together; the older had his arm around the younger and both smiled at the camera. The older man wore a tweed sports coat, the younger a denim jacket slightly too big for his shoulders, a patch on the chest pocket. Their eyes were a similar shape and there was something familiar in the shape of their mouths.

"The photo was in the wallet," he said.

"They look like father and son. Or maybe uncle and nephew. Definitely a family resemblance."

"That's what I thought."

"Could the body be the older man? Or the younger?"

"I don't know but I'm guessing the older from the clothing in the grave."

"There's something sort of familiar about the younger man, like I've seen him somewhere."

Garrett brightened. "Really?"

I shook my head, uncertain. "I don't know... maybe."

"If he lived here years back, could you have hung out?"

I shook my head. "No, definitely not. He's not someone I was friendly with. I'd recognize him if that were the case. I can't put my finger on it except that he seems familiar." I thought about it for a moment. "Maybe it's the patch on the jacket. It looks like it might be a high school's emblem."

"It's not local. I would recognize it."

"Same. Those jackets were popular back when I was in high school. All the boys had them. The patches were sewn on."

"Is that a regional fashion choice or was it a thing? I don't remember having one."

"You were long out of high school by the time I was a student," I reminded him. "I think it was a generational thing, not regional. Sorry. I know that doesn't help narrow it down."

"It gives me a time period to look at. This kid would be in his mid-thirties now. That makes the older guy, let's see—" Garrett paused in thought while I took the opportunity to count on my fingers "—Sixties or seventies now at a guess, maybe a little either way. I'm going to run both their faces through missing persons, but missing adult white males aren't exactly a rare thing so I'll be surprised if I get anything beyond whittling the numbers down to a few thousand."

"Maybe you'll strike it lucky with DNA or the skeleton has a titanium plate or something like that with a serial number."

"Maybe," agreed Garrett.

I studied the photo again. "I still think there's something familiar about the younger one. Could he have played on a sports team perhaps? Like, his school team came to play our school in a tournament? He's cute." But even as I said it, it didn't feel right. I turned the baggie over, hoping something might be written on the back of the photo but there was nothing, not even a printer's mark. "What else did you find?"

"I think I've told you enough," he said, scooping the baggie from my hand and depositing it in his pocket, "given that you're a mere bystander."

"Lieutenant!" A woman hopped out of the ME's van and jogged across to us. She held overalls in her hand, along with booties. Two men followed her, carrying lights and more equipment. "Where do you want us?" she asked.

"Follow me," said Garrett, starting to step away.

"Call when you have some information," I said.

"Unlikely," snorted Garrett. He stopped and turned back to me, leaning in. "You're not on the case, remember? Don't you have something better to do than hang around here? Maybe something to do with multiple thefts." He sucked in his cheeks and held his lips firm but I knew from his amusement he'd heard about my calamities earlier. Terrific.

"I solved my most recent case and the thieves were caught red-handed. Not quite as exciting as Maddox's jewel heists unfortunately."

Garrett stilled. "Say again."

"Jewel heists. He didn't say who or what, just that he's looking into it."

"Well, that's interesting."

"Isn't it?"

"No, I meant... that's *interesting*."

"Yeah, you said." Then I caught the hint of something else, something Garrett hadn't told me. "Why?" I asked, my eyes narrowing.

"Because when I extracted the wallet from the deceased's jacket pocket, I also found this," said Garrett. He pulled another plastic packet from his pocket containing what looked like a scrunched cotton handkerchief. He opened his palm and shook the bag.

Several jewels, shiny in the moonlight, tumbled out.

CHAPTER FIVE

"Are they real?" I asked as I gazed at the array of cut diamonds, sapphires, emeralds and a very large ruby, that now lay clustered in Garrett's open palm. The stones were mesmerizing, their beauty not at all diminished despite being buried in the dirt for so long.

"If not, they're excellent fakes."

"So, they could be paste? It's hard to tell the difference. I'm not sure I could."

"Me neither. At least, not without knowing what I'm looking for, but an expert can easily determine their authenticity and there's a world of difference in price."

"If they're fake, they could be bought online or at any craft store. But if they're not..." I reached for one but Garrett moved his palm, leaving my fingers pinching the air.

"If they're not, I can't begin to imagine how much these are worth." Garrett wrapped the jewels in the cloth and slipped the package into a plastic baggie that he tucked back into his pocket. "I'll need to get them appraised."

"We had a jeweler client a few months back. I could ask if they would do it, or if they know someone who will."

"Thanks. I'll need to check with the department first in case we have an approved expert, but I might take you up on that."

"I can't believe you showed me the jewels, and not the driver's license."

"I think I showed you out of sheer surprise, although I'm not sure why anything you say surprises me. I must have had a senior moment."

"Lieutenant?" At the fence line, the ME was halfway into her white suit and pulling the upper half over her shoulders. Lights had been set up in the yard and her deputy was assembling a canopy over the body. "Would you like to join us?" she asked.

"Gotta go," said Garrett, abruptly turning on his heel.

"But..." I started to protest, but he was already gone, leaving me hovering by myself with the uniformed officer eyeing me uncertainly. I waited a moment, watching the ME and her colleagues zip closed the canopy sides, completely removing the burial site from view. That had to be a good thing because along with the arrival of Garrett and the ME came several bystanders and the steady hub of low, excited, chatter was growing. With every passing minute, news was spreading and it was only a matter of time before the mawkish masses showed up to gawk.

I moved around a couple of neighbors who lived down the street and headed for Solomon and my mom. "Where are the Dugans?" I asked.

"One of the officers took them inside to pack a bag. They've decided to get a hotel for the night," said Solomon.

"I said they could stay with me and your father but they were adamant they didn't want to put us out," said Mom.

"Sensible on all counts," I said, imagining how my mother's interrogation would go once she had the Dugans in her home. I could already imagine the Dugans' shell-shocked faces tomorrow morning. "What did they have to say about Garrett's questions?"

"Nothing unexpected came up. He asked them about their home ownership, the renovations, who had access to the site, who were the previous owners. Where did they previously live, where did they grow up. Everything we would ask."

"He's a very good detective," said Mom, looking pleased.

"What about you?" asked Solomon, addressing me.

"Lexi tries her best and we're very proud of her too," said Mom.

"Thanks, Mom." I restrained the sigh threatening to leak out.

"Lexi is an excellent investigator but I actually meant what had she found out from Garrett," said Solomon.

"Oh," said Mom. "*Oh*. Of course. What did you find out, darling?" She patted me on the arm and I jumped.

"Garrett found a few things on the body that could help with the identification. He wouldn't show me everything," I said, skirting around the big reveal as I tried to brush off her hand. That would be something I told Solomon later when my mother wasn't hovering and ready to tell the entire neighborhood, no matter what she said.

"Figures," said Solomon.

"It's so nice of your brother to help you out," said Mom. "He always was a good boy. So smart. No wonder he's made such a career for himself."

I ignored that. "So what do we do now?" I wondered.

"I've left our cards with the Dugans and suggested they call us tomorrow if they want to, after they've thought things over. For now, I think we should go home and resume our evening plans," said Solomon.

"You don't want to stay and watch the body being exhumed?" asked Mom. "I only saw part of the skeleton. I wonder how long it'll take to dig out the rest? Or do you think they dig it out with tiny spades and brush it off with toothbrushes like they do on archeology shows? I wonder if the adult education center runs an archeology course? I almost finished making my basket."

"We can only see the tent," pointed out Solomon. Two men brushed past us, craning their heads to see. "Plus, it's drawn attention."

"Such busybodies," said Mom, without irony as she continued to stare. "Rubbernecking like that isn't a real-life tragedy in there."

Solomon raised his eyebrows just barely and I held back a smile. "We'll walk down the street with you, Mom," I said.

"No need. I'm staying. The Dugans need to know they have a friend," she said, folding her arms and planting her feet like we were about to tackle and carry her off the field.

"Okay," I said, and turned to leave with Solomon.

"Wait! You're really going?" Mom's face fell.

"We are. There's nothing we can do and we haven't been officially hired. For that matter, we haven't even accepted the case. So we're going home. We have stuff to do."

"Oh. *Oh!*" Mom's wink was exaggerated and I wasn't dignifying that with any further comment. Instead, I took Solomon's hand and headed down the street to the car.

"Do I want to know why your mother winked at you like she was having a stroke and couldn't control her features anymore?" Solomon asked as we got into the car.

"You do not."

"I thought not. It's kind of a turnoff."

"You said you didn't want to know! See what happens when you think about it!" I threw my hands in the air, exasperated. So much for baby-making if one half of the team was in a timeout thanks to my mom.

"I'll be in the mood by the time we get home." Solomon smiled.

"How?" I wasn't sure I'd be in the mood again this decade.

"I'm a man."

"Then drive and prove it."

"Prove I'm a man?" Solomon glanced at me, as if he wanted to know if I genuinely expected him to do such a thing. I didn't. I knew he was a man. He'd proved it sufficiently. As for the promised enthusiasm? I was eager to see that evidenced.

"Don't be pedantic," I said and pointed ahead, away from the flashing police lights, the corpse, and most importantly, my mom. "Let's go!"

~

I yawned a near jaw-disengaging yawn and reached for the coffee Delgado had plonked on my desk only moments ago. "Late night?" he asked, eyeing me warily.

"Something like that," I said, and yawned again before I could even put the mug to my lips. After an enthusiastic evening where Solomon had definitely been the man, I'd subsequently had a poor sleep, amid constant thoughts of corpses and jewels whirring in my mind. Then there was the boy staring into the camera. Who was he?

I'd given up on sleep around five AM and lay there, wishing for the day to start, which just went to show how out of sorts I felt.

"Cranky?" asked Delgado.

"Nope, just tired."

Now it was almost nine, and Solomon had been called out only minutes after arriving at the agency, leaving me alone with Delgado, and an assortment of tasks to research.

Behind me, the door crashed open and I glanced over my shoulder to see my fellow PIs, Steve Fletcher and Matt Flaherty, walk in, carrying brown paper bags that emitted a tantalizing scent.

"Why do you both look so pleased?" I asked.

"We got bacon sandwiches to go," said Fletcher.

"And the counter girl flirted with me," said Flaherty.

"She asked if you wanted sugar for your coffee."

"She said I was sweet already." Flaherty's

smugness increased.

"She gave you the check," said Fletcher.

"She did it *flirtatiously*," said Flaherty. "She looked me dead in the eye as she slid it towards me. I've still got it." He flexed his biceps.

"The receipt?" I asked.

"No. *It.*" He pumped his arms again.

"Where's the boss?" asked Fletcher.

"Called out," I told them as they dropped into the seats at their cluttered desks and began unwrapping their rolls.

Delgado followed with, "Are you off the warehouse surveillance case?"

"As of today. The youths causing all the trouble got arrested and the warehouse is officially open for business. They've got a clean-up crew in there today making it right before they move their people in next week. Plus, they hired a team from us for 24-hour security until they get their own guys hired. We're helping them vet the applicants," explained Flaherty. He stretched out his leg, rubbed his hip and grunted.

"Pain?" I asked.

"Both of us," said Flaherty, thumbing in his partner's direction. "It's all that sitting in the car, not moving beyond reaching for snacks or binoculars. We're a pair of stiff, old dudes."

"Didn't stop you bigging up your duty wounds to the waitress," said Fletcher with a snort. "I thought you were going to pull out a medal."

"I'm saving that for next time," said Flaherty. "Can't wow her with all my stuff in one go."

Since both men had been injured in the call of duty — Fletcher taking bullets in his CIA days while busting a drug cartel, Flaherty in his former life as a police detective — I saw no reason for them not to be proud of their service. Plus, I'd noticed both had been moving sorely over the past weeks, and since Fletcher had been even more stony-faced than usual, it was nice to see them joking around.

"Did you hear about that body found last night in West Montgomery?" asked Flaherty. "Some guy got a fright digging up a body in his yard."

"It happened on my parents' street," I said. "Solomon and I talked to the homeowners."

"Your mom called Serena late last night and now she wants your parents to move to our neighborhood," said Delgado. "I'm not against that per se but it seems an overreaction. She's already sent your parents several listings in the area."

"Don't tell her about granny suites," I said and Delgado paled.

"Did we get hired?" asked Fletcher. "I gotta admit, I'd like to take a crack at a case like that. It's like those cold cases on TV or that new-fangled radio thing everyone keeps talking about."

"Radio thing?"

"Podblasts."

"Podcasts?" I asked.

"That's right. Some journalist or snoopy citizen goes investigating a cold case no one can remember and unveils the story. There's some wild stuff and they make crazy money. We should do one."

"I'm not sure anyone would listen to two guys like us talking about cracking cases," said Flaherty.

"Who said anything about it being you and me? I was thinking me and Lexi," said Fletcher.

Flaherty stopped chewing. "Why Lexi?"

"She brings in the sexy. She brings in the pep.

People want to listen to that," said Fletcher with a shrug.

"It's true," I said. "I do bring the sexy."

"She brings in the crazy," said Flaherty.

Delgado snorted and turned back to his laptop. I wasn't sure which bit he was responding to and if I wanted to know.

"Did you not see the way the counter girl looked at me?" asked Flaherty.

"She wanted a big tip," said Fletcher. "What'dya say, Lexi? You want to collaborate on a cold case podblast-thing and then tell the public all about it for money?"

I was saved from answering that by answering the desk phone, and cut from their view as Delgado got up and walked past.

"It's Jim," said the doorman, as if I wouldn't know. He'd worked in the building for years and I was half convinced he lived here too. "I've got a Mr. and Dr. Dugan here asking to speak with you. They say they don't have an appointment but that you know them."

"I do," I said. "Send them up to the interview rooms and I'll meet them there."

"You got it," said Jim and hung up.

"The owners of that dead body just walked in," I told them as I stood.

Fletcher got to his feet and punched the air. "We're in business."

"Who said you're invited?" I asked.

Fletcher pretended to be shocked, then hurt, as he turned to Flaherty then Delgado, who was standing in the boardroom doorway, his arms crossed, watching us all with amusement. "Do you remember when she was new and eager to prove herself and barely said boo to a goose? Now look at her. Practically telling me to sit down," he said.

"Sit down. You're in pain," said Flaherty.

"True," said Fletcher as he sat with a wince. "I think I need a massage or physiotherapy."

"Or a new body," said Flaherty.

"That too."

I left the three men together and jogged down the stairs, arriving as the elevator doors opened and the Dugans stepped out. Both looked tired but they'd taken effort with their appearance. Pete was clean-shaven and his striped t-shirt and jeans were pressed. Carrie wore a floral summer dress, minimal makeup, and her dark blond hair was tied in a loose bun. For the first time, I noticed the rounded bump of her abdomen.

"Thanks for seeing us. I wasn't sure if you would as we weren't exactly at our best last night," said Carrie.

"You'd had a shock. I wouldn't expect you to be at your best, Dr. Dugan, but you were nothing but polite," I said. "Come through and you can tell me more about any developments." I led them to the nearest interview room, a small room with little more than a table, chairs and a console, which held stationery and paperwork.

"Oh, Carrie, please. We're really not ones for formalities," said Carrie, continuing, as she dropped into a chair. "Your mom was so kind to stay with us until we could leave. She really was insistent that we stay at her house overnight but we decided on a hotel. We thought we needed space to really decompress and talk."

"Sensible choice," I said. "Have you been back to the house yet?"

"No," said Pete. He took the seat next to his wife and sat, folding his arms, his discomfort evident. "We called Lieutenant Graves this morning and he said they took the body away last night but the police needed more time in the yard for their investigations. I guess they want to check to see if anything else was buried with the body."

"Or if there are any more bodies," said Carrie, pulling a face.

"Do you think that's a possibility?" I asked.

"I don't know what to think! If you asked me this time yesterday if I thought there was any body at all, I would have laughed in your face and said there was nothing but weeds in the yard."

"What if there *are* more bodies?" asked Pete.

"Let's find out before we make any decisions," I said. There was no point worrying the Dugans further, although I knew they would no matter what I said, until there was conclusive evidence as to what happened.

"I keep having the horrible thought that we bought a serial killer's burial ground," said Carrie.

"You'd think the price would have been reduced," said Pete, his joke falling flat as Carrie grimaced.

"I'm pretty sure that's not the case," I said. "I grew up down the street and I think someone would have noticed." Even as I said it, I struggled with the conviction. Plenty of serial killers lived in plain sight for years until they were caught. Their neighbors usually spoke of them as friendly, helpful people. Their victims couldn't speak at all.

"Plenty of other cases didn't get noticed," Carrie

persisted, echoing the thoughts I'd thought wise to keep to myself. "Look at all the times a serial killer got caught and all the neighbors said he was such a nice guy. People don't notice everything. We're all too busy with our own lives."

"I can make some calls and find out if there was any sign of strange behavior over the years," I said, hoping to reassure her. "I know it's hard but there's no point worrying about this. You can't control it. It's out of your hands. If anything worse comes up, we can deal with it then."

The Dugans exchanged a look and I thought both of their faces softened. "So you'll take the case?" asked Pete.

"It depends on what you'd like me to do," I countered. "What do you think we can do to assist beyond what the Montgomery Police Department is already doing?"

"I'm not sure I trust the police entirely... oh, I don't mean it exactly like that. It's just, I want to know *someone* believes us, right from the start. I'd like to know who the body is... *was*... and how it came to be in our yard," said Pete.

"And I'd like someone to work hard to prove it wasn't us," said Carrie. "I've heard about people being railroaded by the police. I'm not saying that's what will happen here, but I want to be sure we take all the precautions."

"If I take this case, I can't make any guarantees about what I'll find," I warned them, "but I think we can prove you have nothing to do with it. I can liaise with the police alongside, making my own inquiries to find out who the body once was and how it came to be in your yard. How do you feel about not liking the answers?"

"Fine by me since it's not personal," said Pete. "Any answers are better than none and I can't help wondering if the police will drop this on their cold case file as soon as any leads dry up. Then we'll always be known as the dead body house."

"It feels personal to have a body in our yard," said Carrie.

"It pre-dates us buying the house," her husband countered. "So it's not *personal* personal. There's no way this body is connected to either of us. I'd like our neighbors to know we had nothing to do with it. It's bad enough what our house will be known as without our names attached to it with suspicion."

"Let me get you the paperwork," I said, standing so I could reach over to the console where the paperwork was stashed in trays. I grabbed a pen and slid it across the table with the form. "If you can fill this in, and pay our retainer, we can get started."

"Is this going to be expensive?" asked Carrie. She glanced at her husband. I was sure this expense hadn't factored into their reno costs either.

"All cases have the potential to be," I said, since I wanted to be as honest as possible, "but we can assign limitations. The retainer will ensure I can make all the preliminary inquiries. Once I have that, we can meet again and go from there. If we're lucky, the police will be able to make a positive identification quickly and share their information, making the process quicker to rule you out. If there aren't any pertinent leads, I'll inform you and you can decide whether to continue or stop."

The Dugans exchanged another glance.

"Is there anything else you'd like to know?" I

asked.

"Well…" Carrie paused, and glanced at her husband. A small flash of guilt seemed to pass across her face. Then she took a deep breath. "Lieutenant Graves said something valuable was found with the body."

"I'm aware of that," I said.

"He showed us the jewels," said Pete, leaning in now, his eyes widening. "Just to confirm they weren't ours and that we didn't recognize them. *Obviously*, they're not, and I'm sure he knew that, but…"

"Could they be?" Carrie continued, leaning forwards, then seeming to correct her eagerness. "They were found on *our* property and Pete *did* find the body so does that make them ours? If no one else claims them?"

"Ahh," I said, leaning back in my chair to consider that. "I don't know what the laws are in regard to finding items like that so I'll look into it. I'm sure Lieutenant Graves told you they need to be authenticated. They might not be worth anything."

"It was just a thought," said Pete. "We don't think they'll be rightly ours but I figured we should check what with the discovery being on our property and all." His shrug was so carefully indifferent, I was sure he was more interested than he was trying to let on.

"I'll keep you updated," I said, standing as soon as Carrie finished writing out the paperwork, and passing it to her husband to co-sign. Then Pete handed me a check.

"Hardly ever use these things anymore," he said, flapping the checkbook. "I'm not sure I even know how to balance it. Everything is tap here, bank transfer there."

"I'll see you out," I said, "and call you as soon as I have any information."

"Thanks, we appreciate it."

"Are you staying at the hotel tonight too?" I asked as I walked them to the elevator.

"We thought it prudent to book another night," said Carrie. "You can call us on our cellphones anytime. I don't have mine on me at the hospital but you can leave a message or call Pete."

I agreed I would and once the doors had closed behind them and the elevator was descending, I headed back up to the PI's office.

"Where is everyone?" I asked Delgado when I found the office empty except for us. Delgado stood at the coffee machine, flicking a packet of sugar while he waited for the fresh pot to heat.

"They got called out to a case," he said. "Something new. How was your interview?"

"Good, the Dugans want us on the case. At first, I wasn't sure why they wanted our help when they could just wait for the police but then I figured they were nervous about getting accused of a crime."

"Do you think they did it?"

"No, it's unlikely, but people do like peace of mind and having their innocence proved unequivocally to themselves and everyone else."

Delgado narrowed his eyes. "But now you think it's something else?" he asked, shrewdly. "You don't think they want to simply clear their names?"

"I think they definitely want that but I think it mostly has something to do with the jewels found on the corpse," I said, filling him in on the scant details. "If they're real, they could be worth thousands. Maybe even more. I think the Dugans think they might have accidentally dug up a terrific payday."

"So the corpse is now the least of their worries?"

I thought about Pete's pretense at indifference, about Carrie's bright eyes as she casually tossed out the question. "I think its significance paled once they were shown the jewels."

"I'm not sure whether to admire their forward thinking or be grossed out by their avariciousness."

"Same here," I said, as I reached for my phone. "But I'd also like to know the answer to their questions."

CHAPTER SIX

"What's the news?" I asked when Garrett picked up the phone.

"Hello to you too," he said. "Let's see now. Mom and Dad are okay so far as I know. Patrick is taking a class for extra credit. Sam and Chloe both got on soccer teams. Traci is going for a girl's night out at the end of the month with her buddies and thinking of starting a book club, although I think it's just a ruse for drinking…"

"Fascinating stuff," I said, "but I'm calling about the case."

"Any case in particular?" Garrett asked a smidge too brightly.

"Ha ha."

Garrett turned serious. "I have fifteen homicides on my desk, which is kinda high. Three are slam dunks the spouses did it so I'm hoping for twelve by the end of the week, presuming no one else gets murderous," he said.

"I meant last night's case." I drummed my fingers

on the desk, trying not to fall for his attempt to wind me up. Delgado placed a second coffee in front of me and I gave him a thumbs up and mouthed "Thank you." He nodded and sat down at his own desk, concentrating on his laptop screen where he appeared to be slowly typing a report.

"And that would be…" Garrett trailed off.

"The Dugans hired me," I told him as I made a poor attempt at stifling a loud yawn. "I hope the case doesn't run into my babysitting time. Gosh, that would be just terrible but you know how these things go."

"Oh! The Dugans! Well, why didn't you say so? Yeah, that's an interesting case all right."

"They told me the remains were removed but they're concerned there might be more. Should they be worried?"

"Thankfully not. We had the cadaver dogs go over the site inside and out first thing this morning and they didn't pick up anything. I'm confident the body was hanging out solo."

"That's good news," I said, making a note.

"Unless you're an extroverted ghost," snorted Garrett.

I forced a laugh since buttering my brother up seemed in my best interests right now. "You're hilarious! What about a cause of death?" I asked.

"Unknown, as of yet. The ME thinks she'll get to preliminary findings tomorrow since they're currently low on stiffs as she already dealt with most of my prior cases. She'll need to clean the skeleton and…"

"Please don't tell me," I cut in, my stomach roiling at the thought of whatever gross things they had to do to a dirt-ridden, mostly-decomposed skeleton before they could examine it.

"I can tell you the driver's license was fake," said Garrett. "I took it over to a contact at the DMV. They said it was very good and suspect it was the work of a forger who was busted a few years ago."

"So no ID." My hopes dropped.

"Not yet but the ME intends to extract DNA from the bones and there's always dental and other markers to look for when she gets to that. Her best guess so far is male, forty to sixty years old, six feet tall, Caucasian."

"That fits with your estimate and the age on the driver's license."

"Which is still currently my best lead. I'm going to put in a request to interview the forger."

"You're being very forthcoming about all of this."

"Yeah." Garrett sighed. "I wasn't kidding about all those other open cases. My team is slammed. I'm intrigued by this one for the obvious reasons but the brass say it's not top priority given how long the body's probably been in the ground. They don't want to waste the manpower on a case as cold as this."

"I understand."

"So, with a whole bunch of enthusiasm…"

"I can hear it," I scoffed.

"Work with me here! *With a whole bunch of enthusiasm*, I would welcome your input in the case. With the caveat that there's no budget for this," Garrett finished quickly.

"Deal," I said. "How cold do you estimate the case to be?"

"I'm waiting on the ME for confirmation, but the remains indicate long past a decade to me. Perhaps two."

"So you're not looking at the Dugans as good for the crime?"

"Nope. It's pretty unlikely they're involved but I still need to run some checks on them. Unless something surprising comes up that narrows the death or the burial to the time frame of the period they owned the house, I'm not interested in them as my perps."

"They'll be pleased to hear that, but they would still like to be kept informed."

"Of course, and I will do that, although that seems like your job too. Of course, there is a big obvious problem with this case."

"That it's so cold?"

"Yeah. I can't say I remember much of ten-plus years ago beyond the big stuff. If that's the time frame we're looking at, it's going to be hard to track down potential witnesses, and even if they can be found, the chances of them remembering anything is remote."

"What about the jewels?" I asked.

"I showed them to the ME. She's not an expert but she took a look under a microscope and thinks they're real. She has no clue of the value other than, in her words, 'a lot.' Our listed consultant in Boston is away at a conference in California until next week."

"Do you remember I said we worked a case at a jeweler's a few months back? Why don't I ask the client to take a look? They could give you the information you need."

"That would actually be helpful, thanks."

"I'll call you back."

"Take your time. The body isn't going anywhere."

It took me a moment to find my jeweler contact's

details before I left a voicemail asking if they could consult on something urgently. I had barely set down the phone when it rang again.

"Hi, Lily."

"I. Cannot. Believe. You. Didn't. Call. Me," she seethed.

"Sorry? I should have texted last night and..."

"You should be! I have to find out from my own husband that my best friend fell through a ceiling! After being attacked! With Maddox! What happened to you?"

"Well, I saw the thieves during surveillance. Maddox and I followed them into the crawl space and then we had to hide and..."

"No, I got all that, except the bit about Maddox being there. Why was he there? Anyway, I meant, where's your girl code? Why didn't you call me immediately and tell me everything? Why does my husband get the juicy deets before me?"

"I had to get cleaned up. I was covered in hair products and a jar of sun-dried tomatoes. I needed a shower. Plus, Jord was there. He made the arrests."

"I bet you smelled nice. What a waste of a wash and cut."

"True, but the case is successfully closed. I just have to fill out the paperwork and I'm done."

"Do you think you'll get salon vouchers as a bonus?"

"Probably not. The salon was a mess when I left. I'm sorry I didn't call. I got preoccupied and..."

"I'm not done being mad at you yet!" snipped Lily.

"Oh. Sorry. Please continue," I said, waiting for it.

"You. Found. A. Skeleton. In. The. Backyard."

Lily's voice was low and staccato.

"Mom found it and it wasn't my backyard or hers," I clarified. "But yes, a skeleton was discovered. Mom called me and said it was an emergency. There wasn't time..."

"Did you drive over?"

"Solomon drove."

"Then you had time to call me! I would have ditched work for that! A body! And you left me out!"

"I was going to call you!"

"When?"

That was a good question. Technically, I hadn't lied, but I had neglected to call Lily. "As soon as I had more news to share," I said, skirting the truth. "I didn't want to give you just the basics."

"Your mom seems to have the basics."

I cringed at that. "That's right! I wanted to really clue you in beyond that."

"So what do you have?"

"Nothing," I admitted. "But Garrett is happy to officially work together so long as MPD doesn't have to pay our fee. He says it looks like the body has been there a long time. More than a decade, maybe even two. I don't remember anyone going missing from our street but I'm not sure I *would* remember. I'm not sure that the person would even be registered as missing if another occupant wanted to conceal the disappearance. Garrett's checking that out too."

"We've been friends for more than twenty years," said Lily. "I'm sure one of us would remember a big event like a missing persons case from your street. I remember when the dog went missing on the next block, and I remember that afternoon when Caleb Telsey got off the school bus but didn't go home and half the neighborhood went out searching for him."

"And they found him in Johnny Lombardi's basement eating ice cream and playing video games," I said, nodding as I remembered.

"Yeah. Caleb didn't even know he was missing! Imagine not knowing you're missing!"

"To be fair, he did know where he was. Just no one else did."

"You know what else I remember? When Mrs. Thurber threw all her husband's clothes out the window when she caught him playing hide the sausage with her cousin that time she got home from work early."

"I remember that too. She put all his books out on the lawn the next day and it rained. They all turned to mush and he cried."

"She yelled at him to get a new library card to go with his new life."

"We definitely would have remembered a man going missing," I decided. "Do you remember any of the people who lived in the end house?"

"The one with all the renovations? That's where they found it?"

"We're calling the corpse Roger," I said.

"Weird, but okay. No. I don't remember anyone from there. I suppose there's no reason for anyone to stand out unless we hung out at their house or they did something heinous. Did we ever hang out there as kids?"

"I'm pretty sure no, never."

"Then no kids our age twenty years ago and we didn't know anyone there when we became adults either," said Lily as I made a note. "I do remember that house going up for sale a few years ago. I remembered thinking it would make a great family home one day. Glad I didn't buy it! Who did?"

"Carrie and Pete Dugan. Carrie's pregnant and they have a little girl. They're in their thirties. She's a doctor at Montgomery General. Pete is a…" I pulled out the paperwork and ran my finger down the page. "Marketing director."

"I guess that rules them out. A doctor would dispose of a body better than that; plus, if it was buried during her medical boards, she'd be way too busy. Plus, I bet they have a five-year-plan. A plan that doesn't include buying the house where they historically buried Roger."

"I was ninety-five percent sure they didn't do it but when I hear you say it all out loud, I shoot up to ninety-nine percent. I think I need to plunder my family's memories and find out what everyone remembers. Between all of us, we should have all the decades covered although Garrett doesn't remember anything distinctive about the house or its occupants ever."

"Whoa! You're calling family dinner."

"I'll even cater if it makes them say yes quicker."

"I'll supply the booze. Let's get those lips loosened."

"I'll send out a message and get everyone together tonight. Your job is to accept and pressure everyone else too."

"I don't think it'll be hard. Everyone wants to talk about Roger."

My phone buzzed a message. Garrett was in touch with the forger's parole officer and he invited me to join the meeting. Then another message pinged through in reply from the jeweler suggesting I drop by whenever I liked.

"I have to go," I said, "I have leads to follow."

"Anything I can do?"

"Not yet. Let's talk later. I might need your help."

"Yahoo!" said Lily and disconnected.

I texted Garrett asking him when we could meet at the jeweler's and immediately the text bubble appeared. *Now*, was his brief message. I messaged the jeweler's, then shot out a family group text suggesting dinner. As the yeses came in quickly from Lily, then my mom, who said we could barbecue at her house, then a long, irritated text from Serena reminding us she had a young child and a business to run and couldn't drop everything on short notice — across the room Delgado sighed and put his phone down — but fine, they would make it but she wasn't bringing a dish, and I grabbed my purse.

"Looking forward to dinner!" I said to Delgado.

"You know she's just worried," he said, pausing his slow finger-stabbing at the keyboard.

"Of course, totally read between the lines," I agreed.

"And she'll be chomping at the bit to find out everything everyone knows about the body," he added.

This time, I grinned. Of course that was why she'd been so prompt in replying. "Then I'm sure she'll want to help too," I said.

Delgado paused. "Do you think she'll have information?"

"Despite how terrifying Serena is, I doubt she had anything to do with it."

Delgado breathed out a sigh of relief.

"You married her," I pointed out. "She's not all

bad."

"She's wonderful," he said, smiling now. "I'm not sure I'd put murder past her though."

"Is her ex causing problems?" I wondered.

"A little. He didn't turn up for two visitations in a row. Then Serena got a shirty email about how life doesn't revolve around her and he'd take Victoria on Saturday instead. She reminded him that he was the one who pestered her for the last two date changes. He said she was being pissy because he's getting married and she's jealous. She had to lie on the floor for a full hour."

I frowned. "Was she sad?"

Delgado shook his head. "No. She was laughing so hard she couldn't get up."

"The idea of anyone being jealous of Ted Whitman's life is pretty funny."

"Did you know Victoria isn't invited to the wedding? They're having it child-free apparently and then a two-week honeymoon in Bora Bora."

"She was so cute at your wedding."

"Wasn't she?" Delgado smiled, his entire face lighting up. "Alongside your sister, that little girl is the light of my life."

"I'm glad to hear it."

I headed out to my car, thinking how lucky we all were to get Tony Delgado married into the family. Plus, I was pleased that the family message group was now abuzz with dinner plans although tonight was apparently a no go so Mom had offered to host at the end of the week when everyone agreed they were free. Lily was right: the Roger gossip had spread like wildfire and everyone wanted an excuse to rubberneck. Fine by me. I was going to ride on their nosy coattails in search of answers.

~

The last time I'd seen Claudius Bridge, he'd been concerned about a light-fingered employee. Fortunately, after a week of undercover work, I'd solved his problem, much to his relief.

I'd found Claud to be warm and friendly, with a fine array of bow ties, and was happy that he'd agreed to help, not only on short notice but also with no information provided beyond requesting a valuation. By the time I got there, there was another message from Garrett to say he'd been briefly waylaid but was on his way so I headed inside the jewelry store to wait.

"We didn't think we'd see you again so soon," said Claud as he buzzed me into the shop.

"Me neither. How's Poppins?" I asked, looking around for the big red parrot that usually occupied a perch behind the counter.

Claud pointed and I glanced upwards just in time to see Poppins swoop from the ceiling fan, circle the room, then descend to land on my shoulder. She bobbed her head and Claud passed me a snack to feed her from a box he kept under the table.

"I'm intrigued about your case," he said. "Not least because I'm hoping it'll help me finish my career on a high note."

"Finish your career?"

"It's about time I retired. I'm seventy-two and my daughter has been talking about it for two years straight," he said. "My sister's husband just passed away and she's living a nice, albeit lonely, life in Florida. She suggested Poppins and I go join her. There's an apartment above her garage that I can stay in until I find a place of my own. My daughter is already out there with her husband and my nieces and nephews too. I don't see any of them coming back here so I thought I'd chase them and the weather. The sun, anyway. We'll see about the hurricanes."

"What happens to the shop now?"

"I'll put it up for sale at the end of the month. I own it outright and the apartments above, so, together with my house, I should get a nice sum to relocate with."

"I hope you have a wonderful new life."

"Thank you, dear. Now, my assistant is due back from her break any moment so when she gets here, we can go back to my office and you can tell me all about your case. It *is* a case, isn't it?"

"It is."

"How thrilling!"

Claud's assistant, Joanne, joined us, and after a minute of exchanging pleasantries, we headed into his office. The room was dark and cozy with a desk I knew had been inherited from Claud's father many years before, and a new ergonomic chair that he settled in, apologizing that any creaking came from him and not the chair.

On top of the filing cabinets was a small security system and a large monitor showing the shop front, the rear, and two angles of the shop. I'd barely gotten comfortable when a buzz sounded and we both turned our attention to the monitor playing in real time. "That's Garrett," I said, seeing my brother at the door. He flashed his badge before he was buzzed in. For Claud's benefit, I added, "Garrett is also known as Lieutenant Graves. We're working together on an unusual case and we need help with a valuation."

"And you thought of me? Well, I'm honored. Let me get my microscope and loupe," he added, drawing the microscope that sat on his desk closer before he reached into his drawer and pulled out a magnifying glass. As he laid it on his leather desk pad, Garrett appeared in the doorway.

"Lieutenant Graves," said Garrett, holding out his hand as he crossed the room. "Thanks for your help, Mr. Bridge. Has Lexi filled you in?"

"Only that you'd like a valuation as part of a case. I can assure you of the utmost discretion."

"I appreciate that," said Garrett. "It's an ongoing case. I also realize it's short notice so I appreciate you finding the time to assist here."

Claud turned on his desk lamp and indicated Garrett should take a seat. "I'm intrigued," he said. "Let's see what you have."

Garrett pulled the plastic bag from his pocket, the cloth package inside. He laid the bag on the desk, extracted the cloth wrap, then unwrapped it in his palm. The jewels spilled delightfully onto the desk pad. "The crime scene techs gave them a light scrub," he said as Claud plucked one of the small gems and held it under his magnifying glass. He placed it on the pad, picking up a second, then a third stone, lining them up as he went. Then he reached for a small blue stone, then a green, setting them all in a row, and finally the large ruby. "You scrubbed these?" he asked, gazing at it before looking up from the microscope, a trace of worry on his face for the first time.

"Not me, personally. The techs did," said Garrett. "They didn't leave any scratches. That's fortunate." Claud rested back in his chair, looking between us.

"Oh? Why's that? Are they real gemstones?" asked Garrett. "Are they worth anything?"

"I can confirm all those I picked up are real," said Claud, nodding. "I'd like to take a look at the rest but so far there are diamonds, sapphires, emeralds and this ruby. They've been cut and polished." He pointed to each with his forefinger as he spoke.

Garrett whistled. "Well, that's quite a find. What do you think they're worth?"

"I can't give you an absolutely accurate value just yet. I'd like to take a longer look, and call an associate whom I consider an expert, but so far, I'm going to estimate ten."

"Ten thousand dollars?" asked Garrett, his eyebrows rising. "Wow."

Claud shook his head slowly, then lifted his gaze to look across us before fixing it on Garrett. "Ten *million* dollars," he said.

CHAPTER SEVEN

"My colleague is being conservative," said Laura Reynolds as she placed the last gemstone on the leather pad. The smartly-dressed brunette had arrived within twenty minutes of Claud making the call and had been introduced as a fellow jeweler, and co-owner of a local family-run business. The vintage tennis bracelet she wore as her sole jewelry was understated but costly. Business must be good. "I want to run some calculations but I think your total value might be closer to twelve million. Maybe more if there's a good buyer for the ruby. The other stones are lovely and highly salable. The ruby, however, is a significantly large size, and a very attractive red color. Stones like it are rarely seen and would be competitive on any market."

"Twelve. Million. Dollars," said Garrett slowly, sounding as stunned as I felt. "I really thought you would both say they were paste. Here I am with them in my pocket and no security detail. Twelve *million* dollars."

"It's possible the ruby alone could double what we quoted you," said Laura. "It is rather remarkable."

"If they were paste, I'd still say you could get a good price for the costume jewelry market but these are the real deal," said Claud. He reached for a sapphire, holding the deep blue gemstone up to the light. "I hope it's understandable that I'm curious about their origins. You said it was a case? Where did you get them?"

"That's right. They were found during our investigation in a case I'm working on," said Garrett, his answer purposefully vague. I wondered if he would have been more forthcoming if the jewels were fakes, and if we weren't in an unsecured room with a fortune on the table. "Is there any way to ascertain their provenance? Or their ownership?"

"To an extent," said Laura. "I've really only taken a glance but if I spend a little more time, I would hope to pick up specifics in the gems' features. That would give me an idea of where they came from. The diamonds are easier. I can see inscription numbers laser-etched on most of them. The numbers will be registered and we can identify the true owner and the jewels' origins that way. I'm guessing you believe they're stolen?"

"That's my first deduction," said Garrett. "I can't think of any other legitimate reason for them to be on a person under the circumstances in which they were found."

"I can," chipped in Claud. "A commissioned jeweler or a jewel dealer would have a number of gems on hand. Plenty of people could transport such items entirely without notice, perhaps to another jeweler to set them."

"What if they were set in jewelry already? Could all the gems possibly have come from the same piece?" asked Garrett.

Both Claud and Laura shook their heads. "It would be a gaudy piece," said Claud. "Individually, the stones are excellent but there're just too many to make one item look balanced and attractive. Let's say it was a necklace. Due to the ruby's size, it would have to be set in the middle and even then, it's really too big. Then it would need to be framed by all the other gems and there aren't the right number to make it symmetrical. Plus, where's the gold it would need to be set in?"

"That's easily melted down," continued Laura. "But Claud is right, it wouldn't be a nice-looking piece. Expensive, yes, but not beautiful. Although sometimes the former matters to the purchaser more than the latter. Multiple pieces, yes. One single piece? I lean towards no."

"So the stones could have come from all kinds of jewelry? Rings? Earrings?" asked Garrett.

Laura cocked her head side-to-side, weighing the question. "I think the diamonds are certainly too big for stud earrings and a little too large for a tennis bracelet, but they could be for rings or necklaces. Drop earrings too, I suppose. The ruby could be used for a necklace or pendant or it could even be for a tiara. I would want a stone like this to speak for itself without any accompaniments. That would be superbly dramatic." She plucked it from the mat and peered at it again through the microscope. Then she repeated the action with two of the diamonds before meeting our gaze again. "As it happens, I don't see any kind of marks that indicate the jewels have been set into anything yet."

"That's interesting," said Claud. "Perhaps the suspect in your case had only recently acquired them."

"Where would you go to buy jewels like this? Cut but not set?" I asked.

"There are any number of jewel merchants all over the world. New York, Amsterdam, London. And more," said Laura. "They might not have even come from the same dealer. The ruby does stand out due to its large size so maybe that dealer was more of a specialist but I couldn't discount anyone. Plus, there could be independent traders with gems from less scrupulous sources."

"Blood diamonds?" I asked.

"Ahh, you've heard of them," said Laura, nodding. "Then you know what a terrible trade that is."

"I only know as much as was in the Leonardo DiCaprio film of the same name," I said. "I got pretty turned off sparkly things after watching that."

"I have no idea what you're talking about," said Garrett, glancing between us.

"Blood diamonds come from nations in conflict zones, or with extremely poor labor and human rights standards. The money from those stones can be used for terrorism, war, all kinds of bad things. We refuse to sell anything of that origin at my store," explained Laura. "It's illegal anyway. We only deal in ethically-mined stones now but like many jewelers who've been retailing for years, we've not been able to prove the source of everything we've sold in the past and there's no way to be sure with vintage pieces. Since I can see numbers on some of the diamonds, you'll get a better idea of where they originated when you trace them. I can record the numbers for you?"

"I'd appreciate it, thanks," said Garrett. "Do you ever hear of jewel merchants getting robbed?"

"It's not unheard of but they wouldn't be easy to steal from. Almost all would have safes, guards, and high security," said Claud. "Like us, they wouldn't go out of their way to advertise either their security or their wares. Is there anything else we can help you with, Lieutenant?"

"No, you've been very helpful," said Garrett, "Can I call you again if I need to?"

"Take my card and call anytime," said Claud. "I'd like to know what you find out, if it's no trouble? I don't often get asked to consult on a police case."

"Same. Would you mind if I did some research on the ruby?" asked Laura. "It's such a beautiful stone. I'm really quite curious about it."

"If you can be discreet, and promise to share your findings, then please go ahead," agreed Garrett. He waited a few minutes for Laura to finish transcribing her list, which she handed to him with a smile. Then she had him watch carefully as she returned every stone to the pouch in which he'd brought them, adding that she would email a valuation to us both. "I'll see myself out," said Garrett as he tucked the pouch into its plastic baggie and then into his pocket, like he was carrying marbles instead of a fortune.

"I'll show you out," said Claud. "And might I suggest you find a very strong safe."

"Thanks for helping on such short notice," I said to Laura as we shook hands.

"I'm glad Claud called. It's really a shame to hear he's retiring and I'm sure he'll love having consulted on your case as a last hurrah. It's been an interesting afternoon. I hope I get to know more about the jewels! In my twenty-plus years as a jeweler, I've never seen anything quite like it. I have a feeling there's an interesting story behind it all." Laura smiled and I couldn't help warming to her enthusiasm.

Although I privately agreed with her that something interesting was going on, I didn't add *and a sad story*. Clearly, Garrett wanted to limit the information about the case and I wasn't sure how Laura would feel about the jewels being found buried with a body under dubious circumstances. That would give most people the ick.

When Garrett and I stepped out of the shop onto the sidewalk, he blinked in the midday sunlight and his hand went into his pocket. "I feel nervous carrying this stuff," he said. "I'm going to take Claud Bridge's advice and return these to the evidence locker. That's the strongest safe I know."

"Are you sure? A lot of people have access to it."

"I think keeping this as quiet as possible is in our best interests. The fewer people who know about the gems, the better. People won't go looking for what they don't know about. Plus, I'm going to double seal the box. However our guy died, someone took great pains to conceal the body. I wonder if they knew what he had on him."

"We don't even know if this is a crime yet. Although it probably definitely is," I finished, my stream of consciousness bringing me around to the glaringly obvious: people didn't randomly get buried in backyards with a pocketful of priceless jewels.

"I see no other plausible reason why a person would carry upwards of twelve million in cut jewels and be buried under dubious circumstances," said

Garrett in echo of my thoughts. He indicated I should walk with him to his car. When we reached it, he paused to lean against it. "What I don't understand is why the jewels weren't removed from the body prior to burial. That seems strange."

"It seems like something I'd want to snatch," I said. "Perhaps whoever buried him didn't have time to search his pockets."

"They had time to bury him in a residential neighborhood. Although that seems more like opportunity rather than design. It might have technically been a shallow grave but it was deep enough to lay undiscovered all this time. It might not have been discovered for even longer without the Dugans' landscaping."

"Then perhaps the gravedigger intended to return at a later date and retrieve the jewels? And for some reason, they couldn't?"

Garrett rubbed his chin. "Also possible," he said, nodding.

"What if they didn't know he had the jewels on his person? Or maybe it's not about them at all?"

"You think it could just be about getting rid of this guy?"

"It could be. I don't think we should rule it out. Oof," I squeaked as a group of young men jostled past. When I stepped back, one of Garrett's hands was pressed against his pocket. The other was hovering over his gun.

"Get in," he said, and pulled open his door. I hurried around the other side and got into the passenger seat before Garrett hit the lock button.

"When did you say the ME was examining the body?"

"Some time this week."

"What are the odds that Roger died by natural causes?"

"Low. If that happened, a person would either call an ambulance or they'd disappear and leave him to be found by someone else. No. Someone made an effort to conceal the body. They didn't want him found."

"Perhaps they wanted him to appear alive so they could claim benefits in his name? Or something else?"

"Also possible. As soon as I've logged these jewels back into evidence, I'll search our databases for anyone missing from the jewel trade. It's a long shot but you never know. It might narrow the search from thousands of missing Caucasian male adults." Garrett's phone beeped and he glanced at it then tucked it back into his pocket. "Gotta go. One of my detectives is ready to make an arrest on another case. What're your plans?"

"I'm going to visit Alice and see if she knows Carrie Dugan. I'd like some background info on my client. Pete Dugan works from home so he doesn't have any colleagues to quiz," I said, hopeful that our sister-in-law would have some useful information.

"Alice and Carrie know each other?" Garrett was surprised.

"Maybe. Carrie's a doctor, Alice is a nurse. Even if they don't know each other personally, they work at the same hospital so Alice might know some gossip."

"The Dugans are in their thirties. If this guy was killed twenty years ago, that makes them teenagers when it happened."

"Lily said even in their twenties, Carrie would have been wrapped up in medical boards."

"True. Do you know how long they've been

together?"

"You mean could they have been teens or young adults bonded through a murder in their youth? This isn't a teen horror movie, Garrett."

Garrett laughed. "Weirder shit has happened. Maybe one is lying to the other. I still don't buy it though. I think they're innocent. All the same, let me know what you find out." Garrett's phone buzzed again and he raised his eyebrows. "This is the parole officer overseeing our forger. He says they're due a check-in at four today. We can drop in and he won't alert him in advance. After that, we'll need to wait another week."

"I can make time this afternoon," I said, knowing I would miss out if not.

"I'll call later with an address."

I hopped out, waving to Garrett as he promptly joined the traffic, and jogged back to my car.

Alice answered after only a few rings. "Are you at work today?" I asked.

"I just finished my shift. Why? Are you nearby?"

"Not far. I wanted to ask you a couple questions."

"I have to run errands so let's talk on the phone. Unless it can wait until later?"

"Now's good," I said, watching Laura Reynolds exit the jewelers and head down the street. "Do you know a Carrie Dugan? She works at the hospital."

"Hmm. Yes, I think so. She's a doctor. Is she pregnant? Blond?"

"That's her."

"What did she do?"

"Probably nothing. Did you know she bought the end house on my parents' street?"

"The one with the body that just got dug up?

Wow."

"News travels fast."

"Your mom called me this morning."

"Please tell me she didn't ask you to take its pulse."

Alice laughed. "No, she didn't. She just wanted to make sure we prepared the kids so they wouldn't be scared. For the record, they won't be scared. Rachel's been watching surgery videos online and seems to have nerves of steel. I see a medical career in the future. So what do you want to know about Dr. Dugan?"

"I just wondered what your impressions were of her?"

"I don't know her that well but she's nice, polite, fairly popular with the staff and the patients too. She's got a good bedside manner. They don't teach that in medical school. I'm not sure what else I can tell you. There's never been any complaints that I've heard of."

"Do you know anything about her background? Did she grow up here?"

"I don't think so. I got the feeling she might have spent some of her childhood overseas. Her husband grew up here though. I think they met on vacation one year." A car door opened and shut and Alice continued, "That's real bad luck to find a body in the yard. Your mom said Dr. Dugan's husband dug it up and got quite the fright."

"He did. So nothing stands out about Carrie Dugan?"

"Not that I can think of. She's always seemed nice to me, and the times I recall her mentioning her husband, she's always been complimentary. I think he came into the ER once. They seemed a nice pair but I can't say I was observing them particularly. I'm sorry, I don't feel like I'm giving you what you're looking for."

"No, you are. This is helpful, thank you."

"I'll see you at dinner?"

"Absolutely."

"I wish it could be sooner but with the kids' schedules and my shifts, we just can't until the weekend."

"I understand."

"Don't go solving the case without our help!"

That call done, and nothing untoward uncovered, I headed back to the office. Delgado was still there at his computer and apparently, I'd missed Solomon by minutes, which was disappointing, yet also useful since I wouldn't be distracted by him.

As I walked through the door, Mom texted me suggesting lunch, which I was sure was simply a politer way of requesting information.

Settling behind my desk, I spent an hour perusing the Dugans' lives and found nothing to suggest they were secret homicidal maniacs who'd started out in their teen years. If anything, they were fairly dull.

A starter home was purchased shortly after they got married six years ago with a gifted down payment from Carrie's parents. The small Harbridge apartment was sold and they made a good chunk of money to put into the new house and renovations. They had rented a small apartment while the bulk of the work was undertaken over the past two months and had given up the lease only last week. I wondered how much they regretted that decision now that their backyard was a crime scene.

Carrie had been to medical school on the West Coast and a few public comments on her social media pages mentioned growing up in Europe before returning to the States in her mid-teens. Pete worked in marketing since graduation and set up his own agency last year. He had attended my old high school, then college locally.

No debts, drove older cars, their last few vacations had been a splurge honeymoon to the Caribbean and then they'd taken several short city and beach trips over the years. There was a charge to a storage unit taken out when they moved into the rental, which I figured had to be for their household goods before they could transfer them to their new home. Nothing extravagant. No wild hobbies. Pete played squash. Carrie liked horseback riding. No arrest records or poor credit markers. They seemed like two regular people.

So how had a body gotten onto their property?

Had they really been so unlucky to simply discover it?

I had to wonder if someone had decided to play a cruel trick on them but it seemed unlikely. Their social media was minimal and non-confrontational. Their relationships with friends and family weren't showing any glaring red flags. Their finances showed no signs of stress.

No, the incident had to pre-date them.

They were just the unfortunate finders of a decades-old secret.

I had to give them peace of mind, just like they asked, but they also wanted answers. Unfortunately, I didn't have any to give.

Before I headed out, I called Garrett.

"I don't have anything for you," he said, "but if you want my thoughts on whether the Dugans did it, I'm still leaning no. I ran a couple of checks and nothing."

"Same here. Everything they've told me so far is verifiable. They didn't own the property until three months ago and haven't even lived in it during that time. It doesn't look like Carrie moved to town until eight years ago, which rules her out as a youthful murderer."

"The ME is saying the body was definitely there before that. I'm not wasting any more time on the Dugans' histories. No hits on missing jewel merchants that fit the profile either. I'm looking at prior homeowners and hoping there weren't any gaps in residencies."

"Gaps mean anyone could have access," I guessed.

"Bingo, and then the case goes from cold to icy."

"Did you speak to the neighbors last night?"

"Some. Mostly for reassurance that they don't have any need to worry. I'll circle back around to them soon when I have a little more info."

"Mom can probably fill us in on the details. I'm thinking of heading over there. She texted me and suggested lunch."

"Now?" asked Garrett.

"Yes. It's lunch time." Right on cue, my stomach rumbled.

"I'll join you."

"Cool."

"Hey, Maddox just called me before you. He was asking some weird questions."

"Oh?" I frowned.

"Apparently, he heard about the jewels on our body. Did you tell him?"

"No, but he has plenty of contacts in MPD," I reminded him. "He was a detective long enough."

"Yeah, I guess. I've been trying to avoid news of the jewels getting out just yet until we figure out exactly where they came from and who might be looking for them. The last thing we need are fortune hunters turning up at the front desk trying to make a claim."

"I don't think Maddox will tell anyone. What was weird about his questions?"

"Nothing about the questions particularly. More about *how* he was asking them. Like he was really interested but didn't want to appear that way. He was less interested when I said the body was a man and how long it had been there. Anyway he says he's going to Germany soon so he'll be out of my hair."

"Germany?"

"I didn't ask. I assumed it was work-related."

"Good to know. Okay, see you at Mom and Dad's soon?"

"See you there," Garrett agreed and disconnected.

CHAPTER EIGHT

Like Garrett, my next best step seemed to be centered on the house's history. I hadn't made much note of the residents at the end of the street over the years, less so once I'd moved into my own place. I was sure I recalled sale signs but I couldn't be sure when. As a teen, I'd mostly been interested in the immediate neighbors or the homes where Lily and I had friends and often hung out.

Yet it seemed my time might be best served knocking on some doors and asking what the immediate neighbors remembered. Garrett planned on doing the same thing, but I could narrow the search. Plus, I could drop in on Mom and Dad directly afterwards.

As I headed to the neighborhood, myriad ideas whizzed through my mind but they were less about Roger the corpse, and more leaning towards the person who'd buried him. Was it one person or more? Would a woman be strong enough to dig a grave, move the body, and conceal it? Or was our mystery gravedigger more likely to have been a man? Why didn't the neighbors notice a missing neighbor? Did the digging happen at night? Were the residents known for night gardening, or had the neighbors turned a blind eye?

By the time I parked at the end of the block — a squad car parked outside, and crime tape spanning the downed sections of fence — I had more questions than answers.

I started with the immediate neighbor but there was no answer and the house seemed still and lifeless. The mailbox had a number of items inside and the small, soft parcel on the porch carried a date from four days ago. All the blinds and drapes were shut. I tried the house on the other side of the empty one but the bespectacled man told me in halting English that they had lived there just five years. Another dead end.

Returning to the end house, I crossed the road and entered the yard of the opposing end house.

"Hello?" The woman who answered the door had a sweep of white hair, a floral housecoat, and was using a walker.

"Hi, I'm looking for some information about the house over there," I said, pointing.

"Oh, yes? The detective last night told me what happened. I sat up and watched them take the body. Imagine that! A body! Probably the most exciting thing to happen in this neighborhood in forever." Her crinkled eyes lit up.

"Have you lived here long?"

"Oh, yes. My husband and I bought this house in the seventies. Brought up our children here and now they bring their children to visit."

"That's lovely. You must remember some of the residents across the street?" I asked, struggling to recall any children. Perhaps they'd been my older siblings' contemporaries, not mine.

"Can't say I was friendly with any of them beyond saying hello. We were good friends with the other side but they're gone now."

"Moved away?"

"In a word, heaven."

"I'm sorry."

"There's a lovely couple of girls there now. I think they're best friends. Raising their kids together too! The kids call both of them Mom. Isn't that the nicest?"

"Of course," I agreed.

"Very over familiar with each other," she added, frowning. "Always cuddling. Sorry, what were you asking?"

"If you remembered any of the residents from that house," I said, pointing to the house across the street.

"No, can't say I do. I think the house changed hands a few times."

"Nothing stands out? No fights? Or anything like that?"

"Maybe. I suppose everyone fights some time, but, no, can't say I noticed anything. I'm not sure I'd remember at my age. I'm not sure what I had for breakfast." Footsteps sounded behind her and young woman in a nurse-style uniform, a navy tabard embroidered with "Home Help" came out.

"It's time we got you some lunch, Miss Pearl," she said, smiling.

"This is Ronnie. She helps me out. I call it bossing

me around."

"I do a little of both," said Ronnie, chuckling now. "Can I help you with anything?"

"I'm a private investigator," I said, showing my license. Ronnie took it, examining it with interest before returning it. "I'm looking into what happened next door."

"I see. Let me get Pearl settled and I'll be back with you."

I waited a few minutes and then Ronnie opened the door again. "Sorry to keep you waiting," she said. "I'm employed by Pearl's children to look after her. She has dementia but we've found it best not to mention it in front of her. It's not too far progressed yet but her memory isn't what it was. She's very lucid today but I'm not sure she can help you at all; and I've only worked here six months so I don't think I'll be any use either. The detective that came by yesterday evening said the body was in the ground a long time."

I thanked Ronnie, and told her a few simple details she could pass on to Pearl's children to reassure them she was safe before saying goodbye, knowing I wouldn't find any information here. As I returned to the street, my stomach gave a low grumble so I figured now would be a good time to visit my parents and their kitchen.

~

I arrived before Garrett. I tried the door but it was locked and when I rang the doorbell, no one answered. Just as I was about to step back, I heard footsteps on the path behind me.

"There you are," said Mom. "I thought you'd be by earlier. Did you come by earlier? We were out.

Your father needed a new drill so we went to the hardware store." My father, coming up the path behind her, waved.

"No, I just came now. I didn't realize you were out. I thought you'd be home. You said to come for lunch."

"Why would you think that?" asked Mom.

"You texted me!" I checked my watch. It was definitely a reasonable time for lunch.

"I do leave the house, you know. Just because we're retired doesn't mean we don't have busy lives."

"Got a great drill," said Dad, holding up a box so I could see. "I'm going to put up shelves."

"Sounds amazing," I said.

"We do more interesting things than buy drills and put up shelves," continued Mom, huffing at my father ruining her attempts to sound interesting. "I picked up a brochure for the archeology course at the adult education center. It doesn't say anything about digging up skeletons. You'd think that would be on the syllabus."

"Thankfully not," said Dad, unlocking the door and stepping inside.

"I suppose you've had enough experience with that," huffed Mom as he headed into the kitchen.

"I have," he called back. "I don't need to see any more dead bodies in this lifetime."

Mom shook her head and continued, "I went down the street to check on the Dugans' house first thing and see what the situation is. They have one police officer stationed outside."

"He looked bored," said Dad, returning. "He said they expect to be finished soon. The cadaver dogs went over the house and yard and didn't find anything else."

"Garrett mentioned that," I said. "There's no need for a police presence once they removed the body and finished examining the yard."

"You tell your father that like he's not a retired detective," said Mom, shooting me a look.

"She's right," said Dad, without specifying which "she" he meant.

"Can you imagine cadaver dogs inside the house?" Mom shook her head as she stepped past me and whacked me with her shopping bag.

"Ow! I can. It was sensible to do." I rubbed my arm and pulled a face at her back.

"Hmph," snorted Mom.

"We're glad we don't have an unsanctioned graveyard on the street," said Dad. "Although I always fancied living next to one, if only for the quiet."

"Absolutely not," said Mom, shaking her head and rolling her eyes. She hustled to the kitchen as we trailed behind her. The house was quiet, cool, and unnaturally still. It felt less like home without the chaos of my siblings, nieces, and nephews, although I was sure my mom probably appreciated the peace. I could only secretly hope that I would contribute to the noisy brood sooner rather than later.

"So, what can you tell me about the former occupants? Did you know any of them?" I asked.

"I told you she'd ask. Didn't I, Steve? Didn't I?" Mom bristled happily.

"Yes," said Dad. "Do you want to see my drill?"

"Maybe later."

"It's cordless!"

"She doesn't want to see your drill. She wants to

pump us for information," cut in Mom.

"And lunch," said Dad.

"Terrific idea," I said. "Garrett is going to come by too."

"I thought you picked a convenient time to drop in," said Dad skeptically. Just as I was going to remind him, again, that Mom invited me, he continued, "I thought our grocery bill would go down once you all moved out but no."

"Shush, dear. Lexi has questions. What were they?" asked Mom.

"The former occupants," I reminded her. "Did you know any?"

"A few yes. You should have asked me last night. Did the Dugans ask you to take the case? I knew it was a good idea to call you!"

"They did, and thanks. The residents?" I prompted again as Mom started unloading her bag onto the kitchen counter.

"When you were a baby, we used to go to barbecues at the Batleys when they lived there. Now I wonder if I was standing on a corpse eating a hotdog. You probably crawled over it. It's tainted the memories somewhat. I must tell them when I send a Christmas card."

I swallowed and resolved to wash my hands more often. "Are you sure?" I asked.

"Yes, absolutely. There will be more information to tell them at Christmas. If I tell them now, they'll only have questions and there are no answers and then what will I have to write at Christmas?" Mom gave me a stern look. "Can you wrap this up by Christmas?"

"It's months away!"

"I'll take that as a yes."

"Roger probably wasn't in the ground when I was a baby."

"Oh, well, that's a relief. I'll tell the Batleys."

"Who's Roger?" asked Dad.

"The corpse. Keep up, darling," said Mom.

"Can you remember any other residents as…" I stopped at the sound of the front door opening and footsteps in the hallway.

Garrett called out, "Hello?"

"In the kitchen," called Mom. "Should I make food for everyone? I got fresh rolls from the bakery this morning. I can do cheese salad. And there're fresh cookies."

"Sounds good," I decided as Mom headed to the refrigerator. "Garrett wants to hear everything too," I told her.

"I feel like I'm the star witness," said Mom, brightening.

"You are," I said and she straightened, making herself a fraction taller, apparently ready to give her star turn in the witness kitchen.

"I'm glad I sprung for the good cookies," she said. "What a treat."

"I was just asking Mom about the past residents," I said when Garrett appeared in the doorway.

"And I told your sister she probably played on the corpse as a baby."

"We concluded I probably didn't. Mom's worried she was standing on the corpse at some point."

"We probably all did," said Dad cheerfully.

"When the ME narrows the dates down, I'll be sure to let you know," said Garrett. "So whom do you remember? Have there been many residents?"

"I helped them tear down a shed one year. You must have been fourteen," Dad said to me. "Do you remember? I think you helped."

I frowned, trying to recall the incident. "No, that was across the street," I said. "They had a three-legged Labrador."

"Oh," said Dad, and shrugged.

"I'm surprised you two don't remember but I suppose you never had friends in that house," said Mom. She loaded the bread board with cheese, salad, condiments, and returned to the fridge for a slab of butter. "Let's see. It's not been occupied since the Singhs sold it to the Dugans but you already knew that. There were the Weinbergs, the Longs, the Singhs, and the Batleys were there when we moved in. The Longs were tenants because a landlord bought it to lease out but the rest were owners. Do you think the Dugans will stay? They seem such a nice family and we do need nice families in the neighborhood or we'll just turn into an old people community and I don't think that will be so nice if all we have to talk about is our aching hips and what kind of buffet we'll have at our funerals."

"Okay," said Garrett, raising his eyebrows at me behind our mom's back.

"And my drill," said Dad.

"We didn't really know the Weinbergs," continued Mom, "but the Batleys were good friends. Do you remember them? Annie Batley used to braid Serena's hair for her and you boys used to play with their boys? David and Matthew. They're both married now. Matthew married a man but he never did like soccer so I suppose that's why."

"I don't think that's why, Mom," I said.

"I don't like soccer so much either and I married a woman," said Garrett. "I remember David and Matt. David was rowdy. Matt spent a lot of time in the greenhouse with his dad."

"That's right, and digging in their vegetable garden. He's a landscape designer now." My mom stopped and gasped, a hand flying to her mouth. "He would know how to bury a dead body! He got a lot of digging practice."

"We all know how to bury a dead body," I said. "You don't need to take classes."

Mom's attention turned to me and she shook her head. "I raised you wrong," she said. "But you are entertaining for the most part. Nothing like your sister."

I held back from agreeing with her but it was an internal struggle.

"I think the body post-dates the Batleys," said Garrett.

"That's a relief. I wasn't sure how to word the news that Matthew might be a murderer in the Christmas card to his parents," said Mom.

"Do you recognize this man?" asked Garrett, taking a plastic baggie from his suit jacket as he stood. He crossed the kitchen in light, easy steps and handed it to Mom. I resisted the urge to finger open his pocket and see exactly how many baggies he stored in there. Were they all fresh? Did he ever reuse them? Did he bulk purchase them?

"Why are you looking at me like I smell?" asked Garrett.

"No reason. Is that the photo from the wallet?" I asked and he nodded.

"Hmm, there's something familiar about him,"

said Mom. "The man more than the boy. Put it on the table and let me think while I make the sandwiches. Stop hovering, Garrett, and sit down."

"Yes, Mom," said my big police lieutenant brother as he promptly pulled out a chair.

"Sit," instructed Mom and Dad and I did too.

Mom set a plate each in front of us and another for herself, then she grabbed a pack of chips from the counter and juice from the refrigerator, directing me to immediately get up and find glasses in the cabinet. As she tipped the chips into a bowl, she said, "So the Batleys sold to the Weinbergs. Mr. Weinberg inherited a house in New Jersey from his parents so they sold it to the landlord. There were only a couple of tenants, I think. A family and then a single man. I don't think he stayed long. The house was probably too big for him alone. No, Long wasn't their name, was it? Let's see. Long? No, that's not right. Lang! It was Lang. Nice family, boys yours and Serena's age."

"Mine?" asked Garrett. He bit into his sandwich.

"No, Lexi's. Nice family but their boys had different interests to our girls so that's probably why we didn't get together much and I remember the parents worked a lot so the boys were often staying with their grandparents, I think. The Langs stayed a few years, then bought a house in Chilton, I think. Then the man moved in a couple weeks later. Just him."

"Do you know why a single man would want a house to himself?" I asked.

"I might have asked at the time but I really don't recall. I do remember he worked away a lot. Always traveling. We had him over for neighborhood barbecues here and there. He was quite the charmer, I can tell you. Everyone liked him. He had a way with words. All the ladies thought he was wonderful; all the men liked him too because he always wanted to hear about their police stories. I'm not sure your dad liked him." Mom paused to sip her juice, then reached for the photo, scooping it from under Dad's reaching hand. "That could be him but his hair was different. A little longer, and he often had a beard."

"Do you remember what happened to him?" I asked.

"No. I don't think I even knew he left until I saw a realtor's 'for sale' sign go up in the front yard. I wondered if he'd ripped off the landlord and gotten evicted, or if he'd run off without paying rent, because we never saw him again after that." Mom continued studying the photo. "I think he did mention having a son that he didn't see much but I don't recall why. His name was Joe. The man, not the boy."

"Joe what?" asked Garrett.

"Brown, maybe." Mom shrugged.

"No, that's not it," said Dad, still trying to reach the photo as Mom moved it out the way, studying it intently.

"What was the name then?" asked Mom.

"I don't remember," said Dad "but it wasn't Brown."

"Anyway, then the Singhs moved in during your senior year, Lexi, and they were there for years. Or was it your junior year? Rav and Charvi. Two girls almost grown."

"I remember them," said Garrett.

"I don't," I said.

"You were in your wild era," said Mom. "And the

girls were all star track athletes."

"That explains why I don't remember them," I said, deciding not to add because I was an all star underage drinking and party champion who used to make fun of the athletes.

"They went to the girls' school," said Mom. "Such pretty girls. Clever too. Someone once tied their car handles with shoelaces and dangled their sneakers from the aerial."

"Now I remember them!" I brightened.

Mom narrowed her eyes. "I always suspected it was you."

I feigned shock. "I would never!"

"Hmm," snorted Mom, apparently unconvinced.

"Why did they move?" I asked, hoping to prod the subject along.

"Rav Singh got cancer a few years ago. He died within months, such an awful shame, and Charvi didn't want to live there anymore. The girls had settled elsewhere and I think she left to be closer to them and the grandchildren."

"That's sad."

"It is, but the silver lining is the house doubled in value since they bought it. Oh, you know what? I think I got the order wrong. Joe rented first, then it was the Langs. Joe Smithson."

"Joe Smithson?" asked Garrett.

"That's right. Yes, I'm sure this is him. Why? Where did you get this photo anyway?"

"From the corpse's pocket."

Mom screamed and dropped the photo. "Why would you hand it to me?!" she asked. She scraped her chair backwards and hurried to the sink, adding a double pump of hand soap, then plunging her hands under the faucet.

"It's wrapped in plastic," protested Garrett.

"Is that who the Dugans found? Was it Joe Smithson buried in the yard?" asked Dad.

"Hard to say," said Garrett. "The driver's license photo is the same man as this photo, but the name you suggested is different. I'm thinking it's an alias."

"Why would Joe need an alias?" asked Mom.

"A very good question," said Garrett.

CHAPTER NINE

Mom seemed to have forgotten all about her sandwich until Garrett's hand crept across her plate. "Hands off, you bottomless pit," she said, giving his hand a smack.

"Ow!" Garrett withdrew his hand and rubbed it.

"Don't even look at mine," I said, starting on my sandwich's second half. "You're the one who freaked out Mom."

"I really need you to think about what else you might remember about this Joe Smithson," said Garrett. His finger hovered over the photo. Mom had only just returned to the table and her information was now paramount. However, the way his finger hesitated, there was a small chance he might want to see Mom freak out again.

Obviously, I would *never*.

"I can't say I remember much. He lived there less than a year. It might have only been ten months or so at the most, and even then, he worked away a lot."

"Did he say what he did?" I asked.

"Sales, I think."

"Selling what?"

"I don't know," Mom snipped in exasperation.

"Hopes and dreams," chipped in Dad.

I frowned, wondering for a moment if that was a brand I hadn't heard of.

"I mean, Joe could sell water to the Atlantic Ocean. He was a charmer all right," said Dad. "He could sell you your own house and you'd thank him and ask if he wanted cash or check. I remember him now." His mouth turned down, apparently unimpressed.

"He was a contractor for some big firm and he liked the travel but he liked being at home too," said Mom. She tapped a finger to her chin thoughtfully. "He said he was looking to put down roots."

"Was he from Montgomery?" I asked.

"I… don't know." Mom leaned over to look at the photo, not touching it and I wondered if she were thinking about the pair in the picture or deep cleaning the table. "The boy went to The Walsingham School."

"So you *do* remember him?"

"No, it's the patch on his jacket. It's a boarding school in Boston. Very expensive. I wonder if I have a photo of him."

"The boy?" asked Garrett.

"No, Joe. I just thought, I'm sure he came to a birthday party we threw for your dad. We got him a new camera so I'm sure he took a lot of photos. Let me see if I can find them." Mom picked up her sandwich and headed into the living room, leaving us with Dad.

"It was a fancy camera back then," said Dad. "I think I still have it. I'll get it." He got up, grabbed a handful of chips, and headed after Mom.

"What do you make of all that?" asked Garrett. He scraped his chair back and walked over to the countertop, reaching for another roll.

"Joe Smithson is as close to John Smith as you can get without sounding one hundred percent like a made up name."

"That's what I thought too. And sales? Not a job people ask questions about. Too generic. Too boring."

"The travel might have stirred up some questions," I said.

"Not if he made up where he traveled to. If it were international, people would remember that. It would sound glamorous, but make it boring, say he's got to go to nowheresville and it's just a dull traveling sales job that no one wants to talk about."

"So he's absolutely charming and asks people about themselves, listens to their stories, praises the men, flirts with the ladies, and everyone thinks he's great, except Dad, but no one knows anything about him," I surmised.

"That's what I would do if I had an ounce of charisma and wanted to throw people off the scent. I just have to figure out what the scent is."

"We," I corrected him.

"The state is literally employing me to do this." Garrett stuffed cheese into his roll, followed by a lettuce leaf and a dollop of mayo, then he took a large bite.

"The Dugans literally hired me to do this," I countered.

"Fine. Whatever. Like I said before, I'm happy for the assistance. I'm overloaded with cases and the priority on this shifted up, thanks to those jewels. The chief has taken an interest."

"Here it is," said Mom, brandishing a thick photo album as she returned to the kitchen. She swept our plates out of the way and the album landed on the table with a thump, on an open page. "That's Joe," she said, pointing to a photo. My father was center, beer in hand, laughing at something. Off to the left, his face partially turned away was a man in jeans and an open-necked, checkered shirt, the sleeves rolled up, a beer also in his hand. "I thought there might be another but he's not in any of the posed group shots. I did remember he offered to take a few of the photos. It was thoughtful of him."

Garrett and I exchanged a look. I wondered if he were thinking the same as me: that was a good excuse not to be photographed.

"Do you mind if I take this?" asked Garrett, leaning over Mom's shoulder.

"Go ahead, but I'd appreciate it if you returned it; otherwise I'll have a gap in this book and I don't know what I'll fill it with."

"I'll make a copy and return it," said Garrett, sliding the photo from its transparent pocket. He retrieved the other photo and pocketed them both. He grabbed our plates and headed for the dishwasher. "Thanks for lunch. I have to head back to the station."

"I have things to do too," I said, standing up.

"Here's the camera!" said Dad, returning. "Oh! Are you going? Don't you want to see how it takes real film? You have to open the case and stick it in the slot."

"I'll check it out in a museum," said Garrett as Dad flashed the camera's cavity at us with pride.

"I found a photo," said Mom. "We did take one with your camera! Garrett, I'd appreciate an update. It's horrible to think poor Joe might have been buried in his own backyard. He didn't deserve that, regardless of whatever he did. What *did* he do?"

"No idea," said Garrett.

Mom turned her attention to me, narrowing her eyes. "Was he in witness protection?" she asked, placing a hand to her chest. "Was it mob-related?"

"I don't know any more than Garrett! Was he close to any of the other neighbors?" I asked.

"I couldn't say. The house next to Joe's was empty for a while around then. Yes, that's right. A tree fell through their roof and they had to move out for months but I don't recall if that was before or after he left... disappeared. Anyway, yes, I think they moved in before Joe did."

"I went by the house earlier and there's a lot of mail and a parcel on the porch. Are the homeowners away?"

"Tom died last year and Bea just moved to a retirement community. Although I'm not sure if she's visiting her son in Maine. Or maybe the other son in New Jersey. Anyway, I'm not sure if the house is sold yet. I'll ask if she wants the mail collected."

"What about the other neighbors?"

"Some of the other neighboring homes turned hands more than once so it's hard to say if he was particularly friendly with anyone. Do you remember?" she asked my dad.

Dad shrugged. "I think he came to some of the neighborhood socials but I was busy working back then and hung out with my cop buddies mostly. He wasn't really my kind of fellow."

"Why was that?" asked Garrett.

"I don't really recall. It could have been because I was just busy more than Joe's personality. I had my career and an awful lot of children coming and going."

"And now he has shelves to put up," said Mom. She glanced at her watch and made a show of shooing us to the door. "I have an afternoon glassblowing class to get to. There's a quiz afterwards and I don't want to be late. I thought I might make something in my free time for the Dugans to cheer them up. I already gave the basket from my basketweaving class to Serena for Victoria's room. She was thrilled."

I doubted that and I didn't dare ask what glassblowing entailed; I was just content Mom didn't try to sign me up too. Perhaps one day my mother's thirst for learning and hobbies might abate but until then, I was glad she found things to do that she enjoyed.

"It looks like we might have narrowed down our deceased to a likely suspect," I said to Garrett as we walked out together. "Joe Smithson could be him."

"Could be. Mom's photo only partially shows his face. It's not enough for an identification but it could be the man in the driver's license. I'll run everything I can on this Smithson guy when I'm back at my desk. He could just have been a tenant who moved on."

"I'll look up property records and verify the list of names Mom gave us. Perhaps the landlord will still be around?"

"Good idea. The ME bumped the corpse up the list so I expect to have something on that tomorrow too. I'll update you when I can."

"Appreciate it. I'll see if I can learn anything out

about the boy. Perhaps I'll find something we can cross-reference, and if he's his son, it might lead to a genuine identity. Joe Smithson has to be a fake name so I doubt I'll find a boy named Smithson at that school."

"I smell a rat about this Joe for sure but Mom's other information about the residents might turn up something. Until we get something concrete, all leads are still on the table."

"Agreed," I said. "Hey, there's something I was curious about. Is there an obvious cause of death or does the ME need to investigate further?"

"The ME needs to investigate for a definitive report but I had a look before they took the body away and I think I can give you an answer. There appeared to be a small caliber gunshot wound to the temple. I haven't seen many gunshot wounds on an almost entirely decomposed skeleton before so I need the ME to confirm it but she seemed reasonably sure at the scene."

"He could have done that to himself," I said.

Garrett shrugged. "Yeah, but he sure as hell didn't bury himself. Even if it were a suicide, someone covered it up. That's a bunch of laws broken. I'm leaning towards homicide."

"Did you find a bullet?"

"No, but it's also possible he was killed elsewhere and transported there. The spent bullet could be as close as inside the house but if so, there have been substantial renovations so it's unlikely we'll unearth the exact spot he was killed. I have crime scene techs going over the house this afternoon."

"I'm glad you didn't tell Mom and Dad that."

"I didn't think it would go down well. Best they

find out for themselves. Then they only have their own nosiness to blame. Although Dad would know I'd call the techs in since I had cadaver dogs go over the house and I left a uniform posted outside."

"I feel like someone would have heard a gunshot in our neighborhood." We'd reached the sidewalk and I looked around, conscious of how quiet it was. Here was your average neighborhood. Kids shouting and laughing after school and on weekends, the sounds of lawnmowers and barbecue parties, cars shuttling residents around. We were not a neighborhood of crime so prevalent it went unnoticed.

"You would think so but it depends on when it happened. July Fourth? Nope. It would sound like a firework. Super Bowl? Over that kind of noise, unlikely. Even if it were just a regular night, they're on the corner lot. Mom says the neighboring house could have been empty, and a small caliber weapon wouldn't make a lot of noise. Maybe the TV was on, or music was playing. Plus, no one is going to remember the sound of a pistol pop from back then."

"What are the chances of finding the bullet at all?" I wondered.

"It's remote, but it might be worth taking another look in the yard once we've gone over the house. The ME took a sizeable amount of dirt with her from around the body so we might strike it lucky. I'm not holding my breath." Garrett's phone buzzed. He checked the screen and stuck it back into his pocket, then pulled out his car keys. "I'll pick you up at three thirty to go see the forger?"

I nodded. "Thanks."

We parted ways, Garrett's lack of confidence in finding further evidence lowered my mood after I'd been so pleased about my mom's stream of information. However, by the time I reached the office, I remained reasonably confident that I could put the Dugans' minds to rest and get them returned to their home relatively scandal free. Garrett seemed to have no suspicion about them or their involvement and I was sure they would be pleased to hear that.

Back at the office, I spent the next hour looking through property records, confirming my mother's memory was extremely efficient. While I didn't find a Smithson or the Langs, that didn't surprise me since they'd been tenants. I did find an owner for the time period named Elsie Greenberg. Further digging revealed she owned four duplexes and a small apartment building, plus a single family home in Bedford Hills. The last address had to be her own home. Clearly, the property business had paid off.

There was little else available online about Elsie Greenberg, which was disappointing, but I found a marriage license to a Leon Greenberg fifty years ago, and birth records of two children, Elon and Naomi. Elsie was close to eighty years old. After scrolling several pages, I found an old business article with a photo of a woman in a dark dress beneath a cloud of graying hair. The article was about home offices being all the rage and Elsie was quoted as saying keeping her overhead low meant she could pass the savings onto her tenants. Apparently, she'd never consider hiring office space and her husband was happy to run his construction business from their Bedford Hills home too.

When my phone rang, I wasn't surprised to see Maddox's name flash up.

"Thought I'd check in and see if you're as bruised

as me," he said.

"I'm barely bruised. The woman who tackled me thankfully broke my fall. You looked okay," I said.

"I felt fine. Then, when I woke up this morning, my wrist hurt like heck. The doc thinks it's a sprain."

"Sorry to hear it."

"Worse things have happened. Did you file your report?"

"Shoot! No, I didn't. Thanks for the reminder."

"No problem. I hear you got a case that distracted you."

"Garrett mentioned you called."

"I didn't hear it from him."

"Jord?" I guessed.

"Nope."

"You're enjoying this."

"Always. Your mom told me. She wanted to know if the FBI should get involved in the case. I said no unless there were more bodies. I'm not sure if she were relieved or annoyed. It seemed to be a mixture of both."

"Garrett confirmed there aren't any more bodies."

"Guess that means I don't have to swoop in. I heard there was a fortune in jewels found on the body. Whatcha looking at?"

"I'm sure Garrett told you that it's supposed to be a secret."

"Sure from the general public. I'm an FBI agent. I'm intrigued. I want to help out."

I frowned, narrowing my eyes. "Do you?"

"Of course! It's not every day a stash of jewels is unearthed from a shallow grave. It's the kind of case we all hope for. So the body was a man? Not a woman?"

"Definitely a man, according to Garrett. I didn't get close enough and even if I did, I'm not sure I could tell the difference without some obvious clues. Like lipstick. Or a beard."

"And it wasn't recent? Is everyone sure?"

"Apparently, but the ME still needs to confirm."

"When?"

"Soon, hopefully."

"And there's no clue who this guy could be?"

"It's looking like he had a bunch of aliases. What we don't know is why."

"Criminal activity," said Maddox decisively.

I held back a laugh. "We figured that. What we don't know is what kind of criminal activity. We do have a possible photo of the guy with his kid. It was in his wallet."

Maddox was quiet a moment then. "A girl?"

"No, a boy. A teenager."

"Have the names Stanley, Underwood, Temple, or Fournier come up?"

"No. Why all the questions?"

"Thought it might have some bearing on a case I've been working on a while but it doesn't sound like it."

"If it involves jewel theft and murder, I'd like to hear about it."

"Jewels and theft, yes. Murder, maybe. It's complicated."

"It's never complicated," I said.

Maddox laughed. "It's an ongoing case so my lips are sealed. Let's get drinks soon anyway."

"Lily's bar?"

"Of course. I've had enough of O'Grady's. The beer is tepid and nothing crazy happens. Although I'd prefer not to fall through anything, get shot at, or lose any clothes in the next few days."

"Maybe we should go somewhere else," I quipped.

"Nowhere's safe with you, Graves. Keep me posted on your case and if you want to cozy up in any dark crawl spaces, let me know." He disconnected before he had a chance to hear my eyeballs roll back into my head.

I sent Lily a text asking her if she wanted to join me on a lead and almost immediately she replied: *Yes! Where are you?*

At the office. Need to go to Bedford Hills.

I'm nearby. Meet you out front.

I grabbed my purse and tossed my phone in my pocket and headed to the parking lot. By the time I'd driven up the ramp to idle outside the building, Lily was walking towards me wearing denim shorts, a t-shirt that bared her midriff, and tennis shoes. She hopped in eagerly. "Is this another stakeout? Do I actually get to see something this time?"

"We're going to speak to someone who used to own the end house," I told her.

"Oh, cool. Should I have brought a flashlight?"

"No. It's daylight."

"I meant for the interrogation."

"We're not interrogating. We're going to ask the landlady a few questions about the house, whom it was leased to, and what do they remember about the tenants. It's not much of a lead but most of the neighbors moved and the one that didn't has severe memory issues, while the other nearest might be away visiting relatives. So far, my mom has been my best source of information."

"It pays to know everything about everyone," said Lily. "If I weren't such a scrupulous bar owner, I'd be keeping tabs on all my patrons, especially the ones sneaking into the restroom and thinking I don't know."

"What's wrong with going to the restroom?"

"In mixed pairs? We don't have unisex restrooms," said Lily. "I'm thinking about how to word it so people stop doing that."

"How about 'stop doing that'?"

"That works. It's succinct. What do we know about our lead?"

"She's eighty. Married a bazillion years. Two kids. That's it. I don't even know if I have the correct address. It's a guess."

Lily kept a steady patter of questions up as I drove and when we parked outside the Bedford Hills address, she let out a low whistle. "Hello, McMansion," she said, as we gazed at the Grecian columns, the neat, formal hedging, and the enormous American flag flying from the porch. Two black limousines were parked in the carriage driveway and it looked like they were having a party inside. A waiter with a tray of canapes moved past the window of what could have been a living room, pausing to hold out the tray to two suited men.

"This doesn't look like a rental," I said, pleased at my guesswork.

"I don't know about that. My parents have had leases at some pretty stupendous dwellings."

"Let's check."

"And if they don't answer, we can break in."

"Lily, no."

"But…"

"No!"

Lily's mouth turned down. I felt like I'd admonished a particularly well-meaning puppy, which filled me with guilt. "We can break in if it's really necessary," I said, hoping it wouldn't be.

We headed towards the house and rang the doorbell. A moment later, a man in black suit answered.

"May I help you?" he asked, looking us over, a small crease between his eyes suggesting disapproval. He paused at Lily's midriff and I was inclined to tell him he had no business judging because could he get abs like Lily's after childbirth? I didn't think so!

"I'm looking for Mrs. Elsie Greenberg," I said. "May we speak with her?"

"I'm afraid that won't be possible."

"I don't want to interrupt the party. It'll only be for a few minutes. It's important," I said, reaching for my private investigator's license.

"I'm afraid you've misunderstood. Mrs. Greenberg can't talk to you."

"Oh?" I felt like I was missing something.

"Mrs. Greenberg passed away over the weekend. This is her wake."

CHAPTER TEN

"If only the Dugans decided to work on their yard last week," said Lily. "We could have given Mrs. Greenberg something to live for."

"Yeah."

We were sitting in the car gazing at the house.

"I can't believe Mr. Greenberg refused to speak to us! Maybe he would have if the butler had been more urgent when he asked him if he could spend a few minutes with us. That would have been nicer than shutting the door on us so rudely!"

"His wife just died," I pointed out. "I don't think he was being rude. Do you know anyone else with a butler? An actual, real live butler?"

"Yeah. My parents and their friends."

"I can't imagine having a butler. I can open my own door."

"But you wouldn't have to. Imagine all the people you don't want to see and could get rid of by making the butler deny them."

"Just like Mr. Greenberg," I pointed out.

"The butler said the office is shut for the foreseeable future. Do you think Mrs. Greenberg was still working right up until…" Lily pulled a face, stuck out her tongue, flopped in her seat, and pretended to collapse.

"Seems so. I'm not sure how to get that background information on Joe Smithson now. I suppose I could ask Garrett to officially request it but it seems a lot to bother the Greenbergs with at this time."

Lily nodded. "We should probably break in."

"They're holding a wake!"

"What? Everyone will be distracted. We can get in, locate the home office, go through her files, get the information and get out. No one will even know. We won't even bother *anyone,*" Lily pleaded, then, as if it would do any good, batted her eyelashes at me.

"We don't exactly blend in." I looked down at my outfit. I was wearing my cutest pastels. I looked more like an ice cream cone than a funeral attendee.

"We could. We could go to your place and get black outfits and be back here in far less than an hour. We slip inside, mingle with the other guests, and then poof! We disappear."

I checked my watch. I had time before my meeting with Garrett and I did want to know what Elsie Greenberg knew. If she were meticulous with her records, then she might have kept all of them going back years. I had to see what she had in her file on her mysterious tenant.

"Okay," I agreed, pulling a U-turn to head for home. "Let's get dressed for a wake."

~

By the time we returned, both in appropriately sedate

black dresses and neat heels, the wake was in full throttle and most of the parking had disappeared. I wedged my small VW in between two SUVs and we followed a trio of women inside, neatly skirting past the man posted at the door, who'd turned us away in no uncertain terms before, as he took the shawl from one of the women and walked away.

Lily plucked two glasses from a passing waiter and passed one to me as we headed into the nearest living room. Most of the guests were in their advanced years. Several people sat on the couches. There was a couple by the window talking softly. A young child charged past us, followed by his mother, who herded her around a couch, over several feet and then past us. "Sorry," she muttered, sighing. "You have to stop running, Dee. This is Granny's wake. Not a playground."

"I feel her pain. I thought it would be exciting once Poppy started walking but it's terrifying. She moves so fast. She climbs too. At breakfast, I went to get her more milk and she was on top of the hallway credenza when I got back. I don't even know how she got up there."

"Can't you tell her no?" I asked.

"Have you met a child before?" asked Lily, looking at me askance.

"Fair point. We should make contact with the mom. She's either the daughter or the daughter-in-law. She might know something about the business."

"Say no more," said Lily, turning on her heel and heading after the woman. "Your little girl is soooo cute," she gushed when we found her in the next room.

"She is, but she's also got a lot of excess energy,"

said the woman. "I ran her around the yard before everyone arrived but she seems to have recovered a second wind."

"You must be Elsie's daughter? Naomi?" I asked.

"That's right."

"We're so sorry for your loss," I said. "I'm sure this is an awful time for you all."

"It is. We didn't expect Mom to... well, you know. We didn't expect it at all." Then she frowned. "I'm sorry. I don't recognize you. Are you a neighbor? Or a business associate?"

"Business associates," I lied.

"We're in property," added Lily. "We flip houses."

"Oh? That's interesting. Usually it's guys. I bet my mom was impressed."

"We were hoping to sell some of our properties," I said.

"To my mom? I didn't know she was looking for houses. She thought apartments were a better investment for her portfolio but I expect she told you that. Dee, don't touch that. Sorry."

"There was actually some confidential paperwork we left with your mom recently," I said. "I'm sorry this is awkward but we need it back."

"Oh. Yes, of course. I could ask my dad but I don't think he's thinking too clearly at the moment. Mom's office is at the back. If you tell me what to look for I can check her desk."

"It's quite old paperwork actually. About a property she used to own."

"Due diligence," added Lily.

"How old?" asked the woman.

"Twenty years ago."

"Oh, gosh. Well, Mom probably wouldn't have

that kind of paperwork in her office. She usually keeps all the old files in the basement. If she needed something old, she'd bring it upstairs and she did bring a few things up just last week. I told her she should have asked me or Dad to carry the boxes but she just rolled her eyes." She stopped, frowning. "But you said you dropped off paperwork last week? So that's probably still on her desk."

"Yes, that's right. It's old paperwork about an old property but it's very confidential and we need to get it back or we could get in trouble."

"But you're the bosses?"

"With the city," I said. "The building inspectors have been a nightmare."

"Permits," said Lily in a knowing, hushed voice.

"Oh, say no more. The battles my mom had to fight when she submitted renovation plans. You'd think they'd have improved over the years but I guess not."

"You didn't follow your parents into the property business?"

"Oh, goodness, no. I'm a teacher. Dee, put that down. There's my dad," she said as a man with dark circles under his eyes and slumped shoulders entered the room. He looked around blankly and walked out again. "Sorry, I should check on him. Sorry."

"What are the odds Mr. Greenberg sees through us?" asked Lily.

"High," I said. "Let's steer clear of him, find the office and leave. I don't want to draw any attention if we can avoid it and I don't think we should linger. The daughter says it was at the back. Plenty of people are strolling around so we'll blend right in."

"Let's go."

We left the room, turning left and heading along the hallway, past a dining room and a smaller den. A man stepped out of a powder room into the hallway, and a waiter with an empty tray walked straight ahead into what I assumed was the kitchen. There were two doors left. I tried one, the handle awkwardly wobbly, finding stairs heading down.

"It must be that one," I said, pointing to the other door. "This leads to the basement." I tried to shut it but it kept popping open so I gave up, leaving it slightly ajar.

"It's a nice house," said Lily as she ran her hand across a mahogany credenza. "But it's got a lot of old people furniture."

"Old people live here."

"I'm just saying a little modernization wouldn't hurt." Lily tried the handle and the door opened. She stepped inside, took a few steps, paused, shrieked, turned around and ran into me. As Lily barreled forwards, I stumbled backwards and Lily just kept on going, hands flapping, horror etched across her face until we were stumbling through the open door opposite.

Before we tumbled down the stairs, I grabbed Lily and held her, forcing her to a stop. She breathed heavily, her eyes wide with alarm as she rested against the wall.

"What the heck just happened?" I asked. Behind Lily, the waiter caught the door and pushed it firmly closed, without glancing inside, as he walked past, leaving us in the dark.

"She was in there!"

"Who?"

"Elsie Greenberg!"

"She can't be. She's dead." I patted the walls, searching for a light switch. Finally I found it, pushed it in, and an overhead light flickered on, then kept flickering.

"I know!"

"So you didn't see her in there. It must have been someone else and now some poor old lady thinks you went nuts for no reason."

"It was Elsie Greenberg and she was definitely dead."

"You're not making any sense."

"She was in a coffin on her desk," Lily hissed.

I paused, uncertain if I'd misheard.

"It was open. I saw her."

"Oh!" I palmed my face. "This isn't just a wake. This is a viewing! Some people do that. They keep the body at home so people can view it before the funeral service."

"That is so weird!"

"Apparently, it's comforting."

Lily stared at me. "Do I look comforted?"

"It's comforting for the family. It's not supposed to be comforting for the two women sneaking in." I looked around. The stairs were wooden, the walls painted a soft cream. No cobwebs. That was a good sign. The basement was clearly accessed regularly. "Did you see anything on her desk?"

"No, I was too busy being horrified."

"Was her coffin actually on the desk?"

"No. Some kind of plinth with drapes in the middle of the room. I don't think there was anything on her desk at all."

"The paperwork we're looking for would have been archived years ago, probably when Mrs.

Greenberg sold the house." I turned to look at the stairs as the lightbulb above started to fade. "Let's head downstairs and look through the files. I bet we'll find info on Joe Smithson down there. We can get what we need and hopefully, we won't have to go back into the office."

"Good because I don't want to go into the office."

"Stick with me."

Lily snorted. "Like I was going to wait up here with a dead body close by."

"Dead bodies can't do anything to you."

"Have you watched *The Walking Dead*?"

"Come on." I headed down the stairs, shaking my head, trying to make sure I didn't make any noise on the wooden steps. The stairs curved to the left, then opened up into a wide storage room with windows set high in the wall allowing a stream of natural light. The room was clearly used for storage. There were two Christmas trees in boxes, and a dozen clear plastic bins with decorations for all the seasons. Two couches were covered in plastic and there were several boxes of children's toys and books and a large rocking horse with a beautiful mane and leather saddle. Across the back wall was a series of filing cabinets. I headed for them, hoping Elsie Greenberg had a coherent system for her paperwork.

"What should we look under?" asked Lily, pulling open the top drawer of the first cabinet.

"The year? Around twenty years ago?"

Lily's fingers moved over the files. "I think everything is filed by address."

"That makes it easier. Look for my parents' street."

I pulled open the drawer of the next cabinet, scrolling through the card files.

"Not here," said Lily, closing that drawer and pulling open the one underneath. "They don't seem to be in alphabetical order."

"I noticed. I'm not sure what kind of system this is." I pulled out a couple of files, flipping through them. "Oh, now I get it. These files are for apartments. I think they all are." I neatly inserted the files back, extracting a couple more, finding I was correct.

"These are for commercial buildings," said Lily, scanning several sheets of paper.

"We need to find the cabinet for houses. Maybe single family units."

I closed the cabinet, and moved onto the next one. "This is it," I said, pleased to find the first two files I pulled were for duplexes. Near the middle of the files, I found the one I was looking for. I pulled it out and lay it open so we could both see.

"What are we looking at?" asked Lily.

"The sales particulars. Elsie Greenberg bought the house from the Weinbergs like my mom said. There's an application from the Langs with some background information. Jobs, former addresses, credit checks, standard stuff. A photo of the family." I ran my finger down the sheet. "Move in date. Move out date. Deposit marked as returned." I turned the page. "Looks like it was rented out immediately to a Joe Smithson. He's listed as a salesman but it doesn't say what he was selling or his employer. Two former addresses. No credit check but he paid three months up front and took out a six-month lease. He renewed it for another three months."

"It says here he didn't pay the last month and left a bunch of stuff so they retained the deposit and no claim was ever made." Lily pointed to a paragraph near the end of the page.

"The year fits. If he didn't make that last month's rent, perhaps he was already dead?"

"Someone made a note to blackball him for future rentals based on the non-payment and abandonment."

"There's something clipped to the form." I turned the page, finding a receipt from a home clearance company. It listed removal of a small amount of furniture, clothing, a TV and personal possessions. "He didn't pay the last month's rent and left everything behind. That does sound like he wasn't in a position to claim anything."

"AKA, dead and buried," said Lily.

"It narrows down a timeline. I'm going to take pictures of this form. There're addresses and phone numbers. They're probably long out of date but I can check."

"Then let's get out of here," said Lily.

"Agreed." I snapped photos of each page of the registration paper, the receipt, and the rental contract, then I slipped all the paperwork back into the file and deposited it into the cabinet.

We headed back up the stairs and I reached for the handle, turning it. "It's stuck," I said, giving it a harder tug. Then another. No matter how I twisted it or how hard I pulled, it wouldn't budge.

"Let me try," said Lily, edging me out the way. She tugged and tugged, pulling a face. "It's stuck."

"Not stuck. Locked." I pointed to the keyhole. "The door kept popping open when I shut it earlier. I bet someone decided to be extra safe and locked it without realizing we were down here."

"What do we do now? Knock and holler?"

"Then we'll have some explaining to do. There must be another way out. Let's check. Hollering is the last option." I headed back down the staircase, goosebumps popping out on my arms. It was very cool in the house and, with a dead Elsie Greenberg upstairs, I now understood the temperature was more than to simply combat the summer heat.

There was no outside door in the room we checked and neither was there in the furnace room or the unfinished part of the basement. I headed for the row of high windows reaching the ceiling but even on tiptoes, I couldn't quite reach the catch. They were wide and not too shallow and I couldn't see any locks, just a lift and push mechanism. "I think we can just fit through. We just need to be able to get up there," I said, looking around for something to stand on. "Do you see a stepladder?"

"No. The rocking horse is the only thing big enough to stand on," said Lily, looking from the window to the horse. "Where do the windows lead? I don't remember seeing any at the front of the house."

"I think either the backyard or the side. I'm a little disoriented. Let's get the horse." Lily and I tried to lift it but it was awkward and heavy so we wiggled it back and forth across the floor until it was under the window. "Hold it still," I said as I climbed up, steadying myself so I could stand on the saddle.

"Ride 'em, cowgirl," said Lily.

I balanced, my arms stretched out. "I think a childhood dream just came true. I always wanted to be one of those flying acrobats on horseback." I beamed, then the horse wobbled and I crouched again, grabbing a fistful of silky mane.

"How about you just stay upright and don't do anything crazy."

"Okay, but I look good, don't I?" I rose again, wishing I'd done the core work that involved working my muscles for balance, and not just to employ them to keep the cake inside me.

"I'm imagining you in a sequined leotard and a plumed headdress," said Lily. "I'm also imagining you looking out the window then trying the latch."

"I was enjoying the moment," I said but she had a point. "It looks like the side of the yard. There's no patio. The window opens into a flower bed and I think I see a path." I tried the latch. It was a little rusty and stiff but with another push, it opened wide. I grabbed hold of the edge and pulled myself up. I dug my hands into the dirt, clawing for purchase, then I felt hands under my heels as Lily gave me a hard shove. I popped through the window, my triceps screaming.

Pop. Pop.

Lily's heels suddenly fired through the window and bopped me on the head.

I turned over in time to see her head appear at the window. "Coming through," she said as she levered herself up. I tucked my hands under her arms and pulled and we fell backwards. "That wasn't so bad. We escaped! Hurrah!"

I grinned, then my face fell as fat water droplets landed on my dress.

Water sprinklers began to fire all over the yard, dousing us in a plume of cold water.

CHAPTER ELEVEN

"What happened to you?" asked Solomon.

I squelched to a stop inside the doors of the PI's office, trickles of water making their way off my hem and down my legs to form shallow pools at my feet, and heaved a deep breath.

"Did a raincloud follow you and no one else?" asked Garrett.

"Did you go to a very formal water park?" asked Delgado.

"I don't want to talk about it," I said, hoping the heat from my cheeks wouldn't turn the water into steam. "Could you pass me a towel?"

"How about a bucket to stand in?" suggested Garrett.

"You left some clothes in my trunk last week," said Solomon. "I'll bring them to you if you head over to the suite and take a shower."

A drip ran down my nose and fell off the tip. "My car needs drying inside," I said, my voice just short of a plaintive wail.

"How about *you* getting dry? We have an appointment to make," said Garrett, tapping his watch.

I pulled a face. "The forger! I'll hurry!"

"What're you forging?" asked Delgado as I turned and slid out of the office. I didn't hear Garrett's answer because the door swung shut behind me. As I pushed the elevator button, Solomon came out and wrapped an arm around me.

"I'm wet," I said as he pulled me into him.

"So am I now," he said, a damp patch forming on his chest. "Do you want to talk about it?"

"Lily and I gatecrashed a wake in Bedford Hills, saw a corpse, got stuck in a basement, and then got soaked by the yard sprinklers."

"That's all?"

"The whole funeral party saw us when we dashed to the car." My shoulders slumped.

"Do they know who you are?"

"No. We made up a back story and didn't include our names. There won't be any comeback on the agency."

"I wasn't worried about that. *Corpse?*" added Solomon, his eyebrows rising a smidge.

"The centerpiece of the funeral."

Solomon nodded slowly. "That makes more sense now."

"It wasn't a random body," I clarified.

"Pleased to hear it. Do I want to know the rest?"

"We got some useful information."

"Glad to hear that."

"Sorry about the mess."

"I'll get it cleared up. You might want to think about leaving a set of clothes here permanently."

"I'm not planning on this happening again." I paused. "I can't see how anything like this could ever happen again."

Solomon smiled. "We'll see," he said.

We parted ways on the next floor and I headed to the small suite the agency had set up in a former interview room. The idea was that we had a place where we could put up the occasional client that needed a secure place to stay; but primarily, it had been used by the staff when working long hours that prevented them from going home. There was a bedroom with a queen-sized bed and bunkbeds, a small couch and a coffee table. Off that was a compact shower room, equipped with a variety of travel products, although I noted someone had left their toiletry bag by the sink with half-used men's products inside.

I showered, washed my hair until it squeaked clean, and wrapped a towel around myself. When I stepped into the bedroom, my bag was on the bed. I grabbed the jeans and a blouse, socks and sneakers and dressed quickly. The only thing we seemed to have forgotten to add to the suite was a hairdryer so I settled for combing out my hair, hoping it would dry quickly in the summer heat. Gathering my wet things, I returned to the PI's office, cleaner, drier, and ready to pursue the new lead.

"Let's go," said Garrett, rising and beckoning me to follow. "My contact says our forger is very prompt. I don't want to miss this opportunity."

"What do we know about him?" I asked as we headed down the stairs.

"Name's Owen Weaver, he's sixty-five years old, sentenced to fifteen years, paroled in ten. Apparently, he's very well behaved in prison and spent time teaching some of his fellow inmates to read and write. Hopefully, not so they could help him out in future forgeries but who knows? Maybe he just has a heart."

"Or else he was bored."

"Or that. Single, no kids. Currently works in a small retail shop. Absolutely not allowed near computers, printing presses, commercial photography equipment, or the internet."

"How does he get through the day?" I wondered.

"Old school style. His parole is in effect so long as he doesn't re-offend and the restrictions are supposed to ensure that, along with him being a law-abiding, productive member of the community. In reality, the parole officers can't monitor everything he does and neither can we."

"So he could have returned right back to forging?"

"Sure, but then he runs the risk of someone finding out and getting sent back to prison. A sensible parolee doesn't risk that. Certainly not on his sentence. Better to do those years outside than inside."

"How sensible do you think he is?" We reached the parking lot and Garrett pointed to his unmarked police pool car in the visitor parking spot.

"We'll soon find out. If he's dry, that's a good sign."

"Dry? Oh, very funny." I thwacked my brother's arm and Garrett laughed.

~

The man walking towards us looked friendly, if not strained around the eyes. He bore a wide smile, thinning blond hair, and his forehead held deep frown lines. His checkered shirt sleeves were rolled haphazardly, one sleeve slightly higher than the other.

"Don Kempner. I kept Weaver as long as I could," he said, shaking Garrett's hand, then mine. "He's one of my few clients whose appointments I can set my watch by. In on time, out as fast as he can. Always prepared to prove anything I want to know."

"Sounds ideal," I said.

"I want to agree with you, but his compliance is so rare, it's suspicious. All the same, he's ticking all the boxes and there isn't a whiff of anything alarming so I'm prepared to give him an easy ride."

"Your other clients are very different?" I asked as Don headed down the hallway, leaving us hurrying to catch him.

"We get them from all walks of life. Some are compliant, some aren't. Some disappear as quickly as they can. Others have just had a bad lot in life and need guidance in turning their lives around. I do what I can but…" Don looked around and threw his hands in the air. "Budgets," he said simply. "We could do more if we had more. It would save money down the line but it's hard to get the powers that be interested once the person you want to help is an official felon."

"Understood," said Garrett. "What else can you tell us about Owen Weaver?"

"Not a lot. Always polite, keeps to himself. Speaks well and is articulate. I don't see him chummy with any other felons although his prison record said he was an unofficial teacher to a number of them. Helped them get into educational courses, things like that."

"What about his residence?"

"Halfway house. He has his own room, shares a

living room and kitchen with five others, keeps curfew. No reported issues. I've done a couple spot checks and I'm satisfied with it. He's only been there a couple weeks as the last one had a termite issue and the whole place needed fumigating. In my opinion, it should be condemned. That said, he didn't have any issues there either."

"Has he spoken about his crimes at all?"

"We spoke about them at the initial meeting when we went over what he could and couldn't do. After that, no. If he's interested in taking up forging again, I'm sure I'll be the last to know." Don paused outside a door, his hand on the handle without turning it. "I know you said your case involves a dead body but, for what it's worth, I just don't see Owen Weaver as a murderer. He's not the type."

"You've met the type?" I asked.

Don turned his attention to me. "I've met the type that'd make your skin crawl. There's nothing 'off' about Weaver. He's just your run-of-the-mill, non-violent criminal. I'm sure of that."

"Good to know," said Garrett as he nodded to the door.

"Owen, this is Lieutenant Graves and…" Don looked at me, apparently uncertain.

"Lexi Graves, private investigator," I filled in as we filed into the room.

"What a treat," said Owen Weaver. "If you were a cop, I'd have been arrested much sooner and more often." He winked at me but it was friendly rather than lascivious, and any tension I thought might have appeared at our introduction seemed to evaporate. "I can guess you're here to talk to me, not Don. How can I help you both?" he asked.

"We're here about a case that recently resurfaced," said Garrett.

"Should I take a guess?" asked Weaver, with a small huff of a laugh. "I can if you'd like us to be here all day but I have other things to do."

"Do you recognize this document?" asked Garrett. He put a baggie containing the fake DMV license on the table. Weaver leaned in and studied it without touching.

"It's a fake," he said.

"We know that."

"And you're assuming I made it?"

"Did you?"

"Maybe. It's hard to say for certain. I'm hardly the only ex-forger around."

"Do you recognize the man in the photo?"

"No."

"Take another look."

Weaver redirected his gaze, taking longer this time. "Still no. But I'm assuming it was a local guy so I *might* have made it. Can't confirm it though."

"Or deny," I said.

He glanced at me and a flicker of a smile appeared on his lips.

"You're not going to get in any further trouble," said Garrett. "In fact, if you're helpful, it'll probably work in your favor."

Weaver's gaze returned to Garrett. "Probably?" he asked.

"Would you take another look, please?" I said.

"For you, anything," he said, winking again at me before he leaned in. "He wasn't a regular but I did create a number of identification documents for him. Driver's licenses, passports, some letters of recommendation, and employment records. They're easy. He wasn't a local guy and from what I recall, he asked for different names, different details."

"What else do you recall?"

"He paid cash but I know that because I only accepted cash. I don't recall him asking for documents for anyone else so it was just him."

"Not a boy?" asked Garrett.

"No."

"How'd you meet?"

"Introduction although I don't remember who. My business was big enough and successful enough, that I didn't need to advertise. My clientèle came from introductions from people whom I'd already assisted."

"Do you remember the names he asked for?" I asked.

Weaver pushed the license away. "My memory's good but not *that* good."

"Did he tell you his name?"

"I doubt it and I wouldn't have told him mine either. Neither of us needed to know that kind of information."

"So tell us how this works," Garrett said. "He's introduced to you. Then what?"

"A new client tells me what they're looking for and pays up front. I take photos and any details I need. I make a note if they can pass for any other ethnicity. You'd be surprised who could pass for whom," he said with a shrug. "I tell them to wait two weeks and give them a key to a mailbox. They get the location once I've made my drop off. We met only for the job. Less risk that way."

"And if they want to commission another job?

Like this guy did?" I asked.

"Then he has a way to get in touch. Back then, I'd use a voicemail box to pick up messages, or an intermediary."

"You said 'back then'," said Garrett.

"Well, I'm not doing it *now*," said Weaver with a shake of his head. "Plus, I saw the driver's license. I know this isn't recent work and I know I haven't seen this guy in years. A decade or two, maybe. Closer to two, I think. Then there's the small matter of my prison sentence. I've been out of the game for a while."

"And will be staying that way," interjected Don.

"Quite right, Don," said Weaver, nodding along, although I wasn't sure if anyone totally believed him. He was too quick, too slick, and too congenial to be totally trustworthy. "I met this guy three or four times, and then nothing."

"Did he give you a reason for not returning?"

"None. He just didn't return."

"What did you think happened to him?"

"I didn't think anything. I wasn't interested in his life story. Unlike you two," he added. "I'll admit to the forgeries but I can't help you any further."

"Thanks for your time," said Garrett.

"No problem," said Weaver. "That *probably* helps, right?"

Garrett nodded, and Don said, "I'll make a note in your file that you were helpful and courteous."

"I'll take it," said Weaver.

Garrett and I filed out, Don just behind us, shutting the door behind him. "I hope you got what you wanted?" he said.

"Unfortunately no, but it's par for the course. Not

everyone's going to have a viable lead for us," said Garrett.

Don stuck out his hand, shaking ours. "Let me know if I can be any more help."

We thanked him again and headed out.

"It was a long shot," I said, hoping to remind Garrett of the fact.

"Yeah. Shame we didn't learn anything useful. A few more aliases could have been helpful in building the movements of this guy. A real name would have been better."

"We do know he didn't commission any identification documents for his son," I said. "Perhaps he wanted to keep the boy well out of anything nefarious he was doing."

"Sounds like he might have gotten one thing right in his life," said Garrett. "Although that does make me wonder about the kid. Given that no IDs were commissioned for the boy, it doesn't sound like he lived with him, so where was he? Who looked after him while Joe Smithson was away on jobs? Who's the mom? Were they even related?"

"You think the boy might be, what? A friend? No way. The age gap is too big. They'd have very little in common."

"Nephew then?"

"It's possible but I'm still leaning towards son," I said. "Let's go back to the kid for a moment. There were no IDs for him so… they couldn't have been on the run. The boy didn't live with him and I'm sure we would have known if there was a teenaged boy being homeschooled in the neighborhood."

"He probably lived with the mom. Dad dropped in and out of his life, kept them out of it."

"So there should be a record somewhere of our John Doe keeping his original name. He would hardly tell the boy to call him by some other name. Imagine if our parents did that. It would be hard to wrap our heads around. Plus, he must have made provisions for him somehow if he were paying towards his upkeep. Mom recognized the school badge. She said the school was expensive."

"It's likely Smithson used his real name for his close personal interactions, but until a name pops up, we don't know what that is. I'm hopeful the autopsy turns up something."

"Any news on when that will be?"

"I'm still waiting for the ME to call. C'mon. I'll give you a ride back to the office, then I'm heading to the station to talk to my captain about these jewels."

"What about them?" I asked, hopeful there was news.

"He wants to know who owns them. Funny that because me too." Garrett laughed.

He dropped me off at the agency, declining to come inside, but with the insistence to call him if anything turned up.

I crossed my fingers and hoped something would because the forgery lead had been utterly disappointing.

When I reached the office, Solomon and Delgado were sitting at the table in the boardroom. Solomon stepped out, asking, "How's it going?"

"Dead end," I said. "The forger recognized the driving license and admits to supplying him with forgeries but didn't have any more to say. Garrett's hopeful that the autopsy might turn up something useful. So far, the body is our best lead."

"Where are you at until then?"

"Mom had a lot of background information for Garrett and me and we might have an identity."

"Already? That's great!"

"It would be if we didn't suspect it to be false. Lily and I got some correlating information from Elsie Greenberg's house so I'm going to work on that. Perhaps something will turn up," I said, wondering if I sounded as despondent as I felt. There were so many jigsaw pieces to complete the puzzle, but I felt like we had three puzzles and all the pieces were jumbled up while the crucial ones were missing.

"Pull Lucas in if you need the manpower."

Solomon's phone rang. He glanced at it then put it to his ear. "Solomon here," he said, turning away.

As I opened my laptop, I remembered in the commotion I'd forgotten to search the school my mom had mentioned. Now I called up The Walsingham School, navigating to the past yearbook pages. There were decades of entries. How long ago did my mother think Joe Smithson had lived in the end house? If the Singhs had moved in during my sophomore or senior year, that narrowed down the time frame. I started with my senior year and scrolled through the photos, disappointed by the time I reached the end.

My junior year yielded the same lack of results.

Disappointed, I hit the *back* button and moved the cursor to my sophomore year, my chin in my hand as I pulled the cursor down.

Halfway down, I stopped and scrolled up.

A boy with dark hair in a uniform smiled at the camera.

Yes, that was the boy in the photo but the smile…

the mouth was what I recognized.

Of course he was older when we met, his features more defined, his youthful good looks having grown into handsome.

Just when I thought the day couldn't get any weirder, it gave me my nemesis, the thief, Ben Rafferty.

CHAPTER TWELVE

The last time I'd seen Ben Rafferty he'd happily escaped me and arrest.

Handsome, charming, and very clever, he'd outmaneuvered me, even used me to steal jewels from an exclusive ball thrown by the woman who had engaged us to catch a thief.

To make matters worse, I'd actually liked him.

I never thought I'd see him again.

Yet here he was, youthful and joyful, smiling in his expensive private school blazer.

"Gideon Black," I read aloud to the empty office. "Everyone's buddy. Played on the cricket team, earned his black belt in karate, fluent in three languages. Destined for great things or great devilry. Hard to tell."

"Sorry 'bout that," said Solomon as he exited the office. He paused. "You look like you've seen a ghost."

"I think I just did." I beckoned for him to join me and he rounded the desk, stooping to look at the screen.

"Who's the kid?"

"You don't recognize him?"

"Should I?"

"Ben Rafferty."

Solomon frowned. "I feel like I should know that name."

"Remember that job we did for the dating agency Million Matches? When I was pretty new on the team? We were hired to find a thief targeting rich women."

"I remember."

I pointed at the screen. "That's him. Gideon Black is Ben Rafferty."

"I see it," said Solomon, frowning as he leaned in for a closer look at the smiling boy on my screen. "How did you find him after all this time? Wait. Have you been looking for him all this time?"

"No! I was looking for the boy in the photo that Garrett retrieved from the body found at the end house."

Solomon straightened. "You have got to be kidding me."

"I wish!" I slumped against the seat back. "How can this be?"

"So Ben… Gideon Black could be the son of the body found in a shallow grave just a few houses over from your parents'?" asked Solomon slowly, like he couldn't quite believe what he was asking.

"The two men are definitely connected somehow," I said. "They're the right age for father and son… and it doesn't seem like he lived with his dad but I don't get it… Ben is a master criminal, a conman, a jewel thief, and he's brilliant at evading capture. And we've got this body in a shallow grave with millions in jewels on him. Does Ben… Gideon… have something to do with this?"

"Are you suggesting Ben… *Gideon*… what are we calling him now?"

"Gideon Black, I guess. That *is* his real identity."

"Let's prove that. Get Lucas on the phone."

I reached for my phone, punching in Lucas's extension. I quickly gave him the rundown and asked him to find proof of Gideon Black as fast as he could. "He's on it," I said to Solomon who simply nodded.

"Are you suggesting Gideon Black killed the man in the grave?" he asked.

"As much as Gideon Black is a criminal, I never thought he was a dangerous one. I just don't see him as a killer. A confidence trickster, yes. Killer, no."

"Let's not count it out."

"Ben… Gideon… heck, I'm not sure I can keep his name straight… is a thief, not a killer. Even if he did murder that man, is it really feasible that he left millions in jewels behind? It doesn't make sense."

"He would have been just a kid then, assuming the body was buried close to twenty years ago, a young adult if not. It could have been his first crime. Perhaps he bungled it," said Solomon.

"Don't criminals usually escalate? He wouldn't start at murder and work his way down to theft."

"Point taken."

"Plus, Gideon would have been set up for life with those jewels. Even if they were worth less back then, it would still have been a fortune. Even if he didn't know how to fence them, he wouldn't just leave them. Anyone with a pinch of sense would take them and figure it out later."

"Unless he knew where they'd been all along and thought he could come back anytime."

"Then why head for a life of crime if you knew there was a payday just waiting to be dug up?" I asked. "He could easily have lived a boring, normal life, waiting for the right time. He didn't need to risk, well, all the risks he's taken." I stared at the photo on my screen, wondering how this wannabe Karate Kid had spiraled into a life of crime.

Maybe because he'd been born into one?

"Plus, why didn't he just dig up the jewels when he was last here? It doesn't make sense. I should tell Garrett," I said, reaching for my phone.

"Call him on the way to the car and then we're heading home," said Solomon. "It's time to wrap up for the night."

I opened my email and sent the school's website link to Garrett first, then I closed the laptop and slid it into my desk drawer, grabbed my purse and followed Solomon out. On the way down the stairs, I called my brother.

"I just emailed you something for the case," I said.

"I'm at my desk. Gimme a minute to get to my emails. What am I looking at?"

I explained and Garrett was silent. "You have got to be kidding me," he said finally.

"That's what Solomon said too. Can this information help identify the body?" I asked as we got into the car. I put the phone on speaker so Solomon could listen in as he drove.

"Maybe, but DNA would be better. I'll look up the kid's records and see if there's anything I can cross-reference."

"We have Lucas running him down too. If this is his real identity, we'll know soon."

"I'd appreciate the info when you get it. The ME says the autopsy is scheduled for the morning so I hope to have more information then. Thanks for this."

"Thanks goes to Mom. She was the one who recognized the badge in the photo when you showed it to her at lunch. I only remembered to check out the school after you dropped me off at the office."

"It must have slipped my mind with everything else going on. Guess we owe Mom a big thank you. Did you ever meet him as a kid? I think I would remember but I don't."

"I don't think so and you would have already moved out by then. Mom said she knew there was a kid but it didn't sound like she met him either. The school he attended was a boarding school so maybe he never came to Montgomery. It's only in Boston so if Joe Smithson is his dad, it's not far to visit without raising suspicion. Or Gideon could have lived with his mother? Mom said the guy she remembers was single but that doesn't mean he didn't have a wife stashed somewhere else. Or, at least, a woman he visited."

"If this guy were up to something like we think, it makes sense that he'd put his family somewhere safe. Boarding school would fit the bill for the kid. Like you said, it's close enough from here to visit but far enough away to put distance between them. Given that it looks like Smithson was murdered, that was a good decision. I'd like to know where the kid's mom is."

Solomon pulled over in front of our house, the

street unusually empty of vehicles for the early evening. He turned off the engine and waited.

"Lucas is running her down too," I said. "I still don't think Gideon killed him, whatever their relationship is. Gideon Black's not a killer. He's a lot of things, but not that."

"I'll bear that in mind. Let's talk tomorrow."

"There's one more thing. The Ben Rafferty I knew had a sister, Madeleine. He let it slip when I last spoke to him but I can't guarantee it wasn't another lie to cause confusion. And Madeleine probably isn't her real name anyway."

"I'll consider that but there's been no hint of a woman or girl so far in this case. Let's catch up tomorrow. I need to update the chief, then I have other cases to review."

"I should tell Lucas about Madeleine," I said to Solomon when Garrett disconnected.

"I sent him a text already." Solomon waved his phone before pocketing it and popping his door open. "What do you make of all this?" he asked when we both reached the sidewalk.

"I have no idea what to think. You?"

"I'm as confused as the next guy, but I do think Ben Rafferty, Gideon Black, or whatever his name is, turning up in this case is bad news for everyone."

~

Solomon's words bothered me all night and, in the morning, I felt unrested and confused about the troubling discovery of the boy's identity.

How had Gideon Black become Ben Rafferty? And what did he know about the man in the photo?

What did he know about the man in the grave?

Garrett sent a text at seven telling me to be at the

autopsy suite at ten. That he was extending me the privilege was more than a professional courtesy, it was an acceptance of collaboratively working on the case, although I'd have much preferred he suggested a nice brunch spot. Dead bodies, sliced and diced, didn't do it for me nearly as much as avocado on sourdough.

Solomon had left almost as soon as he awoke, citing an emergency risk assessment, leaving me sipping coffee on my own and wondering how I could find out more information about Gideon Black and how he had become Ben Rafferty.

Then, like a lightbulb pinged in my head, I realized there was someone who knew as much about that man as I did.

I fired off a text suggesting breakfast and within an hour, I was walking into a chic café full of velvet chairs and bleached wooden tables near the FBI's field office.

Maddox waited for me at a window table, a coffee in one hand, a menu in the other. Seeing me walk up, he smiled, set both down, and stood, greeting me with a quick hug and a kiss on the cheek.

"This is a nice idea," he said as we took opposite chairs. "I'm sorry to hear about the divorce."

"Divorce?"

"You've come to your senses and are finally divorcing Solomon?"

"No! Where did you get that idea?"

"I figured you were celebrating and wanted to share the moment with me." Maddox gave me the most unsympathetic smile as he touched both hands to his heart. A bandage peeked out from under his shirt sleeve.

"No!"

"I think you protest too much. It's okay, Lexi, you don't have to be ashamed. Not every marriage works out." He patted my arm reassuringly.

"I'm *not* getting divorced."

"So you want a recommendation for a lawyer?" Maddox reached for his phone and ran his forefinger across the screen, scrolling through his phone book.

"Have you finished having your fun with me yet?" I asked, sighing and taking the menu the server offered as she walked past.

"I'd rather wait for the divorce to be finalized. I'm a man of principles."

I shook my head and ignored him as I contemplated crepes or waffles.

"Okay, fine. You're not about to make all my dreams come true. Why are we eating together? I know it's not because you want to stare at my dreamily handsome face. But, on a side note, you can still do that."

"I want to pick your brains on my case."

"Our neighborhood robbers? I thought we wrapped that up nicely. It wasn't even my case but we nailed it!"

"No, my other case. Dead body on my parents' street."

Maddox winced. "Did your parents do it?" he asked.

"No!"

"That's what your mom said but I figured I should ask a more reliable source. I can't find one so here we are."

I narrowed my eyes at him, wondering how I was going to get him back for his teasing. I would, somehow, someday, and definitely enjoy it.

"Okay, because I would have still helped if they had. Especially your mom. She's great."

"I'm not putting in a good word for you."

"No need to. She loves me. Wait until she hears we've hung out twice in one week! Let's order, then you can ravage me for information."

"I'm not ravaging you for anything."

"You used to for nothing." Maddox winked.

"You're incorrigible!"

"You like that about me. Handsome, charming, witty, *incorrigible*... and that's before we get to the good stuff."

I swatted him with my menu, then continued to browse it as I said, "You love taunting me."

"I love all kinds of things about you but taunting is definitely one of my favorites." Maddox waved for the server and we placed our orders, distracting me from closely examining what he said. "You could have picked a dive but instead, we're at this romantic, little setting."

"It's the nearest nice café to your building."

"I know. It's my regular spot now. Beats the dive nearest the police station in my detective days. Anyway, stop playing around with my heart, and tell me what you want to know."

"Do you remember Ben Rafferty?"

"Name rings a bell. Who is he?"

"One of your cases when you were a detective. He was one of my targets at a high-end dating agency where our client suspected someone was targeting women for their cash and valuables, not their hearts."

Maddox nodded, smiling. "I remember. You were parading around town in a Ferrari as a super-rich, hot, single woman in need of a man. Did you keep any of the stuff?"

"Did you see me drive up in a Ferrari?"

"No."

"There's your answer."

"You have a terrible job."

"Says the man in government service. Although you do get trips to Europe."

"Currently postponed. *Again*. So Ben Rafferty?" Maddox sipped his coffee thoughtfully. His eyes widened and his eyebrows rose, and I knew that had to be the exact moment he remembered the case clearly. His lips hovered over the cup before he put it down. "Shit! He was the guy who escaped our custody!"

"That's him."

"Aided by a woman posing as his lawyer."

"The same woman who was a plant in the dating agency's office. Madeleine, his accomplice."

"Yeah, I remember now. What's he got to do with your case?"

"He might be well acquainted with our dead man."

Maddox blinked. "I can't even fathom how Ben Rafferty and your dead guy are connected."

"I'm not sure either but with the evidence as it stands, I'm leaning towards father and son. I wondered what happened after he escaped your custody? Or if you discovered anything about him after that?"

"I wish I had more to tell you but Rafferty was a slippery bastard. We searched his apartment and it was scrubbed like a professional. Not a scrap of information and no fingerprints. There was literally nothing we could use to find him. Of course, we had a decent photo and prints from booking him into custody and we sent that out to the agencies but we didn't get anything for a while. Then a hit came in that he might have been involved in a love scam in Phoenix."

"A love scam? Like the dating agency scam?"

"Very similar. In Phoenix he was courting rich, older women, then swindling them out of their cash."

"That's horrible."

"And something he has form for so not unexpected. I spoke with Phoenix PD and they told me they didn't have anything concrete, only the complaint from one of the women that he'd made off with at least a hundred thousand dollars."

"A hundred grand!"

"Small change. Apparently, this woman had money to burn but it was the principle of the thing."

"Wait… you said one of. How many women did he rip off?"

"Hard to say because none of the others came forward, but we think there were several targets. Whether he was successful with them all, I don't know. But I can say he didn't go for any personal, irreplaceable possessions, just generic stuff or cash."

"Are you trying to say he has a heart?"

"Maybe. Maybe not." Maddox shrugged as he took a sip. "Anyway, there was no direct evidence to connect him to the crime in Phoenix, no prints, and no photos where we could definitively identify him as the same guy. Even the plaintiff couldn't be sure from our mug shot. This guy had longer hair, a beard, and a tan. He said he was from Connecticut but his target didn't see any proof of that."

"What about a sister?"

"From what I remember, their perp claimed to be an only child."

"Any female friend or colleagues that could have been an accomplice?"

"Nothing that stood out to the complainant."

"So what happened next?"

"Phoenix PD didn't have any solid leads and without an identification, we couldn't confirm it was our guy so they shelved the case." Maddox paused as the server placed our plates in front of us. "The only thing that stood out to me was the guy was calling himself Tom Benedict."

"Benedict," I repeated, considering the odds. "Ben. It could be a coincidence."

"It could. There was one more hit, right before I left the force, but this was overseas and a different MO." Maddox forked egg and toast into his mouth, chewing. "This time, it was a heist from an old, aristocratic family in Europe. They were throwing a party and someone used all the commotion as a distraction, then got into their safe, making off with two gold ingots and a bunch of paperwork. They clammed up pretty quickly about the paperwork, claiming that was an error and nothing was missing but they were steamed about the gold."

"Where's the connection to Ben Rafferty or Tom Benedict?"

"One of the catering staff was found tied up in an outbuilding, minus his uniform. After reviewing the footage of the event, all the catering staff could be accounted for except one man. He was caught on camera once and it's only a partial facial, but he looked a lot like our man. Again, nothing definitive to tie the two men together, and, before you ask, no sign of a female accomplice, so I made a note in our file and left it. I was leaving anyway and there was nothing more I could do. We hit a dead end."

"Safe cracking doesn't sound beyond him, although he obviously prefers people just handing him the money."

"My thoughts exactly. How's your breakfast?"

A waft of sugary heat rose from my pancakes. "Perfect."

"That's as much as I can tell you from my detective days. It would be great if you could fill in a few blanks, like his connection to your dead guy. You must have come across something that directly pointed to Ben Rafferty, otherwise we wouldn't be talking and you'd just be staring at me dreamily."

I couldn't see any harm in telling Maddox after he had so openly explained the aftermath of his case. "The dead guy was carrying a photo in his wallet. The ID was fake but the photo showed an older man and a very young Ben Rafferty. That's why I think the older man might be his father, but we're not sure yet if the man in the photo and the dead guy are the same person. I didn't even recognize Ben at first."

"I don't suppose there was an inscription? 'To my son, Ben, love, Dad' or anything like that?"

"No. And his name, unsurprisingly, isn't Ben either. I tracked down his real name," I said, enjoying my moment of smugness as I forked a piece of pancake into my mouth.

"Don't leave me in suspense!"

"Gideon Black."

For a moment, Maddox was very still, his eyes calculating, but then he shrugged. "Can't say I've heard that name before."

"Do you think you could try running it? Maybe through one of your super-duper databases? Lucas is working on it now, but the more eyes the better."

"Sure. I'll let you know if anything comes up although I can't imagine we'll find anything Lucas can't and I still don't want to know exactly how he conducts research. Do you have any more information on this Gideon Black?"

"Just his school. An expensive boarding school in Boston. Interests were cricket, karate and languages. Garrett's looking into him too. The more the better, I think, given how slippery he is."

"I seem to remember you had a good rapport with him."

"When he was masquerading as Ben Rafferty? Sure. I thought he was charming and he was, but then he thought I was loaded and he was looking to lighten that load."

"He probably enjoyed taking on the challenge of seducing a young, attractive woman. A nice change of pace for him."

"I'll take the compliment. Is that what he does? Seduces these women?" Privately, I wondered if that was a worse betrayal for the women he stole from. Taking their things and their money was one thing, but their bodies? That was personal.

"More courting than seducing. Claims he's an old-fashioned man who wants to wait and not rush the romance. I think they fall for it hard."

"So... not a total cad," I decided.

"I'm not saying he doesn't, just that no one has *said* he'd gotten them into bed. There could be a reason."

"Such as? Oh! You think he's gay."

"Maybe that, but maybe he's got a woman of his own and some morals."

"He didn't come off as gay to me. I don't know that I can equate someone who steals with someone with fidelity values."

"Could his female accomplice be a wife, not a sister? She was a similar age to him from what I recall."

"Could be, but I didn't get the impression he was harboring any longing for anyone. Although, he would hardly make that obvious since he was trying to be my perfect man while calculating my net worth." I paused to eat, reflecting on what I did know. "I wish there was more I could tell you but I have a feeling I'm not going to come up with much. Gideon Black appears and disappears and he's careful. He must have a regular home, or people somewhere, but he definitely isn't advertising it. He's got access to identity documents, travel… he invests in his business such as it is and he knows how to charm his way into people's inner circles. He knows the right people. Or the wrong ones. Plus, he has no problem moving in elite circles."

"So what if he is the kid of this dead guy in the shallow grave? What are you going to do about that?"

"I guess Ben/Gideon needs to be informed but I don't know how we'll go about doing that. Garrett isn't entirely convinced he isn't involved in the death."

"And you?"

"It seems a stretch to start a life of crime with murder and work your way down from there."

"There are easy ways to draw him out. Publicize the discovery and he might come out of the woodwork," said Maddox.

"Assuming he wants to. I don't know if the relationship between him and this guy was good. No one remembers Joe Smithson having a kid around but that doesn't mean they didn't keep in touch." I thought about the jewels but didn't mention them. They could attract all kinds of people.

"Do you mind if I liaise with Garrett?"

"Go ahead. Maybe check in this afternoon? We're due at the autopsy suite at ten."

"You're going there after eating that?" Maddox pointed at my plate and I nodded. "Amateur," he snorted.

"I don't think Garrett intends for me to be *in* the room!"

"Just take a hair tie."

I frowned, then I caught his drift. "He's been in the ground for a long time. It can't be so bad. They'll just poke around his bones and tell us the cause of death."

"I'd love to fill you in on procedure but I'm eating too and I don't want to. Good luck. Remember, it happens to all of us."

"What does?"

"You'll see." Maddox grinned.

CHAPTER THIRTEEN

After breakfast, I went directly to the morgue, arriving early enough that I could sit outside under the cloudless blue sky and pass the time plugging Gideon Black, Ben Rafferty and Tom Benedict into my phone's browser. I'd known the search would be largely fruitless but I did find a couple of team sports photos from Gideon's teenage years. As I zoomed in on his proud, smiling face, I was more certain than ever that I'd found my charming thief.

Some more searching and I found mention of Gideon at a small, private university where he'd majored in art history with a minor in finance. He'd gone onto a master's degree and then seemingly dropped off the face of the earth.

No work history, no social media, no LinkedIn profile.

Nothing to suggest that Gideon had done anything with his life since the age of twenty-two. It was like he graduated and vanished into thin air.

Except I knew he hadn't.

Somehow he had turned to a life of crime… and it had paid off.

Gideon Black. Ben Rafferty. Tom Benedict. Could they really all be the same person? How many more aliases did he have?

I searched for each name and then in various conjunctions with each other and found nothing. That didn't deter me. The man had to live somewhere. He had to pay some kind of property tax or utilities. He couldn't just not exist in between targets.

"Have you been waiting long?" A shadow fell over me and I jumped, my heart thumping. "Sorry for startling you!" said Garrett.

I pressed a hand to my heart, willing it to slow to a more reasonable speed as my brother looked at me with concern. "I didn't notice you coming towards me," I said, then waggled my phone. "I was concentrating."

"The case?"

I nodded and as I got up to join him to walk to the morgue, I filled him in on Maddox's chat.

"I'll expect a call from him," said Garrett when I'd finished. "This case is getting weirder by the day but I suppose I shouldn't be surprised. I might pay Phoenix PD a courtesy call."

"Any more news about the jewels?"

Garrett shook his head. "I'm waiting for something to come back in reference to the diamond serial numbers. If they weren't registered, we might never know where they came from."

"Surely, no one could write off that kind of cost?"

"We're assuming all the jewels came from the same place. It's possible they're from several different places. It could even be that our body is the rightful owner."

I raised my eyebrows. "Really?"

"Unlikely," said Garrett. "I plugged Gideon Black into the missing persons database after your call but there weren't any hits."

"So no one reported missing him?"

"Apparently not, or at least not under his birth name. I pulled his birth records. Mother deceased when he was a child. Father listed as Charles Black. Known as Charlie. The search on him came back with a missing person as of twenty years ago. Last known address in Rhode Island. I checked and it was a rental that's changed hands a bunch of times. I don't need to tell you that's easy driving distance to here or Boston. The missing person case file was thin and the detective on it passed a few years back so that's a dead end."

"Any sign of a sister?"

"I didn't find any other kids registered to either parent, but that doesn't mean there aren't unregistered siblings or half-siblings. I contacted the school too but no one remembers him, which isn't surprising, given staff turnover. They could confirm his fees were paid in advance, covering until the end of his senior year, and he was a boarder. Tracking down classmates will take time and there's no guarantee anyone will have remained in touch since our guy seems to have taken great measures to disappear. That's if he really is connected to this case. Let's find out what the ME has to say and circle back."

We'd arrived at the entrance to the morgue and Garrett pressed the buzzer, announcing us both into the speaker. A moment later, a technician appeared and let us in.

"Dr. Barnes is waiting for you in the autopsy suite," he said. "I'll take you through."

I'd been in the basement morgue's office a few times, rarely by invitation. When we entered, the room was quiet, and only one metal table had a white cover on it. The room smelled of bleach and something unidentifiable and unpleasant. "Lieutenant Graves, nice to see you and your associate. It's a slow day," said Dr. Barnes as she entered via another door. She adjusted her big, round, spectacles and smiled. "But I'm sure it'll perk up!"

"Let's hope not," said Garrett just as the implications of that hit me. "What have you got for us?"

"We don't often get unauthorized burials like this so everyone was interested in taking a look," she began, reaching for the sheet.

I recoiled as the skeletal remains were revealed and had a moment of indecision where I badly wanted to run out while my morbid curiosity made me want to stay.

"I thought I'd go ahead and get the bones all cleaned up before you dropped in," she said. "Afraid there wasn't anything useful for you there unless you want some extra worms."

My stomach heaved.

"No, thanks," said Garrett.

"Okay then. Well, cause of death was a bullet to the skull. See here and here?" she said, manipulating the skull and pointing with a gloved finger. "Entry wound here, exit wound here. Small caliber weapon. No bullet. The trajectory suggests he would have died instantly. Your shooter would have been no more than a few yards away when he or she fired. Make of that what you will."

"Homicide," stated Garrett.

"I believe so, yes. The skeleton belongs to a man, Caucasian, approximately fifty years old, in good health. No abnormalities. Two fractures to his fingers on his right hand, which hadn't healed so possibly from a fight close to his death."

"Could be with the killer," I said.

Dr. Barnes rocked her head, uncommitted. "It's possible and it fits with a theory of trying to defend himself before he was shot, but I can't definitively say that was the case. I'll leave that to you."

"What else can you tell us about him?" asked Garrett.

"Some good news. His left leg had been broken and the pin used to set it had a serial number. I ran it against our database and we got a positive match. I just sent my junior ME to collect the print out."

"So we have an identification?" Garrett flashed a smile at me.

"We do. Here's Dr. Kimura now," she said as a younger man came towards us flapping a piece of paper. It was then I noticed what was tucked underneath his arm. A severed head. The eyes seemed to focus on me.

Before I could even fully register what was happening, I turned, my stomach heaving and lost the contents of my stomach on the tiled floor.

"There's always one" said Dr. Barnes as Garrett pulled back my hair. "Is she a rookie?"

Whatever was said next was lost to me as the world turned upside-down and then I winked out of existence.

~

"Lexi?"

"No heads, thank you please."

"Lexi?"

"No. No heads. *Iz nawt halloweeeeen!*"

"Lexi?"

"I'm *schleeping*. Night night."

"Lexi!" snapped the voice.

I opened my eyes, an acrid taste filling my mouth and blinked under the uncomfortably bright lights in the paneled floor. Or was it the ceiling?

Garrett's face loomed over mine. "Where am I?" I asked, blinking, the words slurring in my mouth.

"The corridor. You fainted."

I struggled to sit upright, finding myself lying across several chairs, and planted my feet on the floor. Garrett pressed a plastic water cup into my hand as I groaned. "Sip," he ordered. "You threw up."

I sipped and pulled a face. "You can never tell anyone," I said, wondering about the small wound to my pride.

"It happens to everyone."

"I will never live this down. Don't tell Maddox!"

"Why would I tell him?"

I grimaced. "He'll ask." No wonder he'd looked so smug when I left him at the café. *Happens to everyone*, huh?

Garrett squatted in front of me. "How're you feeling?" he asked.

"Fine." I touched my head, surprised to find it didn't hurt.

"I caught you before you kissed the floor."

"Thanks."

"Let me know when you feel up to moving and I'll fill you in on everything."

"So long as everything doesn't include that severed head, I'm good to go."

"Apparently, it was just a joke prop. It wasn't real."

"All the same, I'm not sure I'll ever close my eyes again." I sipped the water until I drained the cup and gave myself a little shake. "Okay, I'm ready. Hit me with it. What did you find out?" I waved at Garrett to hurry up and fill my brain with new information so I didn't have to think about that head, real or not.

"You were only out for a couple minutes, so not much but we do have a name. Our body is confirmed as Charles Black. The same man as our missing report. Before you ask, yes, he's definitely Gideon Black's father. The ME is going to confirm the identification through dental records once she has them but she's given me a ninety-five percent certainty verdict based on the plate from the leg."

"So Joe Smithson *was* an alias."

"Yes, we were right on that, but the big question is why?"

"Because he was up to no good," I said, wondering if maybe I'd had a little knock on the head after all. I ran my hands over my head, reassured to find no bumps.

"Okay, that is probably why. The ME had some more information."

"I like all this sharing!"

"Don't get used to it. I'm only telling you because I'm overworked and need another set of eyes on this case, and, even better, your consultancy fee isn't coming out of our department budget."

"I wasn't aware we were charging a fee."

"Precisely."

"And there I was feeling all warm and fuzzy about us working together. What's the extra information?"

"Based on the decomposition, the ME estimated the burial to have taken place between fifteen and twenty-five years ago. His clothing matches the fashion of around that time and when they tested fibers, she was able to confirm the jacket he'd been wearing was from a manufacturer that went out of business eighteen years ago. That narrowed the time frame. The leasing information you sent me reduces it further. The missing person report clinches it. I don't think Joe Smithson ever left that house willingly. I think he was killed there and it was covered up to look like he'd left or skipped out on the rental."

"Who filed the missing person report?" I asked.

"Looks like his son filed it from Boston. But it doesn't look like he ever followed up."

"So either he knows what happened to his dad and was trying to hide his part in it, or something happened that made him lose interest in finding answers. Or scared him off."

"I had the same thoughts. No one reported a Joe Smithson missing, but I also can't find a record of anyone by that name paying taxes, utilities or anything else from that time. I think we should assume Charlie Black used more than one identity."

"Father and son are starting to sound alike." I thought about it for a moment, then said, "I was about to suggest we should come at this from two sides and meet in the middle. You take Charlie Black. I'll take Gideon Black, but now I think about it, I have no idea how to find Gideon now. He just disappeared last time. If it weren't for Maddox's intel about two possible sightings, I'd say he'd ceased to exist. Or turned law abiding. The first seems more likely."

"He probably goes to ground between jobs. That could be what the father was doing too. Biding his time and checking in on his son before he picked up another scam."

"We're sure Charlie Black was running scams?" I asked. "It couldn't be anything simpler like he just wanted to change his name to run from, I don't know, debtors? A gang? Drug lords?"

"You have a fanciful mind. I'm thinking scam but I'd like evidence to confirm."

"But how did he get those jewels? Everything seems to come back to them."

"The twelve million dollar question."

"I think we should focus less on the two men and go straight to the middle ground. The jewels. Gideon is a thief. We know that. We should assume his father is too. He might have even taught his son how to steal. If Charlie Black stole the jewels, someone probably wants them back. Might have even killed for them." I stopped, stumped again. So why not take the jewels? Why leave them behind?

"I'll let you know what comes up as I poke around. What are you going to do until then?"

"Inform the Dugans that they're definitely not going to be arrested." I side-eyed Garrett. "Are they?" I asked.

"They are not," he confirmed.

"And then I'm going to focus on the rental records and Lucas's findings."

"What are the odds that we have two thieves already in the mix? One who steals jewels, one with a pocketful of 'em?"

"I don't know, but it's starting to sound like the family business is a dangerous one."

Garrett and I walked outside and after he retrieved me a bottle of water and a candy bar from a vending machine, and checked several more times that I was okay to be by myself, he left for the police station with a promise to call me as soon as he had an update.

Since I had time to kill, I decided to walk back to the office so I could gather my thoughts. More than once as I tried to separate my thoughts about Gideon and his father, I found them sliding together, only to struggle to wrench them apart.

It had to be a coincidence that these cases had dropped onto my lap. Charlie Black had been dead for around twenty years. Yet now I had a solid connection between this town and Gideon Black, I had to wonder if swindling rich women and theft were the only reasons he came here under his Ben Rafferty guise? Or had he also come to search for his father? Gideon had been the one to register his father missing all those years ago so that implied they had regular contact until the older man's disappearance and premature death. That contact had to be regular enough for Gideon to find his father's absence concerning. Did he know his father lived under an alias? Was that how he knew how to assume identities too?

If the forger, Owen Weaver, hadn't been imprisoned for so long, I would have asked him if he gave family referral discounts.

I had more questions than I had answers and by the time I reached the agency, I was deeply frustrated.

Lucas hadn't sent any information to my inbox or left me any messages, which was disappointing.

I called the Dugans, leaving a message on their voicemail that there was nothing alarming to report, but that there had been developments on the case and that the evidence strongly suggested they had nothing to do with the death or burial. I asked them to return the call so we could discuss the next steps, feeling certain that they wouldn't want to invest any more of their money. The thought was disappointing. Not the agency's fee but if they terminated our contract, once I'd sent them my report, I would have no reason to continue digging and I really, *really* wanted to.

Garrett might be a lot less sharing if he knew I didn't have a finger in the pie, and I doubted Solomon would want me stuck in if the agency weren't being paid. I could take the occasional pro-bono case but that involved having a client in need. The Dugans weren't in need, they were simply inconvenienced.

Despite using every database I had at my disposal, I couldn't find any variation of Gideon Black's names with the ages and variables in active use in the area, or any historic references for Charlie Black or his aliases, and there were far too many hits across the States to feasibly check every one. That made me sit back and assess the case.

I had wondered if we were looking at this all wrong.

What if I'd been right when I said to Garrett we should look into the middle ground. What if it weren't the people that could crack the case open but the jewels?

We had initially assumed all the jewels came from the same place but the jewelers and Garrett had cast a shadow over that. What if the jewels were a hoard made up of multiple thefts and deceptions? The smaller jewels would be the most marketable as desirable stones for all manner of jewelry but it was the large ruby that was by far the most valuable.

There couldn't be many rubies like that.

It had been hidden for near twenty years so that was where I started searching.

That the jewels were in Charlie Black's pocket felt significant. Had they recently come into his possession? Or was he preparing to offload them at the time of his death? Otherwise, why not hide them in a safe place?

A search for jewel thefts in the state returned a handful of articles. Broadening my search to nearby states offered a few more pages but none referenced anything as valuable as the ruby. Was that because there was nothing to find? I doubted it. I just hadn't hit on the right lead yet.

I closed my laptop and headed over to Lily's bar, determined to clear my head with another walk. Plus, I wanted to check in on her after our unfortunate sprinkler jetwash and maybe avail myself of some nice snacks to appease my empty stomach.

When I arrived, the bar was quiet with just a handful of patrons dotted around the booths and tables furthest from the bar. Lily was serving a couple while her employee, but also our friend, Ruby Kalouza, was polishing stemware. The music was low and upbeat, soft conversation easily flowing over the top, and the scent of leather and polish hung in the air.

"I thought you'd be out chasing bad guys," said Lily as she returned to the bar. Her hair had been washed and her curls freshly set. Yesterday, she'd been drenched, her curls plastered to her face. "Or did you catch them already?"

I slid onto a bar stool and hooked my bag under the bar. "I'm at an impasse," I said.

"That doesn't sound ideal," said Ruby. Dark-haired, pretty, and with an hourglass figure, Ruby was more trendy than elegant in her crew-neck Lily's Bar t-shirt and apron. She personified exactly the kind of customer Lily wanted to attract: cool. "Would wine help?"

I shook my head and my stomach gurgled. My mouth tasted gritty and my day's calorie intake was at the morgue. "Maybe a soft drink and snacks," I decided.

"Coming up," said Lily. "If I throw in ice and a lemon slice, will that help?"

"Supremely."

"What's the impasse?" asked Ruby.

"My dead thief is related to my arch nemesis and I can't figure out if he's committed a crime or was the victim of one." I let out a sigh.

"Your arch nemesis committed a crime?" asked Ruby, frowning.

"No. Well, yes, he definitely has, but probably not this one. My dead guy is related to him and it looks like they might both be criminals."

Lily and Ruby exchanged looks and Lily shrugged.

"Ben Rafferty," I said to clue her in, waiting for realization to dawn on Lily's face.

"That rat!" she spat. "He's back in town?"

"No, but it looks like my cold case dead guy might be his dad."

"Shut! Up!" squealed Lily.

"Okay," I said, and rested my forehead on the bar. Lily tapped on my head and I lifted it expectantly.

"Do not shut up," she said. "Is this the guy with all the jewels that we nearly got drowned for yesterday?"

"Jewels?" asked Ruby, looking between us. "Drowned?"

"Long story," I said.

"I'll tell Ruby later. You better fill us in," said Lily. She slid a tall glass across to me, a wedge of lemon over the rim, followed quickly by a small bowl of peanuts and a larger bowl of chips. "You have to earn your keep if you want that on the house."

I repeated what Garrett and I had discovered, leaving out the part where he had to hold my hair back before catching me. "So you see," I said as I finished, "With the Blacks' aliases making it tough to research them, my best lead is the jewels. I think they're stolen and Garrett is looking into it but there haven't been any leads so far. There's no way someone isn't missing a huge ruby!"

"Did you hear about the Queen's Ruby?" asked Ruby. She reached into the dishwasher under the bar for the next set of glasses to polish. "Now that was an audacious theft!"

"No. Did it happen here?"

"No, it was in New York. I remember because my dad was working in New York at the time and only coming home on weekends and he said there was a lot of fuss about it. Apparently, it was the big centerpiece of an exhibition at the New York

Museum of History and poof! They showed it off at a big, fancy party on opening night, then the next day it was gone! Like magic. No one saw a thing. Every time I went anywhere, all the kids at school called me The Disappearing Ruby for two weeks," she added with a laugh. "You must have heard about it. It was big news."

"What happened?" asked Lily. "It couldn't have simply disappeared!"

"I think there was a break-in overnight or maybe someone hid in the museum after hours? Or maybe it was stolen during the party? I don't remember. All I know is everyone at the party claimed they never saw a thing."

"Was it ever found?" I asked.

Ruby shrugged. "I have no idea. I don't think so, but this was twenty something years ago so I really don't remember. You mentioning a ruby made it pop into my head."

I sat up a little straighter. "Twenty years ago?"

"Thereabouts. Not just the Queen's Ruby but a whole bunch of jewelry too. It was like something out of *Ocean's 11*. Well, I imagine it was anyway."

"What kind of jewelry?" I asked, reaching for my phone.

Ruby pursed her lips. "Necklaces, earrings, rings, I guess. I'm trying to remember the name of the exhibition. My dad bought my mom a replica necklace from the gift shop and I was really into being a princess at the time, so he got me a little paste ruby tiara. So cute. I think it was called something like…"

"Treasures of Rachenstein," I said, reading from the screen, which had returned several results following my quick search for the Queen's Ruby.

"Yeah, that's it!" Ruby said. "Did you find a picture?"

I scrolled my forefinger down the screen, skimming the article about the incomprehensible theft, the baffled statement from the museum, the determination of the police chief to apprehend the culprit, the discreet refusal to comment from Rachenstein, and then there was a picture.

The ruby rested on a velvet cushion, so large and dazzling that I just knew it was the one unearthed from its decades of concealment only days before.

CHAPTER FOURTEEN

"Ruby, you just blew my case wide open."

Ruby beamed. "You're welcome! I think?" She frowned, apparently uncertain if I were serious.

"You did," I insisted, my excitement rising. "I think this is it. I think this is the ruby!"

"My dad didn't do it," she said quickly. "I swear."

"Is he a criminal?" I wondered.

"Only occasionally," she said. "And never jewels. It's pure coincidence he was in New York at the time that ruby was stolen. Plus, he's not smart enough. Whoever stole it is a hundred times smarter than my dad."

"Maybe not," I said, thinking about the shallow grave.

"What does the article say?" asked Lily. "Does it name any suspects?"

"It looks like the ruby was the centerpiece of an exhibition of the state jewels and treasures of a small European country called Rachenstein. The jewels were on a year's tour of major museums, in celebration of the crowning of their new king." I paused to read ahead, then continued. "New York was their penultimate stop in the US, having already exhibited in Los Angeles and Chicago. Its final stop was due to be in Washington DC before the tour returned to Europe, then home. It seems like it was also a way of encouraging tourism for Rachenstein."

"Look how cute it is," said Lily, turning her phone. She'd opened to Instagram and ran her finger down the screen, showing picture after picture of pretty castles surrounded by spring flora, quaint cottages against an array of snow-capped towering conifers, and cobbled streets bordered with pretty boutiques.

"Girls' trip?" suggested Ruby. "Look here, we can get rooms in a renovated library that has wild deer visiting its gardens. How romantic!"

"I'd feel like I was in a Disney film," I said. "And I'm not complaining. That sounds dreamy."

"Wait until you see the cocktail menu," said Ruby, "and they serve afternoon tea."

"Tell us more about the ruby and then ask Solomon if we can take an all-expense paid trip to Rachenstein for research," said Lily.

"I don't think he'll go for that," I said.

"*Research*," said Lily slowly.

"All three of us?"

"I can take notes," said Ruby.

"And I'll drive," said Lily. "Although it seems they have horse-drawn sleighs in the winter." She sighed.

I laughed and returned my attention to the article. "So the jewels had their big opening night in a society gala thrown by the museum and the very next day they were gone."

"How?" asked Ruby.

"It doesn't say. Only that the museum director was incredulous and the police are following a number of leads. Let me see if I can find more." I hit the back tab and scrolled to the next article. "Okay. Oh, wow! Here it says the theft caused a huge diplomatic incident with Rachenstein and the exhibition was immediately closed with the announcement that every exhibit remaining would be returned to their country at once."

I was ready to read through several more articles when the agency number flashed on my phone. "Gotta take this," I said, half-turning and expecting Lily and Ruby to entertain themselves for a moment. Only they didn't move an inch. Instead, they waited expectantly. "Hey?" I said.

"I have results for you," said Lucas. "Not a whole bunch but I have your Gideon Black's birth records. Mom and Dad listed. Philippine and Charles Black. Mom deceased nine years later, accidental drowning."

"That much I know from Garrett," I said. "Not the drowning part, but the dad bit."

"Yeah, it wasn't hard to find. No siblings. You asked about a Madeleine and I couldn't find any in the family history. Mom was French, no family left. She immigrated here a few years prior to her marriage. She worked as a teacher at a private school. Dad has a very patchy work history, nothing of note."

"So Madeleine is not his sister," I said, contemplating that. Of course it was another lie. No surprise there.

"Not legally. Definitely not via the mother. Could be unregistered to the father."

"Or simply a lie. You're sure there's definitely no

siblings?"

"None, unless they're unregistered. If I had DNA, I could do some more poking around."

"Sorry, I don't have any lying around. The work history… Patchy how?" I asked.

"Black was born into a wealthy family whose fortunes took a nosedive after bad investments and big purchases. Private funds ran out in his early twenties, prior to his marriage. Not through his fault; the dad was profligate. He had a heart attack and died and the widow was left to sell everything to settle debts."

"Would there be enough money left for Black to put Gideon through boarding school and a private university?" I asked.

"No. When I say there was no money, I mean *no money*. The widow had enough to buy a property for herself. Grand to most people but it would've been a huge downgrade for her, and a moderate pension until she passed. She wasn't much better with handling money. The house was mortgaged heavily and she ran up debts. Black inherited very little when she passed a few years later. He was married by then.

"I didn't find any arrest records for Charles or Gideon Black. A driving misdemeanor for the dad twenty-five years ago that he got a slap on the wrist for. That's it. I have sales records of the Black homes and there are a couple articles about their fall from grace in the finance and society sections, which probably embarrassed the heck out of them back in the day. I've forwarded them to your email."

"Thanks."

"I wish I could say I had more recent news but Charles Black pretty much disappears while the kiddo is young and I hardly find anything after Philippine dies. I've got school records for the boy but nothing to indicate where they lived and then records show he's a boarder from age thirteen. The costs were paid through a trust that paid the school directly and also deposited an allowance into the kid's account at the start of every month. After graduating, the school fees stopped and university fees were drawn. The account was almost drained after Gideon graduated with his master's degree. Here's what's interesting: the account was paid into semi-regularly until the kid was seventeen, then all payments stopped."

"That fits with when the ME thinks Charlie Black died."

"Yeah, I'd say this corroborates it."

"Any idea where the money came from?"

"Some cash deposits. Some wired in from offshore accounts. One in the Caymans. One in a European country known for its extreme privacy in banking."

"Rachenstein?" I wondered.

"No."

"What about Gideon Black? Do you have anything else on him?"

"I found a man of the same name registered for a master's degree in Paris and then a postgraduate program on his return to the US. That's it. He disappears too. Do you want me to keep digging?"

"Please," I said, "but let me know if it's fruitless. And can you check his aliases too? Ben Rafferty. Tom Benedict. Also Charlie Black instead of Charles Black. Can you send your research to Garrett too, please?"

"Of course. Ben Rafferty I did and cross-referenced with Gideon Black. Asides from the arrest you already know about, there's nothing that connects to the man we're looking for. Do you want me to play around with the name combinations?"

"Yes. It's a longshot but maybe there's a reason he chooses particular names.

"I'll get back to you," said Lucas and disconnected.

"Good news?" asked Lily. When I turned to face her and Ruby, they were already leaning across the bar. I was pretty sure they'd heard everything.

"Frustrating more than anything. Our suspect knows how to cover his tracks but we do know a few more things about him now, and the timeline for our dead guy's disappearance is becoming more conclusive. It seems like Black, regardless of aliases and who knows what else, really cared about his son. He made sure he was looked after."

"What about the documents we found yesterday? Were they any help?" asked Lily.

"That's my next task. Want to come?"

"I can cover the bar," said Ruby.

"Then you bet I want to come! Let me grab my stuff," said Lily, grinning broadly. Then she stopped and asked, "Should I get an umbrella? Or will a poncho do?"

"Neither I hope."

"Both then," said Lily as she disappeared around the corner of the bar.

"I hope it *is* the ruby," said Ruby while I waited. "It would be the find of the century and it sounds like you'd solve a mystery that's kept people guessing for decades!"

"If it is, I'll make sure you're credited."

"Thanks! Dibs on any tiaras they might give you

in their undying appreciation and gratitude."

"We'll have a long way to go to prove their ruby is *our* ruby but even if it isn't, you've given me some ideas to broaden my search for stolen gems. There's no way someone isn't missing a stone that size."

"And if they are, then it's probably of dubious origin anyway," said Ruby. "Or what if they already collected a huge insurance payout? They might not want it back."

"I wonder how a person even insures something like that?" I pondered, not expecting a reply.

"Beats me. I'm just a bar manager. Rubies and diamonds are a whole different world to mine, despite my name."

"Ready!" called Lily, coming around my side of the bar. She'd tied her curls into a poofy ponytail and removed her apron and "Manager" pin. "Where to first?"

"I tried all the phone numbers and they're long dead but I have two addresses to check out," I said as we left the bar.

"Maybe they can give us the skinny on this guy."

"I'd like to think so but I assume our expectations should be in the gutter. I expect to find they're fake. One is a past address and the other two are for references and our forger admitted he could make those."

"Wouldn't he have been found out at the time if he'd handed over a forged document?"

I beeped my car unlocked and we climbed in. "Security was a lot more lax twenty years ago. I think it would be easy to fake references and not have anyone check up on them, especially if you were the kind of handsome, charming, guy Charlie Black parading as Joe Smithson apparently was. I think he would have an answer for everything. 'Oh, you can't get through on the phone? Let me pick up a letter of reference for you! It's no trouble!'" I mimicked. "'What's that? They don't remember me? Whom did you speak to? Mabel? She's a hoot! Always messing with people. I'll get them to give you a call,' then pay a woman twenty bucks to call and give a reference over the phone."

"That's how we used to give each other glowing references," said Lily, cracking a smile.

"And that's why I know how easy it is to get a fake reference."

"We could have taught this guy a thing or two."

"Yeah, and he could have taught us a hundred."

Our first stop was the three thousand block of Glenhaven Road but I couldn't find 3406. We double-backed, then on the third pass, I pulled over at a disused scrub of land with six-foot-high fencing and bold "STAY OUT!" signs at regular intervals. "This is why we can't find it," I said, pointing. "It's been knocked down."

"Strike one," said Lily. "A lot of the neighboring businesses look like they're going or are already gone out of business."

I followed her gaze to the boarded-up windows and the "Everything Must Go" signs on neighboring properties. "I don't think we're going to find anyone who remembers a business here twenty years ago, much less, a man who once needed a reference. Next!"

The second address on my list had been turned into a grocery superstore with a sprawling parking lot more than ten years ago.

"I remember this now," said Lily. "There was a campaign to save the neighborhood but the grocery store had bought up the land rights on either side and were steadily buying all the houses in the middle. I think a couple of households refused to move until the grocery store made them a big offer and that was it. By the end of the year, the street was flattened and the store was being built."

"I remember the store being built because Mom was irrationally excited about it but I don't remember the fight about the land. Black couldn't have foreseen the development so many years before."

"The original homeowners might still be local."

"Yeah, but he listed this address as a former rental residence. They might never have met him. You know what would be interesting? Finding out what happened to his stuff when he disappeared."

"The things he left in his house?"

"Yeah. While we drive to the next place, can you look through the pictures I took and see if it says what happened to them? I think there was a receipt for a house clearance company. Did the Greenbergs keep any of his stuff? Or toss it all?" I passed Lily my phone and unlocked it to the image folder. As she scrolled up, I pulled a U-turn, heading back the way we came. The final residential address listed was in Chilton, only a couple of streets from my home. A number of the residences on that street had been divided up into apartments but Black had only listed a number.

"Found it," said Lily. "Oh, no."

"They tossed his stuff?"

"As good as. They made a note here saying all his belongings were kept for six months by the clearance agency, then donated to Goodwill."

"That's all long gone," I said.

"You're not disappointed?"

"No. It was too much to ask that they kept the stuff. I'm surprised they stored it for that long but I'm not surprised it was later donated. They kept it long enough to consider it a good deed to a former tenant that skipped out."

"I hope the next place isn't knocked down too. I feel this trip would be more enjoyable if we got some answers."

"Such is the life of a PI," I said although I agreed with her. "But I do know that street is fully intact so the house will be there. We'll find out about the owners when we get there."

"What happens if that's a dead end too?"

"Then I'll have to stop searching in the past and see what I can do about the future," I said, thinking about something Maddox had said.

"What does that mean?"

"It means we need to lure out Ben Rafferty-slash-Gideon Black. Out of everybody that could have been in Charlie Black's life, I figure Gideon has to know his father best." However, as I said it, I wasn't sure that was true. Gideon had been in boarding school for a large chunk of his childhood. Would a child really know what nefarious and illegal activities his father was potentially engaged in? Or did Gideon grow up thinking his father was the salesman he purported to be? The more I thought about it, the more I was certain Gideon knew the real story behind his father. The question was: did he know at the time of his father's disappearance? Was it possible the jewels weren't anything to do with Charlie's death but a son angry at his father? I wished I knew.

Tilden Street was a tree-lined street of brownstone houses with steps leading from the sidewalk up to the front doors, giving them an imposing look.

We parked at the end of the block and walked back, finding our target to be neatly kept with a small magnolia tree in the front yard.

I knocked on the door and waited, Lily hovering behind me.

The man who answered was portly, balding, and holding an excessively fluffy dog with fur the color of gold. If he'd told me it was a lion cub, I would have believed him. "Can I help you?" he asked.

"We're looking for a man who lived here around twenty years ago," I said.

"You're looking at him." The man eyed me over and frowned. Then the dog did the same. His tongue flopped out and a dribble of drool hit the front stoop. The dog, not the man.

"You lived here twenty years ago?"

"I have. My wife and I bought this house thirty years ago."

"Then perhaps you had a lodger named Joe Smithson?"

"No, we've never had a lodger. We would never have had space for one between the kids and the dogs, and that one time we had a goat."

"A goat?" asked Lily.

"It lived in the backyard. A whimsy of my wife's. Good for lawn mowing apparently, although our goat ate everything else. I recommend a lawn mower."

"Good to know. So you never rented a room or sublet to anyone?"

"No. Like I said, we always had a house full.

What's this about?"

"I'm a private investigator," I said, pulling out my license to pass to him. He held it between his thumb and forefinger and nodded. "I'm checking into the background details of someone who once listed your address as a previous address of theirs." The dog stretched his muzzle towards me, took a long sniff, and then continued to stare at me. The man put the dog on the floor, then lifted the glasses resting on a chain around his neck and gazed at the card.

"A PI, eh? Well, that's interesting. All I can tell you is we never had any tenants. Not now, and not twenty years ago."

"Can I show you a photo?"

"Of course. I have nothing better to do," he said dryly. The dog slumped to the floor and rested his jaw on the man's slipper.

I pulled out my phone, swiping to the one good photo I had. The photo Charlie Black had in his pocket on his death.

The man took my phone in his hand and consulted it. A small furrow appeared on his forehead. "It's been a long time but I would recognize him anywhere," he said. "You say his name is Joe Smithson?"

"That's the name he was using."

"Yes. Joe. I remember him. He tried charming my wife."

"Oh?"

"Oh, she knocked him back but it didn't stop him trying. From what she said, I think he was scouting around for a well-off woman who would either house or help him. He wasn't too impressed when he realized I was around but it didn't stop him from keeping the sweet talk going. My wife always did like helping people."

"Did she help Joe?"

"Only with little things. Treated him to lunch here and there, introduced him to people. I think he was new in town. It wouldn't surprise me if he convinced her to give him a reference. What was it for again? A job?"

"A rental house in West Montgomery."

"Right. Yes, I doubt she'd see a problem with telling a white lie for that."

"Could we speak to her?" I asked.

"Unfortunately not. She passed two years ago."

"I'm very sorry."

"Us too," he said and the dog yapped and thumped its tail. "It's like all the warmth went out of the house with her."

"May her memory be a blessing," said Lily.

"Very kind of you, young lady," he said to her as he returned my phone.

"You have a good memory to recognize Joe from so long ago," I said.

He nodded. "I haven't thought a single thing about him in years but that photo brought it all back. I remember how very charming everyone thought he was, so erudite. Not me though. I thought he was loathsome. There was something very unpleasant and oily behind his charm. I was glad when he seemed to disappear."

"Disappear?"

"He stopped coming around my wife and her friends. There was a rumor of something stolen, I think. I'm not sure whether that was hearts or jewelry or something else, but he became persona non grata with our crowd."

"Do you remember who was involved? Whom he stole from?"

"I'm afraid not. Even if I did, I doubt anyone would talk about it. They all like gossip but not if it's about themselves," he added with a wry smile. "Dare I ask what Joe has done?"

"We're not sure yet," I said.

"That's what we're trying to find out," added Lily.

"Well, whatever it is, it can't be good," said the man. From the ground, the dog lifted his head and whined.

"I wonder what he stole," said Lily as we headed back to the car. "Like father, like son, right? I bet he tried to make off with jewelry and someone's wife."

"In terms of people, you can't steal someone who doesn't want to be stolen," I said.

"Did you get that off a fridge magnet?"

"No!"

"Motivational quote of the day?"

"No."

"Fortune teller?"

"No!"

"We're having a fortune teller afternoon next week at the bar. You should come."

"Ooh, okay."

"I knew you'd say that so I already put you on the list. What now?"

I paused to think. "Now I tell Garrett we enact Plan B. It's time to draw anyone who knows Joe out of the woodwork."

"Can't wait to find out what mayhem that causes," said Lily.

CHAPTER FIFTEEN

I dropped Lily off at the bar so she could get her car and pick up Poppy from daycare, then I headed over to my parents' street. Not that I was planning on visiting them but I'd had a missed call from the Dugans and a voicemail saying they had returned home and I could either drop by or call them when it was convenient.

Speaking to them directly would give me an opportunity to gauge their reaction to the case's developments. I expected to see only relief, and maybe some curiosity about the identification and the jewels. Both would be natural reactions.

Instead of pulling up at my mom's and walking to the end house, I took the approach from the other end of the street and pulled around the corner, out of sight.

The fence had been partially filled in with wood panels, held in place with twine. Only small fragments of yellow tape pinned to the right panel indicated crime scene tape had been tacked there recently.

Someone had gone to great pains to try and remove any evidence of it and it was understandable why. The sooner the neighborhood forgot about the body buried in the yard, the better. Soft scrapes sounding from the other side suggested someone was at work.

A car was in the driveway so I headed up the path and knocked. Footsteps sounded from the other side of the door and there was a long pause where I felt I was probably being scrutinized through the peephole.

Carrie Dugan opened the door, wearing an apron and drying her hands.

"Thanks for coming by," she said. "Pete and I are eager to hear what the news is. I'm hoping you have something to tell us?"

"I do," I said.

"Come into the kitchen. I was in a baking mood and needed to keep my mind off worrying. Melissa is at Pete's mom's and Pete's outside tackling the yard. He's grimly determined to make it look as different as possible."

"That's understandable."

"Excuse the mess. We're still unpacking," she said as I followed her into a light and airy kitchen that overlooked the rear yard. "Can I get you anything? Coffee? Juice?"

"I'm okay, thanks."

"Then I'll call Pete." Carrie hurried off, leaving me alone in the kitchen. The interior renovation looked almost complete with the kitchen and dining room one big room. A sofa was against one wall with a large rug and a wicker basket of toys. A tray with an artfully arranged posy and glossy hardback books had been set on the coffee table. Several boxes were stacked against the wall. Over on the kitchen island, mixing bowls and utensils were paired with a large recipe book held open on a clear stand. The oven made a soft hum.

"Hi there," said Pete. He wore faded jeans, the knees rubbed with dirt, and socked feet. "Carrie and I are eager to know how it's going. Do you know who the dead guy is yet? I called Lieutenant Graves but he wasn't available."

"We do. The ME was able to confirm him as a Charles Black." I watched them for any reaction but there wasn't a spark of recognition.

"I don't know anyone by that name," said Pete. "Do you, honey?"

"No."

"He was a former rental occupant of the house. At the time, he was going by the name, Joe Smithson."

Carrie looked at Pete and he shrugged. "That name isn't familiar to us either."

"I think it's just a coincidence that you bought the house twenty years after he lived here."

"And was killed here," said Carrie with a shudder.

"We don't know he was killed here for certain, but it's likely he was."

"How awful!" She pulled a chair out from the kitchen island and sat, letting out a breath before rubbing her pregnant belly.

"What about the jewels?" asked Pete. "Has anyone claimed them?"

"We haven't been able to track down anyone close to the deceased yet. I was with Lieutenant Graves when the jewels were appraised and some additional checks need to be made," I said, purposefully vague.

"What kind of checks?" asked Carrie. "Are they very valuable?"

"Yes," I said, "it looks that way but until we can be sure of the provenance, and their ownership, it's unlikely the police will release them. The good news is: you're both absolutely in the clear. The police aren't interested in either of you as suspects."

"That's certainly good to hear," said Carrie. "I guess that wraps up the case? I suppose we were a little hasty in hiring you but I'm glad we did. Is there any paperwork we need to fill in?"

"No. I'll send you a report and your check covers the fee. There might be a small reimbursement but I'll confirm that with the remittance slip I'll include."

"I guess all we do now is register our claim with the police and wait and see," said Pete.

"You can do that," I said. "I'm sure Lieutenant Graves can advise you further."

"I'll walk you out," said Carrie after they both shook my hand. "I can't tell you how grateful we are to get some answers."

"I'm glad I could help," I said, then I left, pleased that at least someone had some answers. *But what about me?* I wondered as I got into my car. I was no longer officially on the case but how could I let it rest when I still had so many questions? Before I started the engine, I called Garrett. "I just spoke to the Dugans," I told him.

"Yeah? How'd that go?"

"They're pleased to know they aren't suspects and it sounds like they'll put a claim in for the jewels."

Garrett snorted.

"You don't think they'll get them?" I asked, thinking about the Queen's Ruby. If it really was that jewel, who had the bigger claim? The finders now, or the real owners?

"Not these kind of jewels. If it were a ring or a bracelet or something like that, sure, they'd have a claim but the Treasure Valuation Committee will want to take a closer look first. They won't give up millions."

"The Dugans won't be happy. I think they think they have a legitimate claim."

"Are they still your clients?"

"No. We're both happy to part ways. I need to write up my report and send it, then we're officially done. I'm going to sit on it for a few days in case any new developments arise that I should add."

"But you're still going to help me out as my consultant, right?" asked Garrett.

I could hardly contain myself. Garrett wanted me to stick around! "Of course," I said as calmly as I could. "I wouldn't leave you in the lurch. I'm happy to help."

"Good because I want to run some ideas with you about gaining publicity for this case. It's about time we drew out the interested parties we don't know about yet."

"I had the same thought. And we need to lure out Gideon Black," I said. "Plus, I have an interesting lead about the jewels that I think you should know about."

"I'm about to head out. Come by in the morning and we'll talk. Can it wait until then?"

"It can. I want to do some more research before I say anything more. See you then."

~

I was outside the police station at eight AM. Garrett

had sent me a text saying he was running late because his son, Sam, had tied all his shoelaces together so I was lingering in my car near a news kiosk across from the police station until he called me again. After spending the evening researching the Rachenstein jewels, I was more and more convinced Ruby had unwittingly provided a brilliant clue and I was excited to tell my brother as soon as I could.

My phone buzzed with a call. "Kinda early, Maddox," I said.

"Some of us have been up for hours," he replied jovially. "Working cases, chasing leads, finding jewel thieves."

"Aha!" I pounced on that. "This isn't a friendly call. You want to pump me for information."

"Sure. I'll settle for information," he snorted. "Any leads on your jewel find yet?"

I rolled my eyes. "Plenty of leads but I hit a dead end on all of them except one."

"Are you going to smoke potential suspects out of the woodwork?"

"We are."

"I thought you'd see the wisdom of that although it could bring more than you expect. Could you do me the courtesy of keeping me informed?"

Maddox was never this polite. Whatever he wanted, he wanted it badly enough not to tease me. "Why?" I asked, my curiosity clutching me.

"I mentioned I'm working a case with a thief? She's responsible for probably a dozen jewel heists. She's a menace."

"She?"

"We know she's a woman and we know this is the sort of cache that might pique her interest. That's all I can tell you. Could you give me a courtesy call if any women show up in your inquiries? Please," he added, politely.

"I can," I agreed, "but I'll need more to go on than just a female menace. Is this anything to do with the names you mentioned?"

"She has a lot of aliases. Caucasian, thirties, American but she's good with accents. It's a long shot. I doubt she's in town but you never know."

"Hair? Eyes?"

"Yes, and two. Apart from that, your guess is as good as mine. She might be bald and wearing an eye patch the next time she turns up."

"So you don't know what she looks like?"

"I do, but I couldn't tell you what she looks like *today*. Or if she'll look like today tomorrow. I'll send you some photos so you can see for yourself." With that, several images came up on my phone. "Take a look."

I scrolled through several grainy photos. "Are these all the same woman?" I asked.

"Yep."

"She looks so different." Long brunette hair and green eyes, a redhead with green eyes, a blond pixie cut, a bob with a baseball hat pulled low over her eyes. Then there was every conceivable fashion choice: skinny jeans, dirty and holey sweater and track pants, an evening dress, a pant suit. She looked different in every picture yet with the high cheekbones and a sweetheart face, I was sure I was looking at the same woman. "I'll let you know if a woman matching that very broad description pops up." I wondered how many of the female employees of MPD that covered. Maddox was crazy if he thought his description would help.

"Cool. I really want to arrest her."

We said goodbye as a man walked past me, stopped to buy a newspaper and walked off with it under his arm without even looking at the cover. I caught one word in the headline: JEWELS. I hopped out, bought a copy, unfolded it, and raised my eyebrows at the headline.

PRICELESS JEWELS FOUND BURIED IN BACKYARD WITH BODY.

"Mystery of dead man living under assumed name. Police have few leads," I read before I grabbed my phone as I settled into my car, the newspaper spread across the wheel. I called Garrett, pleased that he picked up straight away.

"Did you see *The Gazette*?" he asked as a door slammed shut on his end.

"I'm reading it now. Did you release that to the press?" I asked.

"No, someone leaked it. I would have given more targeted quotes than their anonymous source. Could have been anyone from the Dugans to the morgue employees to my team. I'm afraid we're going to get calls from a thousand fortune hunters all with a compelling reason why the jewels should be handed to them forthwith."

"I have a lead that might help you cut the numbers."

"Are you anywhere near the station?"

"I'm outside."

"I'll be another twenty minutes. Bring donuts."

"On it," I said and hung up. The Donut Delights drive-thru was less than ten minutes away so I killed time by heading there and ordered a mixed box. As to why I was buttering my brother up with donuts remained a mystery but since I planned to eat some too, I was okay with that.

"That was quick," said Garrett when I walked into the station, waving to the desk sergeant. "I only just got here."

"I'm incentivized." I held up the box.

Garrett peeled back the lid and said, "You took a bite out of the sugar glazed ring."

"And it was worth it."

"I'm surprised you didn't taste test the rest."

"Me too!" Gosh, I was good to my brother! Helping him pro-bono and bringing donuts. If only he were a sheriff, he could deputize me immediately.

Garrett shook his head, sighed, and motioned for me to follow him. We headed to his office, keeping the donuts under guard, and he dropped the box onto his desk. As he sat, he reached for a triple chocolate and bit into it. "What have you got for me?" he asked.

"Have you heard of the Queen's Ruby?" I asked.

"No."

"Twenty years ago, there was a big exhibition in New York with a jewel named the Queen's Ruby as the centerpiece of a whole bunch of other jewels and jewelry. Right after opening night, the ruby was stolen and never seen again." I passed Garrett my phone, the browser open to the page with the ruby's picture. Since my searching the night before, I felt I knew as much about the theft as anyone at the time did. The ruby was stolen, and there were no concrete leads only theories and rumors. I'd even found a website dedicated to crimes that listed it as one of the most audacious thefts of the century.

"That does look a lot like our ruby," Garrett said,

nodding as he contemplated it.

"It also explains why no one's seen it in all this time and why it's never turned up. It was buried in Charlie Black's shallow grave in a minor city where no one would ever think to look."

"It's going to be hard to place Black in New York at that time. We already know he used at least one alias and I'm not drawing any luck tracking his movements under his real name or the one he used to live here in town. He could have used any number of names in his lifetime."

I settled in my chair, the glazed donut in hand. "I hadn't thought of that."

"And security wasn't as good then as it is now so I doubt we'll get much from the robbery file. Let me see if I can track down the detective in charge of the ruby case. It's the kind of crime that would stand out in your career so he or she should have something to say."

"There's another thing," I said. "I got a weird call from Maddox earlier. He says he wants to know if any female thieves turn up in our case. Something to do with a jewel thief in *his* case. I doubt the two cases cross but Maddox thinks she'll be interested in this." I tapped the newspaper's front page. "He said he doubts she'll be in town but there was something about how he said it that makes me think she might be familiar with the city."

"That's a lot of thinking," said Garrett. "The jewels are locked up tight. Let's deal with one thing at a time." He shoved the donut into his mouth and turned his attention to the computer screen. He tapped at the keyboard, frowning with concentration. That was funny because back in my temping days, I used to frown hard at the computer screen when I wanted my employers to think I was doing something productive instead of playing my seventy-fifth game of online solitaire. "Okay, I got a Detective Phipps who was assigned the Queen's Ruby case but he retired six months ago. There's a good chance he's still alive."

"That's good news."

"For now. Let's hope he didn't have a heart attack in the last six months. Odds are good though. I'm going to give the department a call and see if I can get a number for him. Do you want to sit in?"

"Duh. Obviously, I do."

"Then hang tight." Garrett reached for his desk phone and tucked it between his ear and shoulder as he dialed. While he went through the rigmarole of getting to Detective Phipps' previous captain, I relaxed in the uncomfortable chair and stretched my legs. Finally, Garrett made a note, smiled, thanked the person on the other end of the line and hung up.

"I have Detective Phipps' number. Apparently, this case was one of his biggest bugbears and he was disappointed to retire without it being solved. His captain says he'll be happy to hear there might be a new lead."

"Can we call him now? I want to hear what he has to say."

"No time like the present." Garrett was already dialing. I barely dared breathe as I waited, trying vainly not to raise my hopes. Detective Phipps hadn't solved the case twenty years ago; I wasn't sure what he could offer us now after so long. "Hi there. This is Lieutenant Garrett Graves looking for Detective Phipps," said Garrett. He hit the speaker button and replaced the handset. "I'm here with Lexi Graves, who's consulting for the police department over here. She brought in the lead."

I said my "Hello" as I bristled happily, thrilled once more to be an official consultant. Who knew that would ever happen? I couldn't wait to remind Garrett about this forever.

"My captain texted me just now. I didn't expect you to call so quickly," said Detective Phipps, his voice warm and congenial. "He probably told you the Rachenstein museum case sat on my desk for years. One of those that just bugs you, you know? I'm hoping a good lead must have lit a fire under you to call me this fast."

"You could say that," said Garrett. "We've got two interesting leads that may have a connection with your case. The first is a body we found."

"A body? Huh! Well, you don't say!"

"Caucasian male, fifties, would be in his seventies now, gunshot wound to the head that our ME ruled as homicide. We struggled to identify him correctly at first since he was found with a driver's license under an alias, Joe Smithson, but we've now identified him as Charles or Charlie Black. Do those names ring a bell with you?"

"Can't say they do. I was going to get my copy of the file out because it's been a while since I looked at it and I'm a little shaky on the particulars. All the same, no, I'm sure I don't recognize those names. I'm sure that's not what you wanted to hear."

"No, all good. We figured if Black used one alias, he may have used more, especially as building a history for him is turning up blank. Can I send you a photo?"

"Of this Black guy? Of course. If you have a pen, I'll give you my email address or you can text my phone."

"Phone would be good, thanks, but I'll take your email address too," said Garrett, scrabbling for the pen he'd dropped only moments before, then giving up and plugging it directly into his cell phone. "I'll send it to you now." The message disappeared with a *whoosh*.

"Got it. Hmm. He's not a standout guy in the looks department. I mean, not memorable in any particular way. Just kind of average. Something's a little familiar about him but I can't think of what. When it comes to me, I'll call you back if that works?"

"Sure does. While we've got you, it would be great to get your thoughts on the case."

"Off the top of my head? Can do. I wish I had a chance to refresh my memory of the minor details before you called but I can give you the key facts now."

"That would be great."

"I don't know what you know already but the Queen's Ruby was a big deal. It was one of those rare jewels that just had to be seen to be believed and it had all kinds of history attached to it. Anyone who was anyone rich wanted to buy it or borrow it. Even big Hollywood starlets wanted it to wear for the Oscars and the like but they were always turned down. The owners didn't want a jewel like that set into jewelry. They wanted it admired for the stunning gem it was. Although there were photos from a time when the former Queen wore it, first at her wedding, then at her coronation. The pieces were dismantled after that since the ruby was too big to wear as a regular piece. Not that I would know. I wear my college ring and my wedding ring and I'm good. I'm not a tiara man."

"Me neither, but Lexi might beg to differ," said Garrett, grinning.

"It's true," I said. "I could handle a tiara."

Detective Phipps chuckled. "This thing has weight to it. I doubt it was ever a comfortable piece to wear. Anyway, it was on its first official tour outside of Rachenstein, and New York was its penultimate stop in the States. It was due to have one more stop in Washington DC, if I recall, before it went to Europe for six months, then back to Rachenstein. I don't follow fashion and that kind of thing, but I was told back then the exhibition was a big deal. This was the first time Rachenstein was putting its state jewels on tour in I don't know how long, and who knows when it would happen again? However, after the theft, the tour was canceled, all the untouched jewels were returned, and none of them have toured again. It was a national embarrassment and caused a diplomatic nightmare."

"How so?"

"Rachenstein weren't happy with the security. They weren't happy with the investigation. They brought their own people in but they couldn't find anything either. There was a big reward too for information that led to the recovery but all that turned up were fortune hunters and liars. Last I heard, the reward was still active." Detective Phipps paused as he took a breather, the sound of sipping reaching us. "The theft spawned all kinds of articles and was mentioned in books, and there was even a film a few years back. It's often featured on those top ten heists TV shows and I heard a rumor there was going to be an investigative podcast, but I think that fell flat. Shame. I fancied myself a pundit, although I wish I could claim I'd recovered it. Now that would be a story, but I guess with no leads and no good ending, there's nothing new to say about it. Unless…" He paused, waiting for us to fill in the blank.

"We'll have to take a look at some of that media," said Garrett. "Did you have any strong suspects?"

"No, that's the thing. Rachenstein cleared all their employees from cleaning to freight to security, and we cleared everyone at the museum. The ruby was in situ in the museum but we still cleared everyone on transport either end too. The museum tech was top of the range for the time and the museum hired in extra security guards as per their agreement with Rachenstein."

"Direct museum hires?" I asked.

"No, they were hired through a security contracting outfit. They went bust after. Although I gather they circled the wagons and started up again under a new name so the new company wasn't associated with the bad press. The company went out of business when the owner died, oh, five years ago now. I never got any inkling of wrongdoing from them then or afterward. Meanwhile, the museum had a surge in infamy."

"Did you take a look at known thieves in the city?" asked Garrett.

"Sure, but none of them were that caliber of thief. I'm telling you, whoever did it was real smart. There was no way they could have done it without casing the place, having the tech schematics, the security rotas, and the building plans. The heist was meticulous."

"Did you ever figure out how it was done?" I asked.

"Yeah. It took me a week. I'd say I was embarrassed it took me that long but it was so clever, I'm just glad I discovered it at all. It was so simple, I laughed when I figured it out."

"That so?" said Garrett, raising his eyebrows at me. "We're all ears here."

"Listen to this. The museum had a crew in for maintenance prior to the exhibition. Part of it was to repair a wall, paint, and refinish the floors. Only they didn't just repair the wall, someone created a concealed room behind the paneling. It was big enough for one person to stand upright or sit. It wouldn't have been super comfortable but it was enough to conceal someone. Get this... it was installed right under a camera, in the corner of the room, completely out of view. The camera was nudged up just a little, enough that the guard monitoring the camera in that room wouldn't see the false door open or close.

"So what I think happened was the contractors finished up their work a week before and took off. No one noticed this little room since it was hidden in the paneling, in an unobtrusive corner. The exhibition pitches up and sets out the display. They host their party with the press and all the fancy people drinking champagne and getting a special talk and that kind of thing. I figured the thief got on the invite list somehow.

"Sometime late in the night, he gets into the room and conceals himself. I figure he put some supplies in there when it was made. Clothes, probably a bag with snacks and water, whatever he needed to get through the night and clean out easy. Anyway, sometime during the night, he gets into the room. He waits for the museum to empty out at closing time, then he leaves this little room and grabs the jewels. He's able to override the security measures, take what he wants and gets back into the room unnoticed. The jewels don't leave the museum for the first few hours after their theft.

"Since he left paste crap in their place and nothing about the display was broken, no one notices at first, and the exhibition opens the next day to the public. It's a Saturday, the exhibition is sold out for the month and it's busy. People want to see this glamorous stuff owned by European royalty. At some point, the thief gets out of the room, dressed as just a regular person, mingles with the crowd, and walks out of the museum, the jewels in his pocket."

Across the desk, Garrett raised his eyebrows.

"Wow," I said. "That's audacious."

"He was a cool cat, all right."

"Did you get a good look at him?" I asked.

Detective Phipps laughed mirthfully. "I wish. He knew where every camera was situated and he had a cap on too. We got a nice look at the back of his head. Figured his height was just shy of six feet. Average build. White guy."

"How do you know it was him?"

"We don't for sure but when we cross-referenced the people who entered the museum that morning, we couldn't spot him. He never entered. He only left."

"And the night before?"

"There were an awful lot of men of average build, around six feet. Even when we got hold of the guest list, there were numerous men from overseas that we couldn't track down, as well as unlisted plus-ones."

"How about the contractors?" I asked. "You must have taken a look at them too? One of them had to have made the concealed room?"

"That's what I figured and we did, but none of them were new hires or contractors and none of them disappeared afterward. Since there were plenty of them, I figured our guy pulled on overalls and just walked in and did his stuff like he was one of them. With everyone working in different rooms, on different jobs, no one questioned him."

"That's ballsy," said Garrett.

"You're telling me. Any number of things could have gone wrong with his plan but he was in and out and no one saw a damn thing."

CHAPTER SIXTEEN

"What do you think of our detective friend?" asked Garrett. We'd hung up while Detective Phipps retrieved his file from a storage bin in his garage so he could answer some more in depth questions, giving us a few minutes of time to kill.

To me, that meant killing a second donut.

"I was fascinated," I said between chews. "We know the why. He figured out the how but he hit the wall on the who. We might have a who. That's assuming the two cases definitely connect." How many rubies of that size were floating around unclaimed? It seemed outlandish to think there might be more than one. Yet even more outlandish to think it had been found here, in an unassuming backyard.

"It might be very hard to connect our deceased man to his suspect." Garrett pushed back in his seat, and tapped his pen against the desk. "We know Phipps' suspect is good. No, not just good, to pull that theft off, he's exceptional. But if it were Black, he fell foul of someone. Something went very wrong and he didn't see it coming."

"I can't imagine the patience of someone who could conceal themselves in a tiny room overnight with millions in jewels and then just stroll out in the morning." If it were me, I would probably fall asleep, lean against the concealed door, fall out, and wake up with security officers pointing guns at me. Not this guy though. He slipped out of the museum like it was nothing. I wondered if he'd even broken a sweat.

"The patience of a man with a huge payday coming. That's a thing," said Garrett, pausing to tap his pen against his chin. "I can't conceive that he'd want to keep the jewels for himself. Black wasn't living a luxury lifestyle, although his son's school fees were a fair whack and the remaining funds covered college too. He wouldn't keep all those jewels for himself, so who was his buyer? It wasn't the person who shot him. If it were a double-cross, they'd have taken the jewels. And what was he planning to do after he sold them? Even with the red-hot discount fee, I don't see someone with that kind of cash retiring here to put their feet up. Where's the thrill in living a mundane life after committing that kind of heist?"

"Whoever killed him was as dumb as rocks not to search his body before they buried him."

Garrett dropped his pen and stroked his jaw. "Perhaps that's what we're dealing with. A killer who wasn't necessarily dumb but didn't know what was right within reach."

"If that's the case, it means Black was killed for another reason."

"There's probably a bunch of reasons to kill Black. A man like that could have made enemies throughout his life. Both direct and indirect."

"You mean, the people who knew him, and the people who didn't know him but knew what he stole."

"Precisely." Garrett contemplated something for a moment. "It's been surprising to me that Black's name hasn't come up in reference to any other high-end thefts but I wonder if I've been looking in the wrong place. I feel like I should put a call in to the Feds. Maddox investigates major crimes like that."

"He was interested in the jewels earlier," I said. "Maybe give him a call. He'd definitely appreciate the heads-up if there are any similarities to his case."

"Any idea what he's working?"

"No, only that it involves jewels and his suspect is a Caucasian woman, and she's in her thirties so way too young to be associated with Black."

"Father or son?" asked Garrett.

"I meant the father, but who knows about the son? Gideon… it feels weird to call him that… is a conman and he didn't only steal jewels…" I mulled it over in my mind, my thoughts not quite connecting, while Garrett watched me, waiting patiently. "I guess they have something in common."

"Or possibly are in competition with each other. Stranger things have happened."

"He could just be trying to steal our case."

"Likely, but I'm not stubborn enough to swat away any help Maddox might be able to give," Garrett said as he reached for his desk phone before stretching. He sat up a little straighter when his call was answered and said, "Hey! Special Agent Maddox, it's Lieutenant Graves over at MPD… No, I don't know why I announced myself so formally either… It *is* work-related though... No, my crazy sister isn't with me. As if!" He scoffed and rolled his eyes. "It's about that high-end theft I'm looking into and I hoped you might shed some light on the name I've got. Charles or Charlie Black. I'm not getting any hits in our databases. Can you run it through yours? That's great. Appreciate it, buddy." Garrett set the phone down. "He'll call back."

"I can't believe he called me your crazy sister," I hissed in indignation.

"Let's assume he meant Serena. That way, I wasn't lying."

"That's fair. She is actually crazy. Unlike me. I'm just average nuts."

Almost as soon as Garrett took his hand off the handset, it rang again.

"Lieutenant Graves?" the voice drifted through the receiver.

"Detective Phipps, thanks for calling back." Garrett hit the speakerphone button again and I scooched closer to listen.

"I skimmed the file and I gotta say, it's pretty thin for anything concrete. Plenty of notes about dead leads. However, I noticed something when I was taking a look at the photos of the contractors who were fitting out the museum. You remember I said, we investigated those guys and didn't find anything? Well, I noticed the photo of your guy looks a heck of a lot like one of the guys on the maintenance crew we interviewed. He's got a few days' stubble in our pictures and his hair is different but it's easy for guys to change their appearance like that. He didn't stand out at the time because he was still working for the company the last time we checked, which was two months later."

"You're sure?" I asked. Waiting overnight in a hideout was one level of patience. Waiting out an investigation for two months was a whole other level. Not only that, it would be ballsy to hang out right under the police's noses, but then who searched for a person who hadn't attracted any attention?

"Not a hundred percent but the eyes and the nose look the same. Our guy's name was Timothy Wright. We would have run everybody at the time and nothing was flagged. Everything must have come back verified but our systems weren't as sophisticated back then. All the same, if that were an alias, it was good enough that no one took a second look. If Wright had jumped out on work the next day or something, then of course, we would have had our suspicions." Exasperation oozed from his voice.

"What do you remember about him?" asked Garrett.

"Not much. The case, I remember. The individuals less so, but I do remember he was good buddies with one of the other guys on the crew. Kelvin Huff. Huff was on the crew first and he put Wright on when they were hiring after getting the museum contract. That was a couple months before the exhibition. Oh, man! Could the perp have been planning the heist for that long?"

"It's likely," said Garrett. "He could have been planning the heist as soon as the exhibition tour was announced and the venues were confirmed. It would have given him plenty of time to put everything in place. Maintenance work prior to the jewels' arrival would be the perfect window in. Can you send me the particulars of these two guys? Photos, interviews, whatever you have on them?"

"Sure, I'll scan and email them."

"What else can you tell us about them?" I asked.

"Nothing much about Wright. I made a note that he was a congenial sort. Moderately interested in the theft, didn't offer up any explanations or theories. Said he knew about the exhibition but was strictly a sports fan so museums were not his sort of thing. Says here he went to the movies on the night of the theft, then home to bed," said Detective Phipps, reading from his notes. "Nothing we could verify but nothing we couldn't either. The theater was showing the movie at the time he said he was there, he had a ticket stub, paid cash, and we can't ask everyone on the planet for an alibi every time they go to bed alone. Said he went to the bodega down the street for milk for his cereal in the morning. The bodega owner did verify that. Work history was all drywall and decorating. Not married, no kids. Parents passed on."

"The ideal kind of background for an alias," said Garrett.

"Yeah, that's what I'm thinking as I read it aloud to you," said Detective Phipps. "The other guy wasn't much more interesting. Kelvin Huff. He lived alone too. Just down the block from Wright, as it happens. Pretty down on his luck. Divorced the previous year, wife got the lot, not that the lot was very much. She was a nurse and seems to have funded everything while he was in and out of low paid work. One kid, a girl, and a bunch of unpaid child support payments. Yeah, that's right. I remember he was real bitter about it too. Said he was dreaming of a lottery win so he could get out of the city, buy a place on the coast, get a boat, spend his life fishing, and flip his middle finger at the ex-wife. He was pretty adamant that was what he was going to do. No mention of a new teddy bear for the kid. He was on his final warning with the contractors last I heard and that's all I have. I can send a picture of him too, but obviously, it's from twenty years ago."

"I'd appreciate it. I'll run some checks on them and see where they are now," said Garrett. "How did the case go cold?"

"Between what I remember and from flipping through the file, I stayed on the case another four months before all my leads went stone cold. We were working with the Feds by that point too. Decent guys, keen to work together, but I don't think they got a whole lot further than I did. We ran down every angle but there was nothing."

"Do you have their contacts?"

"I wish I did. One got killed on the job ten years ago. The other died from cancer last year. Rough luck."

"Sorry to hear that," said Garrett."

"Thanks. They were good guys. I can tell you we all came to the same conclusion. The thief was damn smart. Everything must've been planned to a tee because not a single trace was left behind. Hey, you really think it might be one of those guys? Did we miss him?" asked Detective Phipps.

Garrett made a non-committal noise, then said, "Our only indicator so far is your possible identification of our dead guy as one of your guys. It's a long shot, but then it was only a passing comment that connected us to your jewel heist. I'll take the odds."

"I'd like to know if you come up with anything."

"Give me the rundown on Wright and Huff," said Garrett, making notes as Detective Phipps read out the information. "I'll keep you looped in. If the ruby and the other jewels are verified as those in the robbery, that confirms our guy was involved. It's possible the case will unravel from there."

"You could talk to the museum curator or someone from Rachenstein. I'll send the contacts I have but obviously they're old news. People move on."

"Appreciate it," said Garrett and after a minute of shooting the breeze about retirement, they disconnected. What do you make of all that?" he asked me.

"Detective Phipps seemed sincere."

"I thought so too. I bet this case has been sitting rent-free in his head all this time. His identification could be pivotal," he said, already turning to his computer. "Let me make some checks, and see if these guys are in the system at all."

I chewed my donut while I waited, wondering when I would get a turn to stick my nose into his computer and maybe search for a few people I knew too. My neighbors, perhaps, or people I didn't like from high school.

"Okay," said Garrett, a few minutes later. "Nothing on Timothy Wright but I got something on Kelvin Huff. He went to prison around nineteen years ago for a grand larceny Class B only five months after the museum theft. He's got a few months left to serve."

"Grand larceny fits the profile."

"Timeline fits too. He was a free man for the museum robbery and possibly Black's death."

"What did he steal? That's a lot of time for theft."

"Several paintings from a house his employers had him working on, to the tune of 1.2 million. He didn't get further than the end of the street and was driving the van the paintings were stashed in. He tried to plead not guilty and the jury disagreed."

"Not guilty? Really?"

"Yeah, seems improbable just reading the notes. One of Huff's colleagues testified he saw him load the paintings, plus, he was the only one in the van when he got pulled over. The kicker is the homeowners had a security camera that recorded everything. He didn't even try to disguise himself. It was a slam dunk."

I pulled a face. "He doesn't sound like a criminal mastermind."

"He sounds like an idiot. I'm going to check with the Federal Bureau of Prisons and find out where he is now. Ah, Detective Phipps emailed copies. I'm going to forward them to you. Take a look while I run Wright through a few other databases." Garrett reached for his computer mouse, staring intently at the screen.

On my phone, I opened the file he'd forwarded me, skimming through the volume of paperwork that Phipps wrote in his email was only a fraction of the file. The images he'd sent of Timothy Wright and Kelvin Huff were black and white and grainy but as I zoomed in on Wright's features, I had to agree. I could see Charlie Black in Wright, but was it enough? There were plenty of differences too although Phipps' comments about hairstyles and facial hair had merit. If he were the same man, we had a starting point and an end point and we knew what had happened in the middle.

Two questions remained: who put him in that shallow grave? And why hadn't they taken the jewels?

"I'm not coming up with anything," said Garrett. "Nothing on Timothy Wright at all."

"How do you feel about splitting the task?" I asked.

"Took the words right out of my mouth. Why don't we reconvene here tomorrow and hopefully, we'll have more to work with by then. Plus, you never know, the public might provide a tip, thanks to *The Gazette's* story."

"It's a plan," I said, rising. I reached for the donut box but Garrett's hand landed on it, even though he was looking the other way. I rolled my eyes and withdrew my hand. "I'll see myself out," I told him.

"Try not to cause any trouble on your way," he said.

I resisted the urge to stick out my tongue. Instead, I crossed my fingers and nodded.

As I left Garrett's office, navigating my way to the exit on autopilot, I thought about the Blacks and how they were the opposite of my family. The Blacks had made a business of lying and stealing. My family had made a commitment to law and order. Could we easily have gone the other way? What would my life have been if we were the Montgomery Mafia? I could see myself as a very glamorous boss lady. However, I could also see myself developing a heart condition before I hit forty and needing to spend a lot of time hyperventilating. I couldn't see myself getting caught and doing hard time in an orange jumpsuit. Some things were just not meant to be so I had to get on with fighting crime in nicer clothing hues.

"Excuse me," I said, sidestepping the two

plainclothes women coming around the corner.

"No problem," said one, barely giving me a second glance as she continued talking. "So there I am staring at my locker, scratching my head, wondering where the heck my uniform went. Did I put it in the wrong locker? Or did I leave it on the bench and the cleaners threw it in the lost property? All I know is my sergeant is going to have choice words for me if I don't find it before the next shift!"

"Someone is pranking you," said her friend. "I'll bet…" Then her words were lost to me as they moved further along the corridor.

"Lexi!"

I looked around for the source of my name, seeing Jord ahead of me, waving. I waved back and we walked towards each other, meeting at the corridor junction. "I've been hearing about your case non-stop."

"Lily?"

"Yeah. And Mom? She's texted seventeen times today already. But also everyone in the building. Are you working on it now?"

"We got a great lead," I told him. "Garrett's doing the heavy lifting with the background research."

"There's a lot of buzz about keeping *that* kind of item in the evidence locker."

"Why? It's the safest place for it."

"That kind of thing brings out all kinds of thieves looking for the biggest payday of their lives. I bet the jewels get an armed escort out of here, wherever they end up getting sent. Although, that said, smart criminals are all about the cyber crimes now. Digital theft is even bigger business and you can do it from anywhere in the world."

"A few million in jewels is small fry to that kind of thief."

Jord nodded. "True. Anyway, we're thinking game night next week. Cards, beers, pizza. Daniel and Alice can't make it. Can you and Solomon?"

"I'm sure we can."

"Cool. Catch up soon. And thanks for not getting my wife into trouble."

"You're welcome?" I said, my intonation suggesting I wasn't sure that had anything to do with me. Nor did it suggest he knew Lily and I had crashed a wake, bumped into a corpse, and received a soaking during our escape. Well, what he didn't know wouldn't hurt him.

"Take care!" said Jord as his cell phone rang in his pocket. He gave me a wave as he reached for his phone, our conversation over.

I turned to head down the hall, colliding with a uniformed woman. She muttered, "Pardon me" as we bumped shoulders in passing, then hurried away. A few paces later, and I stopped and turned, frowning at something I couldn't quite put my finger on. Then I shook my head. She was probably someone I'd gone to school with and forgotten, or someone who'd dated one of my cousins. It was hard to tell in a small city with my big family.

"Always," I said. Yet, as I stepped out into the sunshine and headed for my car, I had the strangest feeling that I was being watched.

CHAPTER SEVENTEEN

My phone buzzed as I reached my car.

"Hi, Mom," I said.

"Lexi, do you have any news?" she asked, her voice reminiscent of the days when she asked why I'd received detention and didn't have better grades.

"Um..." I thought about it but before I could answer, Mom continued, "I went to see the Dugans and they told me they're in the clear, because of course they are. No one could possibly suspect such nice people. You should probably give them the jewels as a thank you."

"They're not mine to give."

"Whom should I call?"

"Garrett, I guess, but he's not going to just give them to the Dugans. We need to trace where they came from first."

"And then they'll get them back?"

"The jewels didn't exactly belong to them in the first place."

"When your father and I bought our house, the

previous owners left a vase. We kept that."

"Uh…"

"It was worth two hundred dollars!"

"Okay?"

"We sold it. It was ugly. But it was ours. The house sale was final."

"I'm happy for you?" I said, frowning and feeling uncertain.

"I went to see Bea today who used to live in the house next door to the Dugans and she was just shocked at all the goings on over there, but do you know what she said? Hmm, Lexi?"

"I'm sure you're going to-"

"She said Joe's son had come by to see her today and had brought her flowers. She said he wanted to make sure she was all right after the horrible news! Wasn't that thoughtful of him?"

"Wait… what? Charlie Black's son is in town?" I frowned hard.

"No. Joe Smithson's!"

"Charlie Black is Joe Smithson's real name! His *son* is in town?"

"Of course he is! Catch up, darling. I assumed Garrett located him and called him. Bea said she was surprised to see him as she didn't recall him ever visiting when his father lived next door to her, but she said he remembered her well and he's obviously a well brought up and successful young man. He was driving a Tesla!"

"Did she get his license plate?"

"No! Why would she do that?"

I resisted the urge to roll my eyes, not because it was mature, but because my mother couldn't see me to get the full effect of my exasperation.

"Did he give his name?"

"Joe."

"The son!"

"Joe! The son is also called Joe!"

I doubted that very much. I wasn't even sure if it was Gideon Black who had made the appearance. The purported Joe Junior could be any man. "Where can I find Bea?" I asked, deciding it was best to get the information from the source.

"At the Harmony Retirement Village, of course. She moved there when the house got to be too much for her. I hear they're ready to wrap up the house sale. If you and John had thought ahead, you could have snapped it up."

"We're not in the market for a house. I thought you said she passed on."

"No, I said her *husband* passed on. I said Bea moved to a retirement village and I was going to ask what she wanted done with the mail that hasn't been forwarded. You really need to start taking notes. The adult ed center does secretarial courses although they call it executive assistant training but we all know it means taking notes and making coffee. I don't think there's a section on making coffee but I suppose all the young folk just order on an app and three minutes later, it's at your door." Mom paused, then added, "I might get one of those apps. Is that short for appetizer?"

"Bea?" I prompted.

"Yes, that's her. Lovely lady. Always so friendly and the social life at the retirement village is very good. I might mention it to your father in case we become infirm, although I'm sure we could live with you. Your house is so big and it's not like you have children in it. We could help with the childcare when you do. Your father can put shelves up in the nursery with his new drill."

"We don't have a nursery," I said before I even started thinking about my parents moving in with me.

"Are you planning on one?" asked Mom.

"Only if a baby comes along," I said, trying not to set myself up for a long line of questioning.

"You do know how babies are made, don't you?"

"Yes, Mom," I sighed.

"Good. I was afraid you'd been sick on the day they gave that talk at school."

I'd figured all the juicy details out before school got around to making everyone squeamish but my mom didn't need to know that.

Mom continued, "I don't suppose you *are* pregnant, are you?"

"No."

"But…"

"I'll let you know."

"And…"

"What else did Bea say?"

"Who?"

"Bea! From the house next to the Dugans."

"She said she should have held out for more when she saw what the Dugans paid for their house. I told her if anyone knew about the body, they'd have gotten less and she said she was sure she didn't have any…"

"No! About the…."

"Some Harmony residents still have their own cars but there's a regular bus service if they can't drive anymore, and there're all kinds of activities at…"

"No, about Joe Smithson's son," I cut in. "Joe

Junior."

"Lovely young man. He bought her flowers and cookies and took such interest in her wellbeing. Wanted to know if she was getting by okay. If she'd invested the money from the house yet? He even said he'd take a look at her investments if she wasn't sure about her pension income. What a thoughtful man. He said he was sure his father would have wanted her to have a few of his things but unfortunately, the landlady cleared the house out. I wonder if he'll stay for the funeral? Do you think there will be a funeral?"

"Of course, once the body is released."

"I hope he gets a nice spot."

"It depends on if he's claimed," I said.

"Oh, my word," gasped Mom. "Of course Joe Junior will claim his own father!"

"I'm sure that's his next step. Did he say anything else? Like where he's staying or how long he's in town or where he's been?"

"I'm not a secretary. I wasn't taking notes. I was just taking Bea's mail over to her. She said the mail carrier seems to forget she had it redirected and occasionally something will turn up in the mailbox or that parcel that was left on her stoop."

"I have to go," I said, realizing my mother had nothing more to add to the useful nugget she'd gifted me. "Tell Bea not to let Joe Junior look at any of her bank accounts."

"Oh, well, okay, I suppose you have better things to do than talk to me. I suppose we'll see you at family dinner whenever that might be. You're all so busy these days. Your father will barbecue and I'll make cold sides," said Mom and disconnected. I sighed, frustrated. I thought about turning around and heading back to the station but since I'd only just left Garrett, I felt sure Gideon Black hadn't contacted him about his father's body or any other aspect of the case because Garrett would have told me.

So if Garrett didn't know Gideon was in town, and Gideon hadn't made it his first step to contact him, what exactly was he doing in town?

The jewels!

It had to be the jewels.

Gideon Black was trying to figure out if Bea knew anything. He had to know that the police had them. So what was he planning? Did he really think his father might have confided in Bea once upon a time? Or did she find another undeclared priceless trinket?

There was only one way I was going to find out and that was by questioning Bea about his visit.

Before I could think twice, I called Lily.

"What's the news?" she asked. "Did Ruby's ruby pay off? Did you catch anyone?"

"Maybe and no, not yet."

"That sucks."

"But I did just get another interesting lead. Do you want to come to the Harmony Retirement Village?"

"You bet I do. Is there a very elderly suspect?"

"No, but a resident might have a lead. I'll tell you about it on the way."

"I'm at home. I'll be ready."

I hung up and slipped my phone into my pocket before beeping the car unlocked. As I reached for the handle, a shiver trickled down my spine. I straightened and looked over my shoulder, then over the other side, but in the stream of pedestrians and traffic passing me, I couldn't identify anyone. Just like a few minutes ago, I had the uncomfortable feeling that someone was watching me.

Pausing for a moment to pretend to rummage in my purse, I kept an eye on the street but I didn't recognize any of the pedestrians. Not the cyclist who pedaled slowly past, nor the guy sat on the bench, talking on his phone.

Perhaps it was nothing.

Perhaps I was just on edge.

I got into my car, still feeling disconcerted. Yet as I pulled out into traffic, I remained on alert for any vehicles pulling out after me but there were none.

I took the long way round to Lily's, despite not seeing any vehicles that seemed to be tailing me. By the time I pulled up out front, I was assured I was alone. I shot Lily a text and a couple of minutes later, she ran out and wrenched open the door, throwing herself into the passenger seat. She pointed ahead, yelling, "Let's go."

"You're eager."

"You bet. I don't get to do this stuff often enough and here we are again! Doing stuff!" She buckled up and relaxed in the seat. "Fill me in."

"My mom visited a woman called Bea who used to live on my parents' street. Not only that, but she owned the house next door to the Dugans. And! Do you know who just went to visit her?"

"The dead guy!"

"No." I frowned. "Lily, he's dead."

"I know but what a twist that would be."

"The dead guy's son. *Apparently*. Gideon Black. Ben Rafferty. He's in town!"

"The rat! I can't believe he showed up."

"If it *is* him. That's what we're going to find out."

"What do you think he wants? Why would he visit Bea? Do you think he's going to seduce her and swindle her?" Lily's questions came thick and fast.

"I can imagine he wants answers about his father's death but I don't know why he thinks Bea has any or how he even knew whom she was or where to find her." I paused. "I suppose he couldn't go to the police and the landlady has passed so Bea was the next best thing."

"He could go to the police. They'd know more."

"No, I meant there're multiple warrants out for Gideon's arrest across the country. If it's him, he must be clutching at any tentative connection to find information and you know how charming he is. Of course he went to talk to Bea. Throw in flowers and charm, and he expected her to sing like a canary."

"He is charming," agreed Lily. "And handsome."

"Annoyingly so."

"I'm surprised he didn't just go straight to you and try hiring you."

"I'm sure he knows I wouldn't be happy to see him. Plus, he can't possibly know I'm involved."

Lily raised her eyebrows. "I wouldn't place a bet on that."

I thought about that. I wouldn't either. Then I thought about the creepy feeling of being watched and shivered. What if Gideon were watching me already? What if he were stalking me, looking for an opportunity to get more information? Of course, I could understand why he wanted to know what had happened to his father but what if he knew about the jewels too? What if he'd always known about them but thought his father had run off with them, abandoning him. If he knew that wasn't the case, then perhaps he felt the jewels were his inheritance. If he knew about them at all.

If, if, *if*.

I needed more than that.

Of course if he were looking for answers, perhaps he hadn't known where his father had been all this time.

I hoped Bea would have some answers for me.

When we pulled up outside the Harmony Retirement Village, I waited a full minute but no cars passed by or drew up behind us. That reassured me.

"Why are you being so jumpy?" asked Lily, looking at me curiously.

"No reason," I said, not wanting to freak her out.

We were almost across the road when several motorized scooters zoomed out of the driveway and aimed directly at us. Lily froze.

"Outta the way!" yelled the man in front. He brandished his cane, pointing ahead. "Charge!" he cried and the others hurtled after him.

I grabbed Lily's hand and leapt onto the sidewalk, dragging her behind me, dropping her hand so we could both catch our balance before we lost our footing.

An orderly in pale blue scrubs tore around the wall and raced after the tearaways. A moment later, another man in scrubs hurried after them, checking both directions. "Which way did the crazy old people go?" he asked, pausing and heaving for breath.

"That way," I said, pointing towards the man in blue as he ran down the street, the cavalcade in sight until they screeched around a corner.

"Thanks," he wheezed and took off after them.

"I hope they make it," said Lily looking after them

wistfully.

"Do you know where they're going?"

"No, but I know they need to make it."

I shook my head, unwilling to enter into whatever fantasy Lily was entertaining. The most important thing was confirming Bea wasn't amongst the marauding elderly. I hoped that meant we'd find her in her apartment or playing something sedate like Scrabble.

"Let's go," I said. "We can find out how this chase ends on the news."

Lily brightened. "I hope so! And maybe we can come back and place bets on them in races."

"We're not starting an illegal betting ring on elderly escapees."

"Fun sponge," huffed Lily.

"Crazy lady," I countered.

The retirement village was a hive of activity as we entered the main building that seemed to operate as a community hub. Two of the employees were arguing and pointing towards the main doors, which I guessed was an argument about what had just occurred with the escapees. Shouts from the recreation room suggested a particularly fiery game of Bingo.

We crossed the lobby, narrowly avoiding a set of Bingo balls that were hurled through the open double doors.

We stopped by the reception desk and asked for Bea.

"She's probably in her apartment and you have to sign in," said the bored-looking young woman, barely looking up. "Are you relatives?"

"Yes," I said. "Great nieces."

"The best," added Lily.

"Sure, whatever," said the young woman. "Do you know where to go?"

"No," I said and she fired off directions, pointing in the direction we should take.

"I think we should exit via the parking lot," I said, perturbed by all the commotion as we passed the rec room to the exterior of the building where the apartments were situated. The Bingo game appeared to involve a lot of finger pointing and shouting. "A fight could break out in there any moment."

Lily snorted.

We followed the directions and spotted Bea's number just a few doors away. "Look! Bea's door is open." I headed for it, knocking and sticking my head through the doorway. A glance around the room suggested the apartment was empty, except I could hear the low buzz of the microwave. A huge bouquet of bright flowers was on the occasional table and a large box of gourmet cookies lay open on the coffee table. "Hello! Anyone home?" I called.

A woman's head appeared from under the counter. She looked familiar and I felt sure we'd found Bea. "Hello," she said, as the microwave dinged. She opened the door and pulled out a large bowl of popcorn. "I was just going to watch a movie. It starts in a few minutes. Can I help you with something?"

"I'm Lexi Graves from down the street. My mom brought your mail."

"Goodness me. The Graves' girl! Are you the clever daughter or the other one?"

"Yes," I said, hoping she wouldn't press for a definitive answer. "I'm Lexi, and this is my sister-in-law, Lily."

"Which one did you marry?" asked Bea.

"Jord," she said.

"Good choice."

Lily grinned. "Thanks."

Bea shut the microwave door and made to lift the popcorn bowl and stabilize herself against the counter at the same time. I hurried forwards and scooped up the bowl and offered her my arm. She accepted and I guided her to the couch.

"It's my hips," she explained. "They're awful sore. Don't block the doorway, honey. Come inside." She waved Lily inside.

"I like your flowers. Are they get well flowers?" I asked, hoping she'd be forthcoming.

"No, they're from an old friend."

"An old *young* friend," said another lady, coming through the door behind us.

"Do you have a gentleman caller?" asked Lily with a wink.

"I do not." Bea bristled but from the turn at the edge of her lips, she was pleased at the suggestion, and trying not to show it. "This is May. She lives next door."

"I think they're beautiful. What a sweet gift," I said.

"It's not even her birthday," said May, waving a finger at the bouquet.

"A 'just because' is even nicer," I said.

"The young man brought the cookies too," added May. "He's a good-looking young man too. Tell them, Bea."

Bea rolled her eyes, her quiet pleasure quickly turning to exasperation. "He could teach a lesson or two to the men of your generation," she said. "Help yourselves, girls. It's sweet of you to visit."

"And ours," snorted May. "Jimmy from Apartment 41 asked if I wanted to have dinner with him on Thursday night."

"What's wrong with that?" I wondered.

"He wanted me to *bring* dinner," said May. "And then stay the night. What am I? Meals and shenanigans on wheels?"

"It is a mouthful," said Lily. "I don't think it will catch on."

"One of these young ladies might be single," said May. "Was he single, Bea?"

"They're both wearing wedding rings," said Bea.

"They might have friends," said May. She peered at us. "Or are you married to each other? One can never tell these days."

"They're my neighbors' girls," said Bea. "Lexi's mom dropped off the mail and Lily is married to their youngest boy. Was there more? Mail that is? I don't want to put out your mom."

"No, no more, we just wanted to ask you a couple of questions about your old neighbor," I said. "I was speaking to my mom today and she mentioned you were Joe Smithson's neighbor."

"Who did you say you were again?" asked Bea, peering at me like she didn't remember.

"Your neighbors' girls you said," said May.

"That's right. The Graves," I added. "I'm Lexi. I'm a private investigator. We wanted to ask you about—"

"Mathilda Graves' daughter?" Bea peered at me now. "Why didn't you say so before? I heard you were a PI. Not quite a detective but good enough."

"I d—" I started.

"I remember you. Oh!" She gasped. "Oh! Yes, I do remember you! I caught you making out with the boy in the baseball jersey on my front lawn."

"That was my sister," I lied quickly. Well, maybe it was a lie. I couldn't remember any boy in a baseball jersey.

"No, wait; it was two boys."

"Definitely my sister," I said and paled as Lily turned big eyes on me.

"I had to chase your sister and those boys off my lawn with a hose!"

That night was becoming a lot clearer to me now. "We got her all straightened out," I said. "Very disappointing behavior."

Lily made a choked sound and clapped her hand over her mouth.

"A family disgrace," I continued. "Now she's a model citizen."

"I remember. She was always climbing out the window and those brothers of yours too, always running off somewhere, up to mischief. You must have been the clever one who always had her nose stuck in a book." Bea looked me up and down then fisted popcorn into her mouth. "You're not as boring as I remember. Probably what with you being a PI now."

"Er… thanks?"

"Which one did you marry again?" she asked Lily.

"Jord."

"Good choice," said Bea, and Lily grinned again.

"You must have known the young man who brought the flowers," said May. "He was Bea's neighbor's son."

"I doubt it," said Bea, "but the flighty one might

have known him." She gave us all a knowing look then made the sign of the cross over her chest. "Although maybe not. I don't ever remember him visiting, but Joe did mention him a couple of times. Very proud of him. Lived with his mother out of state, I think. Or was it at school? Such a nice boy. I suppose I must have been extra nice to him for him to remember me so well."

"He said you were always so lovely to him," said May.

"He did," agreed Bea.

"I vaguely remember," I said feigning attempts to recall. "What was his name? Something biblical, I think. Gideon? Ben? Joe?"

"That's a good memory you have there. Joseph. Goes by Joe like his dad. I'm surprised you remember him at all. What happened to your brothers? Aren't they all detectives now?"

"They are," I said. "And one has joined the FBI."

"And the flighty one? You're the investigator so I seem to think your mother said she was.... what was it now? Was it an accountant or lawyer or something like that?"

"We're so proud of her," I said. "She really turned things around. So, it was nice of Joe Junior to visit you after so long."

"Such a charming young man," said May. "I was here when he came to visit."

"Such a sweetheart," agreed Bea. "He said I was always the nicest neighbor and he'd always had a soft spot for me. He couldn't believe it when he heard I'd moved here. He said he could have sworn I was twenty years younger!" A pink blush appeared on her cheeks.

"You must have heard what happened from your parents," continued May. "They found his father in a shallow grave. Buried right there in the yard!"

"My parents told me," I said. "It's shocking. Joe Junior must have been terribly upset?"

"He said it was a relief to know what happened to his father. He said he was never really sure and since his father traveled a lot, he couldn't be sure if something had happened to him abroad. He reported him missing, of course, but he said nothing came of it until now. He was so grateful to the police."

"Do you remember Joe Smithson well from that time?"

"Some. He was always friendly and helpful but we weren't friends and I recall he was away a lot. Truthfully, I don't really remember the boy at all but my memory isn't so good. I do remember that the house was near the end of its lease because I'd had words with the landlady about fixing the fence and she said she was waiting to find out if the lease would be renewed to decide how much to spend on it. She fixed it a month or so later and the Langs moved in so I didn't really think much of it. Oh! You know, I do remember the landlady had to clear out a lot of Joe's things. Not that there was much left behind but they had to cart it all away."

"The young man asked where to and it was all thrown out, wasn't it, Bea?" asked May.

"I think the clothes went to charity and a few other things too but I'm not sure about the rest. I don't think there was much. The house was leased furnished so all of that stayed of course, but it will all be gone now. Joe's son didn't seem too surprised. He said he never really understood his father's life here.

He had all kinds of questions about whom he made friends with and what kind of people came to the house. Things like that. I so wish I could have told him more but it was an awful long time ago."

"I'm sure he was glad to hear whatever you could tell him," I said.

"That's nice of you, dear. Yes, he was a nice young man, wanted to know all about the neighborhood and where everyone was now. I told him your parents had a PI for a daughter and he was just agog with interest. Asked all about you! If only you'd been here a little earlier, I could have introduced you. It sounds like he needed some professional help, although I suppose a lawyer could serve him just as well. Or maybe the police."

"Oh? What for?"

"He said he was going to claim his inheritance and wasn't going to let anything stand in his way."

CHAPTER EIGHTEEN

"Garrett, we need to talk!"

"We can do that soon. I found Kelvin Huff."

"That's great news. I think. When are we going to see him?"

"Now."

"I'm with Lily."

"She can't come."

"I heard that," said Lily.

"Am I on speakerphone?"

I darted a glance at the phone, just to check, then to Lily. "No?"

"No," said Lily.

"Ears like a bat," said Garrett. "She still can't come. I only got you and me on the schedule and I only got that because I really piqued the warden's interest."

"What am I supposed to do?" asked Lily.

"Can you watch the Dugans' house?" I asked.

"Surveillance?" I thought Lily's face would fall with disappointment but her mouth split into a broad smile. "I can do that! I have snacks and water already in my car. Drop me back at my house and I'll head over."

"Okay," I said, confused at how easy that was.

"Your mom can help," she added.

"Great idea!" I gushed. Not only would my mother love that but she would also feel involved in the case she'd landed in my lap. Plus, she knew everyone in the neighborhood so if a single stranger stood out, she'd notice. Even better, Mom would be involved in the case far from where she could do any damage.

"You can tell me why Lily and Mom are doing that when you get to me. Meet me at the station," said Garrett.

"Police station?"

"No, the train station. Of course the police station," Garrett grunted before he disconnected and before I could tell him about the fake Joe Junior's lies to Bea.

"Glad I'm not spending all that time in a car with Detective Grumpy," said Lily, pulling a face.

"You volunteered to be with Mom."

"And a bag of candy," Lily reminded me. "And I already have my binoculars in my car so I'm good to go. Can I borrow the fancy camera the agency loans you for these kinds of tasks?"

"Yes."

Lily beamed. "My day is made."

"Do you know how to use it?"

"I will by the end of the day."

I wished my day had been made but so far, it looked like it was unraveling. The possibility that Gideon Black was in town was disconcerting and I knew he had to have more up his sleeve than simply finding out what happened to his dad. Of course, it could be that he just wanted to bury him but I'd met Gideon in his Ben Rafferty guise. I'd read the dossier Garrett put together of his other identities. If there was a sniff of big money, there was no way he'd disregard it.

No, he had to be here for the jewels.

They had to be what he'd told Bea he was here to claim. Since he'd made up a ruse to visit her, I had to wonder if he'd try and infiltrate the Dugans' home too.

Thankfully, the jewels were safe in MPD's evidence locker where Ben couldn't get to them. Or could he?

He'd stolen from under my nose before. There was no way I should underestimate him.

Yet I was certain he was up to something and I was going to stop him.

Right after I found him.

Right after I got back from my trip with Garrett.

I returned Lily to her house so she could get her car, and passed her the camera with its fancy zoom lens that I'd stored in my trunk since I last used it, along with instructions of whom to look out for. By the time I pulled away from the curb, she was already on the phone, breaking the good news to my mom.

Garrett waited in his car outside the police station, the engine idling at the curb. He barely moved a muscle as I hopped in, only breaking away from staring at his phone screen for a moment.

"We need to get going," he said, reaching for the parking brake. "Tell me your news."

"Charlie Black's son is probably, almost most

definitely, in town," I said, filling him in on Mom's comment and my subsequent visit to the retirement village.

"Probably almost most definitely?"

"One of those. Let's go with *definitely*. At least the man Bea met with is purporting to be him. I don't have a recent photo of Ben/Gideon so I had nothing to show Bea. Bea used to live next door to the Dugans' house but she says she doesn't remember the boy even though he claims to remember her."

"I feel like you told me that story back to front. Should we look at Bea for any of this? Perhaps as an accomplice?" asked Garrett.

"No, I'm sure of that. She's got sore hips and memory issues but she doesn't strike me as a mastermind jewel thief."

Garrett raised his eyebrows. "Did you show her the high school photo?"

"No, I wouldn't trust a recent identification from that. It's too old and Bea's memory is a little hazy." I paused, thinking. "I keep wondering if Gideon knew about the jewels before the newspaper story was published, and, if so, does he want them? Bea made it sound like the police contacted him about the discovery but you didn't mention anything. Has he come to see you?"

"No."

"Made any kind of contact with you?"

"Also no."

"If he were here purely for his dad, I would think he'd make contact with you," I said.

"Not if he's afraid we'd arrest him."

"For you to arrest him, he would have to know that we know who he is, and that would mean he had insider info. I can't see how he would have that connection."

Garrett shook his head. "I can't see him ever planning on coming back here after that case where you nearly caught him. I can't rule it out but I can't see it either. Even if we didn't know a thing about Gideon Black, we do know about Ben Rafferty."

"That's fair," I agreed, "but it's still suspicious that his first action in town is to track down his father's neighbor and not check in with the coroner or you. What kind of son doesn't claim his missing father's remains?"

"If it's really him," Garrett reminded me, "we need to get verification. I'll alert my team to be extra cautious about any contact or tipoffs. The tip line has already been ringing off the hook since that newspaper article was published. We've had a few claims to be sons or siblings but when challenged, they didn't even have the basic facts."

"I guess people will always try. Garrett, I wonder how Gideon got here so fast. Even if he were tipped off, do you think he was nearby?"

"Could be. He might maintain ties to Boston. Maybe here too if this was the last place he knew his father lived before he disappeared. Or he could be in any number of cities within driving distance." Garrett paused to navigate a turn, his fingers tapping the steering wheel in the way that told me he was thinking. "He might try and find out what we know before he dares to approach. I'm not entirely sure I know what to tell my team to look for. A Caucasian male in his thirties or appearing to be in his forties, possibly dark hair, doesn't narrow it down by much."

"I have Lily and Mom parked outside the Dugans'

in case he goes there," I said. "Bea told him everything was thrown away so he knows there's nothing left there of his father's."

"Can't imagine he will but at least we know where Mom and Lily are." Garrett cracked a smile.

"He might suspect something else is hidden there. After all, his dad's body was secretly buried there for years and the article revealed the jewels. I'm surprised we don't have fortune hunters digging up the Dugans' whole backyard."

"We've had plenty of hopefuls call our tip line with descriptions of anything from a bag of diamonds of undetermined number to missing engagement rings. According to the tip line, this guy could have been responsible for every jewel theft across the state in the last fifty years."

"He probably was responsible for some of them," I decided. "Where are we headed anyway? You said we're going to see Kelvin Huff?"

"I did. As we thought, he's still serving time but officially only has a few months left to go. Since he's been a model prisoner these past few years, he's getting a few months shaved off and will be out next week. He got transferred to a facility closer to his girlfriend, preparing for release. Took me a while to find him as his name was spelled incorrectly in the system. Or we had it incorrect. I don't know. Anyway, good news is it will only take us ninety minutes to get to Barnham Correctional Facility and the meeting has been cleared with the warden. I asked him not to give Huff a heads-up as I don't want him over-thinking his answers before we get there."

"Or lying."

"That too. The warden says Huff's not all that

smart and mostly keeps his head down. He's not violent and looking forward to getting out. I don't think we'll have any problem interviewing him. He's probably been stewing on his misdemeanors for years so I hope we find him chatty about his life before. There's a file on the backseat with his info. I didn't turn up anything on Timothy Wright." Garrett nodded over his shoulder without taking his gaze off the road. "And there's an appraiser coming from Rachenstein in a couple days to take a look at the jewels to see if they're the real deal."

"What happens if they are?"

"They'll eventually be repatriated."

"And if not?"

"Come up with a convincing enough story for the tip line and they could be yours." Garrett winked and I laughed. "Apparently, the bounty for any leads resulting in their return is still active." Garrett named a figure and I whistled.

"The Dugans will be interested to hear that," I said, "and Ruby too."

The drive to the jail was uneventful and not long after we hit the freeway, I stopped looking over my shoulder for possible tails. Eventually, with the traffic flowing and the radio turned up and pumping out pop songs, I relaxed. By the time we arrived, turning into the parking lot and showing the guard our credentials, I was in a positive mood. If Kelvin Huff knew anything about the jewel heist, and how he might have been used as a chump, I felt sure he would tell us.

Instead of the general public's visitation room, a guard showed us into a small meeting room with a table bolted to the floor and a window eight feet high in the wall. Probably at the time of building the facility, the room was painted cream and now it had a smattering of scuff marks, a panic button, and was entirely devoid of anything pleasant to look at.

As Garrett placed his file on the table — the only thing we hadn't logged into the guard's possession — he indicated I should take a seat and he did the same. Then we waited.

Finally, the door opened and a ratty-looking man with a receding hairline, dressed in a gray sweat-suit, entered.

"You must be Kelvin Huff," said Garrett, extending his hand to the man as soon as the guard removed his handcuffs.

The man shook his hand, eyeing us both wearily. "I am. And that would make you?"

"Lieutenant Garrett Graves and this is Private Investigator Lexi Solomon," said Garrett as he flashed his badge.

I opened my mouth to correct my surname then realized Garrett had omitted half of it purposefully, not giving our sibling relationship away.

"Take a seat," said Garrett. "Can I get you anything? A coffee? Soda? Candy? Cigarettes?"

"Yes to the soda and candy. No to the cigarettes. Never could stand the things and I don't care to use them as currency either."

"I'll be right back," I said and headed to the door to retrieve the items, pleasantly surprised that no misogynistic comments followed me. I knocked and the guard unlocked the door, watching me as I slid money into the vending machine further down the corridor. I retrieved a Coke and two candy bars and he let me back into the room.

"Thanks," said Huff when I deposited them in front of him. He reached for the Coke, snapped open the ring pull, and took a long glug. "To what do I owe this pleasure? I know I'm not in trouble for anything so I guess you're looking for information on something or someone?"

"Smart guess," said Garrett, nodding congenially. "You're right."

"Go ahead. If I can answer, I will. I figure you know already that I'm getting out soon so I don't need to trade for any favors but if you feel like adding to my commissary account, I'd be obliged." He leaned back in his seat, his hand wrapped around the can, looking entirely at ease.

"I'll see what I can do. Have you got somewhere to go?" asked Garrett, his voice far more casual than his question but Huff didn't appear to notice as he nodded.

"Man, I have plenty of places to go. I've been locked up a long time and I'm looking forward to seeing the world again." He gave me a tight smile before returning his attention to Garrett. "So what can I help you with?"

"We're looking at a cold case from New York, almost twenty years ago," said Garrett.

Huff held up a hand and nodded. "The museum," he cut in. "That was a big story back then. How come you're asking about it now?"

"How'd you know that was what we were asking about?" I asked.

"Ah, she speaks. Figured you might be the bad cop," said Huff with a wink. "Literally nothing else of interest happened in my life there except all that to-do with the museum and that unfortunate incident of grand larceny. I've almost done my time on the second so it had to be the first."

"You're a smart guy," said Garrett.

Huff nodded sagely, his face serene like he'd heard that all the time. "I've had a lot of time to reflect on my life and get a little education in here," he said, spreading his hands like he was a guru talking to a rapt assembly.

"What can you tell us about the museum theft?"

"I'm sorry to waste your time but not much." He reached for a candy bar, peeling the wrapper slowly like he wasn't so uncouth as to rip it off and eagerly devour the contents. I would have if I'd served as long as he had, with little access to the commissary. I'd have bitten my hand off for it. "A detective interviewed me back when it happened. I don't remember his name but there will be a file somewhere that's better than my memory."

"Detective Phipps?" asked Garrett.

"Could be," said Huff. He shrugged and refocused his attention on the candy bar, savoring every bite.

Garrett opened his file, appearing to read, although I was sure he'd memorized all the pertinent details. "I have here that you were on the maintenance crew the museum hired for a refresh prior to an important exhibition."

"That's right. I was on the painting detail. Walls, ceilings, woodwork, I can do it all."

"And you worked with a guy called Timothy Wright."

Huff shrugged. "I'm not so good with names unless they're on a paint can." He laughed.

"Says here you got Wright the job." Garrett

tapped the file.

"Nice of me."

"So how did you know him?"

"Who?"

"Timothy Wright."

"Oh, hardly at all, I think. It's coming back to me. I think he lived down the street from me. There was a bar on the corner, crappy, little place but the beer was cheap. Probably a Starbucks now. We got to talking one day and Tim asked what I did for work on account of the paint splashes on my hands. Said he was looking for a job if there were any openings. Figured he was an okay sort of guy so I told my supervisor and Tim got called in. They didn't want to put him on the museum job and he was kind of grousing about it, then the day before the job starts, one of the guys had an accident and they needed to fill his spot."

"An accident?" I asked.

"Got jumped. Broke his arm. Can't paint with a broken arm."

"That's unfortunate," said Garrett, glancing at me.

"Right." Huff nodded and shrugged as he swallowed the last bite. "That tasted so good," he said, heaving a sigh while he crumpled the wrapper. "When I get out, I have to avoid going nuts on these things or I'm gonna end up the size of a house in six months."

"So Timothy Wright gets the job in the museum. Did you work with him the whole time?" I asked, moving Huff along before he forgot what we came here to talk about.

"I don't recall. I guess so. He was painting, just like me."

"Were you working in the same room?"

Huff shrugged and his gaze shifted to the remaining candy bar. "Maybe. Some of the time, for sure. I think he did some woodwork stuff too."

"Did you notice him leaving for any lengths of time or doing any tasks he wasn't assigned to be doing?" asked Garrett.

"No, I don't think so but I was concentrating on my work. It was a high-end job and they pay better so at the time, I suppose I was seeking more of them and wanted to do a good job."

"What can you tell us about Timothy Wright?"

"Nothing much. Okay guy. Put his hand in his pocket so he was popular with the guys. You could rely on him to get you a beer or stand you lunch if you forgot yours. He'd take an extra shift if one of the guys needed to swap too."

"Sounds like a nice guy."

"Yeah, I guess."

"What happened after?" asked Garrett.

"What do you mean?" asked Huff.

"After the robbery at the museum. You all got interviewed. Did you stay in the job?"

"Yeah, I did. We didn't get any more high-end stuff though, what with the hit to the firm's reputation. Just shop fitting and house painting and stuff like that. Easy in, easy out."

"What about Timothy?"

"I don't recall. Hey, maybe I remember he got a job out of state a couple months after, said he was looking for a change. Gave his week's notice."

"Did he say where he was going or anything about the job he took?"

"No, I don't think so. Or maybe he did, and I

don't remember."

"Did he show a lot of interest in the jewels at the museum?"

Huff took another long slurp of Coke. "I think everyone was a little curious but I don't recall Tim being any more so than anyone else. There was a lot of specu.. Speckle… what's the word?"

"Speculation," I supplied.

"Yeah, that. A lot of *spec-u-lation* afterwards," he said, careful to pronounce the word. "I gotta write that one down. I'm trying to improve my vocabulary."

"The file says you were talking about leaving and buying a boat somewhere," said Garrett.

Huff laughed and spread his arms out. "How do you like it?" he asked, then shook his head. "A pipe dream. I talked a lot of crap back then."

"Where did you plan on getting the money for a boat?"

"I didn't really think about it much. Like I said, my pipe dream. I don't even like the sea that much but I did like playing the lottery." He unwrapped the second candy bar and bit into it, making "Mmm" noises. "So why all the questions about Tim? Did he have something to do with it?"

Garrett ignored that, asking instead, "Did he ever mention having a kid?"

"I have no idea, man."

"You had a little girl, right? You never spoke about your kid?"

"My little girl is all grown up now. You know how many times she's come to visit me? None. Her mom poisoned her against me a long time ago."

"Sorry to hear that," said Garrett. "So you never sat around chatting about the kids?"

"I don't know, maybe. It was too long ago. I couldn't tell you what I asked the guard twenty minutes ago. I sure as heck can't tell you what I had a conversation about twenty years ago."

"Did Timothy leave you a forwarding address?"

"Can't say he did. He never came back to the city to visit either but we weren't best buddies. I don't think I'd even seen him for a while before I got pinched."

"So he left the crew some time between the museum robbery and you getting arrested for the paintings theft? That was, what…" Garrett flicked through the pages casually, "a few months later?"

"Uh… I don't know. I guess so? Maybe? You should try asking one of the maintenance crew supervisors. Even better, ask Tim!"

"We would but we recently found a body that we believe to be his."

Huff stopped chewing. "How'd you know it's him?" he asked, his mouth full.

"We were able to make a match from a medical database as he had a pin in his leg."

"How'd he die?"

"He was shot."

Huff pushed out his jaw, pursing his lips, and nodded. "That's rough. Like I said, he never visited so I can't tell you what he's been doing or who he's been hanging around with. You know, now I think about it, he did have a few rougher friends. Those loan shark kind of guys. Fancy themselves as the mafia. Yeah, I reckon I saw him hanging with some guys like that back in the city. Maybe he owed them money or something. Or had a thing with one of their wives. He was a charming guy. My mom, rest her soul, would say he was the 'smooth-tongued sort.'"

"And you didn't think to mention it earlier?" asked Garrett.

"It's been a long time and I'm telling you now. Guess you just jogged my memory." He seemed to remember the candy bar he was holding and took another bite, pointing the remainder at me. "Mighty nice of you to get this for me. Wish I could be more helpful. Sorry to hear that about Tim. You said he had a boy? Can't be nice for him. Can't say I know why you're asking me all this stuff though. I've been inside for a long time. Maybe you should find someone who knows him now."

"Timothy Wright was killed a long time ago."

This time, Huff's head shot up. "Say what now? That so? Guess those Mafia guys caught up with him. Yeah, I think he might have taken out a loan with them or maybe he was gambling down in Atlantic City. Yeah, that's right. He'd taken a loan out and they kept hiking the interest. The crew and I went down to Atlantic City a couple times after we got our bonuses. Maybe Tim came with us. I know I didn't have any luck. Guess I never do." He shrugged. "So I'm here thinking you're asking me about Tim and the museum robbery for a reason. Do you think he did it?" He studied the candy bar like he was calculating exactly how many bites he had left, apparently more interested in that than the question. Yet I was sure he watched us from under his lashes.

"It looks that way. He was buried in a shallow grave," said Garrett.

"Horrible way to go."

"A pouch of jewels was found on him."

Huff froze. "Uh huh?" he forced out.

"They look very similar to the stolen, unrecovered jewels from the museum."

"That so?"

"We think whoever killed him didn't realize Timothy had the jewels on him."

"Then they're a damn fool," said Huff softly before he crammed the rest of the candy bar into his mouth.

CHAPTER NINETEEN

"What did you make of that?" asked Garrett. "You were awfully quiet in there."

The door sounded loudly as it opened and I winced. Then it was shut, leaving us in silence once more.

"He was lying," I said.

"Which bit?"

"Most of it. The Mafia guys, the convenient loan, the gambling, the kid."

"I wondered if you picked that up. The kid."

"You didn't say our dead guy had a boy, just that he had a kid. Huff knew though, even though he said he didn't remember. He gave us the loan shark story to throw us off and then he made a slip-up. Or he thought throwing a few red herrings at us would give us other avenues to explore and waste our time."

"At first, I didn't see him as a killer but the longer he spoke... I'm seeing him for it now. I thought he was just a patsy Black took advantage of to get into the museum so he could pull his real job, and maybe he *was* at first. Now I think Huff either knew about the heist or had an inkling about what was really going on before it happened or maybe soon afterwards. Perhaps he wanted a cut for keeping quiet."

We had our backs to the prison as we passed through the final checkpoint, and walked towards the parking lot. Garrett was playing with his keys. I was thinking about Charlie Black's last moments. Black knew he had the jewels in his pocket but did he think about handing them over to his killer to potentially save himself? Or was keeping them his last defiant act?

"Did you see his face when you said the jewels were found on Black's body?" I asked.

"Yeah, he was startled."

We paused to get into the car and pulled the seatbelts around us. As I popped the buckle in, I said, "More than that. I think he was shocked. Like it would never have occurred to him that Black had the jewels on his person."

"What're you thinking?"

I thought harder about it, puzzling out probable events in my mind. "I think Huff knew Black was dead and he knew about the jewels. He thought he was being poker-faced and drawing out information from us. My guess is he figured out what Black did, tracked him down and confronted him. Black probably told him the jewels were someplace safe to get rid of him and that he'd cut him in, when what he most likely intended to do was abandon his life here and start over somewhere new.

"For some reason they fought. Maybe Huff realized it was a double-cross and wanted his cut now for keeping quiet. Black gets killed and Huff buries him in a panic. Huff decides to lie low for a little bit until he can get the jewels. Or figure out where they were, not knowing Black had them on him all along. Unfortunately, he doesn't keep his nose clean and gets pinched for the robbery. He's probably been sitting inside the whole time, waiting for the day he can collect. He now thinks he's only got a week left until he can retrieve them. He must think he knows where they are but now he knows we have them. Well, you do in MPD's evidence room."

"It could mean he was in on Black's theft. They did it together and somehow Huff gets double-crossed. Black told him a lie about where the jewels were or told him they had to lie low awhile."

"Or maybe Huff really didn't know anything until long after. Timothy Wright stuck around for at least two months after the heist, remember? In trying not to draw any attraction, Black made a mistake. Huff figured it out and followed Black to Montgomery where Black had his nice, new, anonymous life far from the grind of maintenance work. Finding Black under an assumed name clinched his guilt in Huff's eyes and he threatened him with exposure in return for a cut of the jewels. They fought and Black was killed.

"Huff panicked, buried him and hightailed it back to New York until he was sure the murder wasn't discovered. Back in New York, thinking he was the new big guy of high-end theft, he plans a heist of his own but he's not as smart as Black. That went wrong and Huff got sent down. He couldn't return to get the jewels or the payout but he thought he knew where they were. Maybe Black told him they were hidden somewhere! All Huff had to do was sit tight until he could retrieve them. He gets transferred here where it's easy for him to get released."

"I like this theory," said Garrett. "But I have no idea in heck how I'm going to prove it. We need the gun, we need to place it in Huff's hands, we need to place Huff in town when it happened. At the very least, we need Huff bragging about coming into money. There's no way he kept that quiet all these years. Wait here." Garrett unbuckled and reached for the door handle.

"Where are you going?" I asked, which sounded better than what I almost said: *sounds like a you problem.* I was pretty sure my brother wouldn't appreciate that. Plus, I wouldn't have meant it. We were a team. Any problems were *us* problems, right up until it went to court. *Then* it was Garrett's official problem.

"I'm going to very politely ask for Huff's phone records. I want to know everyone he's had contact with. Apparently, there's a girlfriend somewhere around here that he wanted to be closer to."

"Will they give it to you?"

"Maybe. We'll see. Wait here while I find out how stringent the prison is on following rules. I'd rather not get a warrant if I don't have to. It adds time more than anything else." Garrett hopped out, slamming the door behind him.

While I waited, I called Lily to check in.

"What's happening?"

"The Dugans are installing a new fence," said Lily. "There're a lot of gawkers, and the temporary panel keeps tipping over, so it makes sense. I'm not sure I'd want my house to be known as the dead body house but I think the horse already bolted from the stable on that one."

"Tell Lexi that the police have all gone," said Mom, her voice as clear as if she were holding the phone.

"The police have…" started Lily.

"All gone," I finished. "I know, I heard."

"They've added a side gate," boomed Mom. "It's got a padlock. That's very wise. They don't want any more dead bodies buried on the property. Do you think they'll have to tear down the garage?"

"They've added…" started Lily.

"I heard. Why would they tear down the garage?"

"More dead bodies," said Mom. "The Mafia do that. There's always a dead body in the concrete foundations."

"This wasn't a Mafia job. It was a one off," I said.

"Lexi says it wasn't…" started Lily.

"Give me the phone, Lily. How do you know? Hmm, Lexi? How?" asked Mom. "This could be a start of something much bigger. We don't know what's in the foundation."

"The police went over the yard and house with cadaver dogs. They cleared it. There are no more bodies."

"If you say so," sniffed Mom. "I suppose Garrett would have said something if there was anything to be worried about."

I wasn't so sure of that but it wouldn't help Mom to tell her I disagreed. She'd whip all the neighbors into a frenzy, hire a digger, and have trenched all the backyards on the street by the end of the week. No one needed that. Least of all, my dad. He'd probably dive into the hole in their backyard and pull the turf over his head for some peace and quiet.

"The Dugans filled the hole and they put turf over it. The retaining wall Pete put in for the patio is very nice and he's added a raised border too. He's done such a good job," continued Mom.

"Put Lily back on," I instructed her before she told me about the new plants too.

"I'm here," said Lily after some considerable huffing from my mom.

"Any suspicious characters lurking?" I asked.

"Only the man across the street. He keeps coming out in his bathrobe."

"That doesn't sound suspicious."

"He's not wearing any underwear."

"How do you… oh." I grimaced.

"Your mom sent everyone on their street a photo of him. He's threatening to sue. She's threatening to have him locked up for public indecency."

"Have you seen Gideon Black slash Ben Rafferty or anyone who even remotely looks like him?" I asked through gritted teeth.

"No," snipped Lily. "And I've visually examined every male pedestrian near the house. Your mom recognizes seventy percent of the lurkers from the neighborhood and the others don't match our man. I'm positive our thief hasn't strolled past or attempted to gain entry. Is that what you hoped?"

"I'm not sure what I hoped for."

"Shall we stay longer?"

"Please. We're out of town, following a lead but we're heading back soon. I'll check in later."

"Who's we?" yelled Mom.

"Garrett and me," I said.

"You can tell us about it at family dinner. This time it's barbecue. We're having Mexican food next time. It's not authentic but we'll do our best. It's Mexican-inspired."

My heart thumped. "Is that tonight?"

"Don't you read my texts?" asked Mom. "No, it's not. You still have time to go to the deli and pretend you made a side dish."

"Gotta go!" I trilled, disconnecting.

Garrett waved a slip of paper as he approached the car. When he got in, he passed it to me.

"What am I looking at?" I asked.

"Huff's phone logs."

"They're all outgoing."

"And? What did you expect? They don't get phones by their bedsides here."

"Ha ha. They're mostly all the same number. Did you call any?" I was already reaching for my phone.

"Not yet. I asked for the visitor logs but apparently, Huff didn't get any visitors since he arrived. They did say he was really chatty about some woman he had here. My guess is that's her number. Amybeth."

"I'll get her address."

"Good. We should visit her on the way back to the station."

"Do you know when family dinner is?" I wondered.

"Jeez. Is that tonight?" Garrett grimaced.

"I have no idea. One of us should find out." When Garrett didn't make a move for his phone, I added, "Guess that'll be me." I unlocked my phone, opened my texts and… nothing. Mom hadn't sent anything. "Mom said she texted but she hasn't so I guess we'll never know when, but we do know that it's barbecue this time and Mexican food next time."

"I love Mexican food."

"It's Mexican-inspired."

"Still food," said Garrett. "Let's get on the road. Mom can let us know what's going on when she's ready. Until then, we're on the clock and it's ticking."

As Garrett drove us down the narrow road and past the checkpoints, I put in a call to Lucas, giving him Amybeth's name, along with the number from the call logs, and asked him for an address. Not five minutes passed before Lucas texted an address and a full name.

"Amybeth Bell lives downtown," I said, reading the message aloud. "Lucas says she's a cook At Tiny Treasures Daycare and they're not related so she has to be the girlfriend."

"What's a daycare cook doing with a felon?"

"You'd be surprised," I said. "Don't serial killers usually amass a big female following?"

"Huff is hardly a serial killer."

"Maybe she's working her way up. Start with a run-of-the-mill felon and eventually marry one of the worst humans on the planet in a jailhouse wedding," I said and Garrett cast a side-eye at me and grimaced. "So he's got a woman in town and it sounds like she's a romantic interest, not a female relative. Doesn't explain why she's not on the visitor logs."

"It could be that Huff needs somewhere to stay while he searches for the jewels. He's been inside a long time. He may well be craving female company while he rehearses his get-rich-quick scheme."

It was my turn to grimace. "Can you monitor his calls for the next few days? If he's here for romantic purposes, he'll keep calling her. If he's really just here for the jewels, and he knows they've been found, he won't call her again. She won't be any use to him now."

"Good thinking. I'll call the warden when I'm back at MPD."

"You know, it could be that he wants both."

"How so?"

"Well, there's no man that falls in love faster than a homeless one and he's potentially going to be that when he gets out. So he romances a woman in the right area in the hopes she'll be desperate enough for a man to take him home when he's released. She puts a roof over his head and gives him everything else he needs while he goes out looking for the jewels. But imagine if he *does* really like her and he's about to get a huge payday. He's got it all then. Money, a woman, and a home."

"That would be something to dream about while incarcerated. Okay, so I'm keeping tabs on his communications anyway. We'll see what happens." Garrett leaned in to his dash and sighed. "I need to stop for gas or we'll be pushing this lump of junk home. Do you want anything?"

"Chocolate," I said as Garrett pulled into the gas station and parked next to the pump. "I'll go in. Do you want anything?"

"Get me a chocolate bar and a coffee," he said. "I'll be right in after I fill the tank."

I headed into the gas station mini-mart and browsed the candy bar counter, then got a water from the big refrigerators spanning the back wall. By the time the coffee was pouring from a self-service machine, Garrett walked in. "I have a deep suspicion of coffee machines that also dispense soup," he said, looking at the machine with mild disgust. "I swear I always get a little bit of the one I don't want in the one I do want."

"Yummy," I said, reaching for a plastic cap. The liquid slowed to a dribble and I extracted the cup, added its cap, picked up packets of creamer and sugar, and carried everything to the counter. Garrett paid, asked for a receipt, and we strolled back to the car.

"What are the other numbers on the call list?" I asked, thinking about another number that had been called a few times. I unwrapped the chocolate and bit into it.

Garrett took a long sip of his coffee and pulled a face. "No clue," he said. "I taste tomato. Or onion. Maybe chicken. I don't know. It's not good."

"Do you want me to toss it?" I asked looking around for a trash can.

"No, I need the caffeine. I'll suffer through it."

Nestled back in the passenger seat, I reached for the call sheet and pulled up a browser on my phone and input the number. "It's a real estate agent's," I said.

"I can't see him buying a house or applying to rent somewhere. He doesn't have a bean to his name. I don't imagine he has any kind of credit either." Garrett buckled his seatbelt and we headed for the road.

"Me neither, but…" A thought occurred to me. I clicked on the website and searched for the recently sold properties. When I found the listing, I smiled and turned the phone to my brother. "Look what they sold."

Garrett glanced at the screen, then back to the road as we left the forecourt. "Is that the Dugans' house?" he asked.

"It is. I think if we spoke to the realtors, we'll find Huff called about it. Probably trying to stall the sale or find out who bought it and what they planned on doing."

"Or seeing if it were empty so he could break in and search. He was trying to cover all his bases." Garrett took the turn onto the freeway back home and accelerated.

"In a clumsy sort of way. He was probably worried the body would be discovered."

"In that case…" A small bang sounded and the car veered sharply. "What the heck!" Garrett wrenched the wheel. The car listed to the side and continued to slide in an arc as the brakes screamed.

Then another pop.

"Garrett!" I yelled as I braced myself.

The car spun onto the opposite side of the road before hurtling nose first off the edge.

CHAPTER TWENTY

"They're all flat," said Garrett. He scratched his head and frowned.

"*All* of them?" I stepped closer, peering at the passenger side tires. The front was flat and the rear was shredded. I moved around to the other side, spreading my arms to steady my balance on the small, grassy bank that bordered the length of the freeway before it descended into a dry ditch. The driver's side tires were equally flat, the wheel rims exposed. "How can they all be flat? And two of them look shredded," I said, stepping around to the trunk. The car was perched precariously where it came to an abrupt stop as the front thumped into the ditch. I was surprised the car hadn't slipped and rolled down as we'd cautiously stepped out. I had no intention of tempting fate — and a ton of metal — now.

"They are. That's what caused the noise before we started to spin. Someone tampered with the tires. One popped and two shredded. The other probably just leaked air and didn't have time to rip. We're damn lucky this wasn't a lot worse!" Garrett glanced at the road. Only a handful of cars had passed in the last hour and we'd been fortunate that the highway was empty as we veered across the oncoming lane.

Steam rose from the engine and I stepped back. I privately agreed with Garrett's sentiment. The car had narrowly avoided flipping. Even luckier, with the almost empty lane of traffic and a long stretch of empty road on the other side, we hadn't hit anyone.

Stooping next to the flat tire, I examined it. The valve cap was missing. Just to be sure, I checked the next nearest tire. "This was deliberate," I said. "The valve caps are gone. Someone wanted us out of the way."

"Or me."

Or me, I thought, but I didn't want to hog my brother's moment of being in the perpetrator's crosshairs. "Where did you park the car before we met?" I asked.

"In MPD's secure lot like I usually do but there's no way it would take that long for the tires to go flat. They'd deflate long before we got to the prison. No, this was done either at the prison or after we left."

"The gas station," I said. "Anyone could have accessed the car there. The prison lot could only be accessed by someone who'd gone through the checkpoint. No one else knew we were going there so I don't see how anyone could arrange to follow us inside. You only got the go ahead shortly before making plans and I didn't know exactly where we were going until I was in the car."

"Yeah. Damn it. We must have been inside the gas station for two minutes." Garrett shook his head, frowning again. "I didn't even clock a tail. I looked out of habit but... Huh." He moved towards the trunk, then stopped.

"What?" I asked, wondering if this were a good time to mention how I'd been looking over my shoulder recently. Yet I'd also been remiss. I hadn't checked for a tail on leaving the prison either.

"Why did you look at me funny just now?"

"What do you mean?"

"When I said tail?"

"I might have been a little on edge, looking for tails of my own. I just have the weird feeling someone's been watching me."

Garrett stilled. "Now?"

"No. Not now. I don't feel it."

"What does it feel like when you think you're being watched?"

"Oily. It makes my skin prickle. But I haven't seen anyone. I might just be paranoid."

"Don't discount the feeling. We have instincts for a reason. They're there to keep us safe. When did you last get the feeling?"

"Outside the police station before I knew Gideon Black might be in town."

"And since?" he asked.

"Not since, and not at the gas station either." I sank into the grass and hugged my knees. Garrett stood over me, his hands on his hips. "What if it were just some stupid punks messing around?" I asked.

"And they happened to mess with our car and *only* our car?" he asked skeptically. "I'm not ruling it out entirely but I don't buy it. Damn it. I'm going to have to take a look at the gas station's camera footage. I noticed cameras over the door and inside. But before we do that..." He stepped towards the car, skidding slightly on the bank. He crouched down, moving around the car, then disappeared around the other side.

"What are you doing?" I called.

Garrett stood up, holding a small box. "Confirming another theory. We weren't being followed. We were being tracked," he said.

"Who by?"

"Good question." He walked around the car to pass me a small, metal box. I opened it, looking at a tiny blinking device inside. "The box is magnetic. All you have to do is reach under the car and stick it onto a bit of metal. Plenty of options on that pile of junk."

"Why does anyone want to know where we're going? Or is it to know where we are?"

"Both is my guess. It does mean we're on the right track. No one would bother about our whereabouts if we weren't following the right leads."

"Then my car is probably bugged too. Here's the cavalry!" I raised a hand as a black SUV slowed and pulled to a stop beside us. I'd called Solomon as soon as we'd calmed down after veering off the road and he'd simply said he was on his way. I scrambled up the bank as the window rolled down, relieved to see him.

"Can I give you both a lift?" asked Solomon. He pushed his sunglasses up onto his head and surveyed us, then the scene. "I see you're in satisfactory condition."

I grinned. "That would be helpful but you have to work on your smooth talk."

"You would not catch me telling my wife she's in satisfactory condition," said Garrett. "That would result in my being in *un*satisfactory condition."

Solomon smiled. "Glad to see you're both in fine health."

"We should take that as a compliment," I said to Garrett.

"Yeah," said Garrett obligingly, "I don't need to hear the kind of makeup talk he gives to my sister later."

"I'll text Traci and she can tell you," I said, my mood lifting with the teasing.

"Please don't."

"Do you want me to send someone to retrieve your car?" Solomon called to Garrett.

Garrett opened the door, tossed the metal box inside, then locked the car. "Nope," he said as he jogged up the bank. "I called it in and MPD are sending a pick-up for it. The car and the transmitter can stay here until they tow it."

"Transmitter?" asked Solomon.

"I'll fill you in on the way," I said. "Shotgun."

Behind me, Garrett tutted, then added, "We need to head back to the gas station at the next exit."

"I have a full tank," said Solomon.

"We need something else," I said.

"I see the candy bar packet in your pocket."

"We need to see some camera footage," I said.

"Sounds like you have plenty to tell me," said Solomon, sliding the sunglasses back over his eyes. "Let's go."

On the way to the gas station, Garrett and I filled in Solomon on the details that led to us coming off the road. By the time we pulled in, Solomon's jaw was tense but he didn't say much. I figured he was too busy thinking about all the ways he was going to hide Gideon Black's body if it turned out he did tamper with our car, and all the ways he was going to do exactly the same to persons unknown if it were punks messing with us.

We trooped into the gas station and Garrett pressed his badge to the security screen. "Can I see your camera footage?" he asked.

"Why?" asked the cashier, barely looking up from the game he played on his phone.

Garrett pointed to his badge, and said, "There's your reason."

"Don't you have to get a warrant or something?"

"Why don't you call your boss and get them down here?!" shot back Garrett.

"Yo, Dave!" called the cashier without turning. A moment later, a man wearing pants two sizes too small and a shirt straining at the buttons stepped through the swinging door carrying a crate of packaged baked goods. "These detectives want to see the camera footage."

"So why didn't you show them?" asked Dave. "Never mind. Let me set this down and I'll help you." He set the crate on the ground and walked to the security door in the interior wall. He pulled it open and beckoned us through, asking to see Garrett's credentials. "We haven't called for any assistance so how can we help?"

"Just need to see the footage from the last hour," said Garrett.

"Sure. There haven't been a lot of customers. Is there anything going on in the area I should be aware of?" he asked, glancing in the direction of the prison.

"No, all's good. We just need to check something, then we'll be out of your hair."

"I'll queue the cameras," he said, waving for us to

follow him into the back room. "We've got one covering the forecourt and one covering the stands in front. There're two inside, one covering the shop, and one covering the cash register."

"Smart," said Garrett.

"The system's easy to run," said Dave, pointing out the controls, but not taking a seat. "I figure I'll leave you to it but I would appreciate a heads-up if I need to take extra care for any reason. I'd like to make sure my employees are looked out for, even that one," he added, thumbing towards the cashier on the other side of the wall. He stepped back, indicating Garrett could take the chair pushed up against the desk.

Garrett sat, rewinding until he saw our car pulling into the forecourt. Then he rewound another minute. The pumps were all empty. A blue sedan was in the temporary parking spaces. A man walked out of the gas station and over to the sedan and climbed into the driver's side. He pulled out seconds before our car pulled in and we slowed to a stop at the pump nearest the shop.

I watched us discuss what we wanted as we remained seated. A red hatchback pulled into the pump opposite and a short black woman hopped out. Garrett got out and unhooked the hose, then I walked into the mini-mart. A moment later, the internal camera picked me up browsing the candy counter.

An SUV pulled into the temporary parking space and a couple got out and headed for the shop, then a motorcycle came in and parked at the pump the red hatchback vacated.

Garrett replaced the hose and headed inside.

Not seconds later, the motorcyclist walked over to our car, stooped and disappeared from view. I counted thirty seconds until he circled the front, taking moments to fiddle with each wheel before strolling back to his motorcycle, swinging his leg over and riding off.

"Can I send this to my email?" asked Garrett, looking over his shoulder at Dave.

"Sure, it's all digital."

Garrett tapped the keyboard, then stood. "Thanks," he said. "Appreciate your time."

"See what you wanted?" asked Dave.

"Someone tampered with our vehicle," he said.

"Sorry to hear it. I don't know if that's ever happened here before. Is the jerk on the motorcycle still around? I don't recall anyone wearing a helmet coming inside."

"No, he's long gone. I doubt he'll be back," said Garrett.

"Glad to hear it," said Dave.

We trooped out, silent until we were inside Solomon's SUV. "Any idea who that was?" asked Solomon.

Garrett looked at me.

"I don't know," I said, disappointed. "I thought it was a man. The shape, the way he walked, but beyond that. I don't know."

"Could he be Gideon Black?" persisted Garrett.

"I don't know," I repeated.

"Seems the right height and physique," said Solomon. "But there are thousands of men in the city who match that."

"So we're back to square one. We know someone tampered with the car. We now know it was a man. We just don't know who or why," I said.

"The why has to be the case," said Garrett. "This

was clearly targeted. He rode in, knew exactly which car to target and did it quickly and efficiently. He's done it before."

"I didn't see a motorcycle behind us at any point," I said.

"Then we should assume we were being tracked before the sabotage."

"That's creepy," I said.

"We should all be careful until we get to the bottom of this," said Solomon. He got out of the car, walked around it, stooping, checking carefully and then returned to the driver's seat. "We're most likely clean but I'll make a more thorough check at the agency. Lexi, are you open to carrying a tracker on your person at all times?"

"I don't mind," I said.

Solomon reached for his backpack in the footwell and pulled out a small box.

"You just happen to have trackers with you?" asked Garrett.

"You never know when you're going to need one," said Solomon, handing me a small device on a keychain. He pulled out his phone and fired off a text. "Attach that to a belt loop and keep it on you at all times. We'll monitor you from the agency."

"What about Garrett?" I asked.

Garrett pointed to the gun holstered at his hip. "I'm good," he said.

"Where am I taking you?" asked Solomon.

"Police station," said Garrett. "I'll check us out another car and we can keep going with our leads. Hopefully, the perp thinks we're tied up for hours waiting on the side of the road. We could get a jump on whoever it is."

"I like that idea," I said. "Let's go."

None of us felt much like talking beyond a smattering of questions here and there and I figured we were all wondering who placed the tracker, and when. It could be Gideon but that would mean he knew we were on the case. Garrett had been mentioned in *The Gazette's* article but I wasn't sure how anyone else could have known I was involved. Unless the Dugans told someone? Or my mom. Or Lily or Ruby. Or Bea. Or someone simply observing the Dugan house. That left infinite possibilities. It could even be a contact of Kelvin Huff, but I couldn't see how he could have called someone and enacted such a plan so quickly after our visit, which ruled him out.

Solomon drove us to the police station, then excused himself saying he had several cars to sweep for bugs, starting with mine since I was parked around the corner. That was far more pleasing to hear than Garrett's theory that we could all be carrying bugs transmitting our location to some unknown person.

"I have an uneasy feeling about all of this," said Garrett.

"Me too," I said.

"If there's an undiscovered tracker on your husband's vehicle, we can hope the perp thinks I've been dropped here and you've gone on with him. "Wait here. I'll get us another car and we can go visit Amybeth Bell and check out the realtors and those other last few numbers."

"I'll research the numbers while I wait. I'll be fine out here. No one's going to try anything in front of a police station," I said and Garrett nodded before he disappeared into the building. I perched on a bench and pulled out my phone and the call log sheet. There were only two numbers left to call. I tried putting them into a browser. The first returned the number of a store that sold recreational vehicles. Not just any old RVs but big, tricked out motorhomes a person could live in very comfortably. My eyebrows rose when I saw the starting price.

The second number was for a jeweler in Boston. What could Huff possibly want to buy there?

When a car horn honked twice, I looked up to see Garrett waving from a silver sedan. I jogged over and got in. "There weren't a lot of options," said Garrett when I wrinkled my nose at the scent of days-old takeout. I cranked the windows down, deciding I'd prefer fresh air instead of cold, stale aircon. When the blast of warmth came through the window I wondered at my choice.

"Huff called an RV sales company and a jeweler," I told him. "You should see the prices of the RVs. There's no way he can afford one right now. A ring is much cheaper if he's planning to propose but even then, I don't see how he can afford one of those either."

"Unless he's expecting a payday. An RV is not what I would buy if I expected to be imminently rich."

"What would you buy?"

"A beautiful place on a corner lot with a big yard and I'd get a vacation place in the mountains somewhere. Maybe Calendar. Traci loves it there. We could ski in the winter and go on fancy hiking trips in the summer."

"What's fancy about hiking?"

"There're wonderful excursions where they take you on the most beautiful trails until you get to your picturesque lunch spot where a gourmet picnic basket waits for you along with a cold bottle of wine, crystal glasses, and no kids."

"I see the appeal." Except the no kids. I could imagine Solomon wearing a baby strapped to his chest while I carried the sandwiches and bear spray. Would that be next year though, or the year after? We hadn't had much chance to put the baby-making plan into action this week.

"The point is, I would not be getting an RV," continued Garrett obliviously.

"A purchase like that suggests Huff isn't planning to settle in town. He's going on the run and doing it in style. He can live anywhere in one of those things. He could even go off grid and he wouldn't lose any sleep on his memory foam mattress."

"He's not on the run if he's a free man."

"Correct. He would be free. All he would need to do is retrieve the jewels from wherever he thought Black stashed them, sell them, buy his RV, and the world is his oyster. Well, North America. And maybe Central America. And Mexico!" I added.

"I get the point."

"Ah!" Another lightbulb went off. "He didn't call the jeweler for a purchase. What if he's scouting for a place where he can make a sale but since he's not so smart, he thought a regular jeweler might buy the gems. What he really needs is a jewel merchant who doesn't ask questions."

"And until he can do all that, he shacks up with our girl, Amybeth. Let's find out what she has to say."

CHAPTER TWENTY-ONE

Amybeth Bell lived in a three family-unit built with a pale brick exterior and windows that were slightly too small and a porch that was slightly too large. It vaguely resembled a child's drawing of what they thought a house looked like.

Bell was written on a slip next to the middle buzzer. "Hello?" wafted her disembodied voice after I'd pressed it twice.

"Delivery," I said.

"Come up! Second floor." The door clicked and I pushed it and headed for the stairs, Garrett on my heels. As I reached the landing, a door opened, and a woman with brassy blond hair and a quarter inch of dark roots poked her head out. "You have a delivery for me?" she asked, surveying us warily.

Garrett held up his shield.

"I didn't order one of those," she said as she stepped back, knocking the door closed with a disinterested slam. I skidded across the hallway and wedged my foot in the frame, wincing as the door hit me.

"Lieutenant Graves, MPD," said Garrett when Amybeth drew back the door. "We have some questions for you about Kelvin Huff."

"Who?"

"Kelvin Huff, resident of Barnham Correctional Facility. He says you're his girlfriend," lied Garrett.

"Oh, that idiot," she snorted.

"So you're *not* his girlfriend?"

"Not anymore. Well, like, not really ever. How can you be someone's girlfriend if you've never been on a date? I don't think so."

"She has a point," I said.

"Thank you! Who are you?" she asked, her attention returning to me.

"Lexi Graves, PI."

"Like a bounty hunter?"

"Like completely different."

"Like a detective?"

"Yes, but without a dental plan."

"Your teeth seem okay."

I smiled. "Thank you."

"You should get Solomon to invest in a dental plan for the staff," said Garrett.

"We have a dental plan. I was trying to make a point that there are some differences between police and private investigators," I said.

"By lying?" asked Amybeth.

"No. Well, yes," I said, "but it wasn't a lie. It was a metaphor. Sort of."

"I don't know what that is but I know what lying is."

"What kind of plan are you on?" asked Garrett.

"Are you two married?" asked Amybeth.

"No!" we both shouted.

Amybeth raised her eyebrows. "Sure act like you're married. Bit of an age gap romance so it must be your personality because cops don't have money," she added, giving Garrett a look that scanned his nose to his toes.

"We're brother and sister," I said.

This time, Amybeth pulled an appalled face. "You two should not be married! That's not legal, dental plan or not. Even being cousins is sketchy."

"We are not married!" we squawked.

"That's a good thing since you work together... and are related." Amybeth grimaced.

"We don't work together either," said Garrett.

"You two are very confusing. I have to go now. I have a hair appointment." Amybeth stepped back. "Tell that no good Kelvin to stop calling me. It's annoying."

"Wait. How did you meet him?" I asked.

"Who?"

"Kelvin Huff!"

She sighed and rolled her eyes but surprised me by staying and saying, "I volunteer with a correspondence service for prisoners who don't have long to serve on their sentences. It's supposed to help them develop friendly relationships to prepare for their life outside. Kelvin sent me a letter. We wrote back and forth a few months and I visited him a couple times at his last facility. He got transferred closer to here and wanted me to visit him again. I said no but he started laying it on thick."

"Laying what on?" Garrett asked.

"Romance?" I clarified and she nodded.

"Yeah. I was being friendly and he was like

'You're the most beautiful woman I ever saw' and 'I'm the luckiest man ever to meet someone like you' and all this talk about how he was going to sweep me off my feet and treat me like a princess."

"That sounds awful," said Garrett.

"Don't mock me," she snipped, giving Garrett a filthy look. "Women know when it's being put on insincerely. At first, the compliments were nice, you know, but then there were way too many. I was happy to put him in touch with some services that could help him out but then he told me he put my address down with his parole officer as his residence! He said we could make a go of things and that he would be ashamed of taking me to a hostel because he just wanted to cook for me in our own kitchen. *Our*! I mean, *please*. He thought I was just going to let him move in with me, sleep in my bed, and financially support him fully, just because he threw a few nice words my way." She snorted.

"Totally get it," I said.

"And when I said no, then he really wouldn't let up. He started pleading, saying I was his only hope of making it on the outside," she said in a mock whine, "and he couldn't make it without me, and it would just tear him up not to make a go of things with a good woman. That he'd never loved anyone like this."

"Playing on your heart strings," I said.

"With the strings of a tiny, invisible violin," Amybeth said, nodding. "It was like he was using every line he ever heard and when he realized none of them were working, then he just tried bombarding me instead. No thank you. I told him I do not want to support a man."

"What did he say to that?"

She rolled her eyes. "He had a big pie-in-the-sky idea that it wouldn't be long, just a month or two. He'd get a basic job and pay his way, and then he knew someone who owed him and as soon as he collected, he'd buy me anything I wanted! He said I could quit my job and we could go on the road and be free spirits. There was no way I was falling for his scheme."

"Who did he say owed him?" asked Garrett.

"Some old friend of his. Apparently, he owed him big time." She spread her hands wide.

"Did he mention how he was going to collect it? Or where?" I asked.

"Some cockamamie story about a safe deposit box and he knew where the key was. I asked him and said your friend just left you a fortune in it, did he? And he said, yeah, and had the biggest shit-eating grin you ever saw. You know what I thought? Hmm?" She looked from Garrett to me.

"No?" I said.

She laughed scathingly. "I thought it was a pile of crap. I told him to stop calling me and I don't believe in one-day paydays. You either have money now or you don't. Anything else, without a solid plan, is just a story you made up for yourself and I'm not falling for another man who makes up stories."

"Sensible," I said.

"Or maybe I'll get a cat," she said. "Either way, I don't want anything to do with that loser and tell him to stop calling me. I've already told his parole officer that he's not moving in with me and I am *not* his girlfriend!" She stepped back and slammed the door shut.

"Well," said Garrett, taking a breath. He raised his

eyebrows.

"I kind of like her," I said. We turned and headed for the stairs.

"Jury's out on her like-ability but her information tallies with everything else we guessed. I have no idea why he thought he was going to get the jewels from a safe deposit box. I haven't found any indication there was one under Charlie Black's name or any other alias."

"I'll bet that's what Charlie Black told him to get him off his back. It makes sense that he would pretend the jewels were elsewhere. Otherwise, why didn't Kelvin just steal them from his pocket there and then? Black probably told Huff that the key was hidden somewhere, maybe even back in New York, and that everyone needed to lie low for a while until the heat died down on the heist. But Huff got antsy and wanted his cut now." I raised my hand, pointing a finger between Garrett's eyes. "He's waving the gun around and it goes off. Now he's got a dead body on his hands and he still needs to track down the make-believe key so he does what Black originally suggests. He lies low, intending to come back."

Garrett gently smacked my hand down. "That all sounds very nice but we still can't prove it. It's not even a case of manslaughter or accidental death or murder. We have nothing that places Huff at Joe Smithson's house then or ever."

As we got into his car, Garrett's phone rang and he answered, listening, then saying quickly, "No, of course not. Why would I authorize that? It doesn't matter. I'm on my way back. Any news on the car? It hasn't? Well, let me know when it turns up. I want a report on it ASAP." He disconnected, grumbling to himself. "I have to head back to the station. I'll walk you to your car."

"No need. Solomon had it picked up to check it over."

"Can you get Solomon to pick you up? I'd feel a lot better if someone came to get you, given everything that's happened."

"I'll call him. Or if Jord is in his office, he might take me home." I checked my phone, unsure whether to be relieved that I hadn't received any further messages after Solomon texted to say my car was now back at the agency. Did that mean Solomon hadn't found anything yet? "Do you really think we should be worried?" I asked.

"Yes."

"I was afraid of that."

"I'm more afraid of Mom. I don't want to tell her you got kidnapped, shot or stabbed."

"That hardly ever happens. Recently," I added.

"Let's keep it that way, and definitely not on my watch."

"Plus, it was your car that was tampered with," I reminded him.

"It shouldn't escape your notice that you were in it."

"You make it sound like I'm a bad omen."

"Not at all."

"Aww, th-" I started.

"I prefer disaster magnet."

By the time we were only a block from the station, the conversation had returned back to tossing ideas around about Kelvin Huff and Charlie Black in his many guises, but we were no closer to a definitive answer.

"Slow down," I said as the light began to turn.

"I can make it through the light!" Garrett protested.

"No, slow down and look over there." I pointed to the SUV across the road from the station as we slowed to a stop. Two men sat in it. "That's Maddox."

"Not unusual."

"To sit in his car, staring at the station?"

"Yup. I do it all the time."

"With your partner? I couldn't quite see but I'll bet Special Agent Farid is next to him."

"With an array of detectives. Depends on who's free and if I mind sharing my snacks. Or if their snacks are better than my snacks."

"But you work there! You have an office!"

"People come into my office. They leave me alone in my car. Anyway, ignore Maddox. He probably has an appointment in the building and it's not with me. Let's go in and you can call for a ride or see if Jord's around. We can get together tomorrow and see if we have any bright ideas overnight because, right now, I'm stumped. It feels like we've got the beginning and the end and enough in the middle to join it together but I want a watertight case. And I want to know who's following us. The only person I can rule out sticking a tracker on my car is Kelvin Huff, but since you're involved, and who knows what the heck will happen with you around, I don't want to go in one hundred percent on that."

The lights changed and Garrett accelerated. I looked back at Maddox's vehicle as we passed it and frowned. I wouldn't rule him out as the culprit either. He'd been acting weird ever since the night we fell through the ceiling.

"Okay, fine," I said.

"I'm switching cars every day until we know what's going on," he said as he parked the car out front rather than heading around to the lot. I followed him as we walked towards the station.

Outside the main entrance, a family were shouting at each other while two officers attempted to intervene and keep them apart. A teenager whizzed past me on a skateboard, then another, forcing me to take a couple of steps behind Garrett. I hurried to catch up, sidestepping the two young women in uniform until I realized one was my cousin.

"Hey, Tara," I said, lifting a hand to wave.

"Hey, you! I'm heading out on a call. Let's catch up later? I hear you're working on that cold case. Can't wait to hear all about it!" Tara grinned as she moved past me to follow her partner.

I turned away, catching the eye of another female officer exiting the building as she pushed sunglasses onto her sweetheart face, adjusting them as she turned away.

Something about her was familiar but then, so was half of MPD. I was either related to them, knew someone who dated them, knew them socially, or I'd dated one or more of them.

A few steps from the entrance and I grabbed Garrett's arm.

"What?" he asked.

"That was her!"

"Who?" He looked over my head.

"Her! One of the women from Maddox's photos. That was her." I paled, the fuller picture filling my head. "And she was wearing a police uniform."

"What are you talking about?"

Garrett's words were lost to the breeze as I turned on my heel, running back the way I came. I reached the sidewalk, looking left and right. The warring family were still arguing, and several people idled, but the uniformed police woman was nowhere in sight.

"Are you sure?" Garrett asked when he reached me. "You recognized someone from a photo?"

"Yes, I'm sure. Maddox showed me photos of the suspect in his case. A thief! It was her. Her hair was different, but she had a police issue hat on and her makeup was different but it was her. I'm sure it was. Garrett, why would someone Maddox is looking for be wearing a police uniform here?" I stopped, a new thought coming to me. "He said she was a thief. What did she have access to?"

"The evidence locker," Garrett and I said at the same time.

We turned to each other and my stomach dropped. "The jewels," we said. As soon as we locked eyes, Garrett was taking off, running to the police station. He created the path as we barged through the main doors, across the lobby and into the building, not slowing down until we reached the evidence locker.

A detective was walking out, staring at her receipt, as we entered. The sergeant on the other side of the thick wire screen was making notes. Otherwise, the small lobby was empty.

"Who's been in here today?" asked Garrett.

"Who hasn't?" asked the sergeant without looking up from his computer.

"Can you narrow it down to women in the last hour?" I asked.

This time, the sergeant looked up. "Now why would I do that?" he asked. Then he saw Garrett and got to his feet.

"We think someone might have accessed something they shouldn't have," said Garrett.

"Give me the box number and I'll check, Lieutenant."

Garrett reeled off the number and the sergeant input it into his computer. He shook his head. "No one accessed this box since you logged it in as evidence," he said.

"You're sure?"

"Positive. Before you ask, yes, I'm the only one on duty. I've been here the whole afternoon and I haven't left the desk in the past hour, and no, no one else could have given someone access."

"This is good news," said Garrett. "Did anyone ask for access to that box and get refused?"

"No, I haven't refused any requests. Let me save you some time here. In the last hour I had four submissions, all from male officers. There were five females, three accessing evidence. One submitting. One brought me a coffee. She was my favorite."

"Did you check all their credentials?"

Sergeant rolled his eyes.

"Sorry I asked. Of course you did," said Garrett. "Can you check the box for me?"

"Must I?"

"Please," I said. "It would set our minds at rest."

"Who're you?" he asked.

"She's consulting on my case," said Garrett. "Now, please, humor me."

"Give me the number again," he said and Garrett reeled it off.

"Wait here. I know where it is. I'll grab it." He pushed off the desk, ambling away and disappearing behind a shelving rack. A minute later, he returned carrying a brown cardboard box. He set it on the desk and made a point of indicating the seals to us. "Nothing's been cut," he said.

"Open it," instructed Garrett.

The sergeant plucked a penknife from the desk drawer and slit the tape open. He set the lid to the side and tipped the box forward. Inside was the plastic bag, the jewels wrapped in tissue, along with the photograph in another bag.

"Open the larger bag please."

"I'll have to log this," said Sergeant.

"Not a problem."

The sergeant reached for the bag, popped it open and tipped the contents into the upturned lid. He unwrapped the tissue and revealed the larger jewels. "This what you expected to see?" he asked.

"It is," confirmed Garrett.

"Good. Now watch me count every piece back in and then I'm going to log it and you can sign off after I reseal the box."

"Thanks," said Garrett. "Much appreciated."

"Anything else, or do you want to get out of my hair?" asked the sergeant as he resealed the box.

"We'll get out of your hair," said Garrett as he signed the paperwork. "Thanks for your help."

I narrowly avoided pointing out the sergeant didn't have any hair as Garrett ushered me from the room.

"I would have had a heart attack if the jewels were stolen from under our noses," said Garrett. "Are you sure you recognized her? It's not your nerves playing tricks?"

"I'm sure. At least..." I hesitated, feeling uncertain now. Nothing had been taken and I didn't know everyone in the building. What if she just looked like Maddox's thief? But what if my gut feeling weren't wrong? "Let's say it was Maddox's suspect. She must have wanted something else. Maybe she wanted to access a file instead? Could she do that?" I asked.

"Not without a password. Maybe you were mistaken? It's been a long day. I'm tired. You're tired. The tracking bug and tires blowing out spooked us. I hate to say it because I know you'll be mad at me, but it was just a face in a crowd. Maybe she looked like a photo but there's no reason to think anything Maddox is working on is directly related to this case. You're spooked. It's natural." Garrett gave me a sympathetic smile. "We have the jewels. That's what matters."

"I'm sure it was her," I insisted softly. "I'm sure it was."

Disappointment weighed on me as I decided against checking in on Jord, and called Solomon instead. Perhaps Garrett was right. Perhaps I was hallucinating. Perhaps I was seeing thieves wherever I looked.

Or perhaps we missed something.

CHAPTER TWENTY-TWO

I'll be outside in five minutes. Solomon's text message flashed on my screen.

"I'll see you in the morning," I said, rising from the chair in Garrett's office. My half-drunk cup of coffee was left on the desk, abandoned. Garrett was on the phone and he hung up when I rose. For the past several minutes, I'd been contemplating calling Maddox and finally ruled it out. Garrett was right. The woman was just a face and the jewels were all there, secure in the evidence locker. It had been a long day.

"You got a ride?" asked Garrett.

"Solomon's picking me up."

"Hey, Rachenstein's representatives emailed to confirm they're coming by in a couple days. Why don't you meet with them too?" he said. "They're bringing their own expert."

"Are you trying to cheer me up?" I asked.

"Yes. I didn't mean to sound like I thought you were making things up. I just know that sometimes I start seeing things that aren't there when I'm worn down by a case. Finding that tracker got us both extra jumpy. We need a good night's sleep and we can talk about our next steps tomorrow."

"Okay," I agreed. While Garrett had answered calls, I'd been pondering the man on the motorcycle who'd tampered with our tires and the name I kept returning to was Gideon Black. It *had* to be him. But why? Why did he want to delay us returning to town? Or did he simply want us to back off? Surely, he knew that wouldn't happen. And why was he tracking us? It didn't make sense.

"I'm going to get the IT guys to take a look at the tracker when the car is brought in and see if they can give us any information about where it's from or who planted it."

"Let me know if anything comes of it?"

"Will do but don't get your hopes up. Night, Lexi."

"Night, Garrett."

I headed outside, saying hi to two uncles and a cousin, and three guys from my high school graduating class on the way. Outside, Maddox's vehicle was gone and Solomon hadn't arrived.

A movement at the edge of the building caught my eye and my jaw almost dropped open.

The man standing there was full of audacity.

Ben Rafferty.

Tom Benedict.

Joe Smithson Junior.

Gideon Black.

He was looking directly at me. His hands in his jeans pockets, his linen shirt open at the neck and sleeves rolled to the elbows, as casual as if he'd caught sight of an old friend while taking a stroll. His dark brown hair was a little longer and he had a few days of beard growth, but trimmed stylishly. I'd recognize him anywhere and I definitely wasn't hallucinating.

Why had that small movement in the corner of my eye stopped me? No, it wasn't because he was moving. It could only be because he was the only person *not* moving, while officers and other pedestrians moved around him.

It was like he was invisible to everyone except me.

For a moment, I was rooted to the spot. Then I stepped towards him.

Gideon stepped back.

I took another step and he turned, glancing behind him with a smile, ensuring I was watching, and walked around the side of the building.

I took off at a run, scared I would lose him but when I reached the edge of the building, there he was again. Waiting.

Waiting for me.

He waited until I began to walk towards him, then turned and speed-walked.

By the time I caught up with him, he was rounding the corner of the parking lot for police vehicles, this side walled from the street.

"Ben?" I called out, wondering if he'd respond. How long had it been since he'd used that name?

He stopped and turned.

"Hello, Lexi," he said, his face even more charming now he smiled. His brown eyes were just as mesmerizing as I remembered. "It's nice to see you again."

"Ben. Or should I call you Gideon?"

If he were surprised I knew his real name, he

didn't show it as he stepped closer, closing the gap between us. "Either is fine. Ben if you prefer since that's how you know me best."

"I don't know you at all," I said. "Ben Rafferty never existed."

"He did for a little while. I've thought about you a lot. You changed me." Gideon reached to stroke my cheek but I stepped back. His face fell, just ever so slightly but I wasn't fooled. He wasn't disappointed; it was just another manipulation. A trickle of disgust slithered down my spine. He wanted me to want him. Or to feel sorry for him. "That was forward of me. I apologize. I hoped I would see you again. Not under these circumstances, of course," he added with a small lift of his shoulder as he glanced around.

"What circumstances would these be?"

"My father's death. Or rather, its discovery."

"I'm sorry," I said. For a moment, it didn't matter what Gideon had done, or his father. He was still a man who'd lost his parent. There was still a man who had been murdered.

"Thank you. It means a lot to me, coming from you."

I ignored that. If Gideon were trying to build a connection, he wasn't going to find me susceptible. His words meant nothing. How could they? He was a proven liar. "Did you know he was here? That he lived here?" I asked.

"No, that was news, but I knew he'd been here. He moved around a lot and he wasn't always honest about where. I figured that out in my teens. I figured *a lot* out in my teens," he said, holding my gaze with a look so knowing that I knew he knew exactly what kind of man his father was. "It took a long time to track my dad's movements but I found out what I needed to know."

"Was that why you came to Montgomery before?" I asked, curious.

"Yes, originally. It won't come as a surprise to you that I ended up in Alabama first. Wrong Montgomery. You'd think the powers that be would call one of them New Montgomery at least." He shrugged. "Easy mistake to make. Only thousands of miles between the two."

"How did you know you got it right when you pitched up here last time?"

"I couldn't be sure at first. I won't bore you with the details but I knew soon enough. The discovery of my father's remains now absolutely solidifies it. I wonder if he liked it here." Gideon cast a look around the street but I knew he didn't mean *here*, here. He meant down the street from my parents, Charlie Black living his life like the traveling salesman he purported to be. Had "Joe Smithson" lived a life here, visiting our museum? Our grocery stores? Did he take walks in the parks? Just close enough to get to his son, but far enough away that his anonymity was guaranteed? "Not his usual sort of place. He liked excitement," said Gideon. "He lived for the thrills."

"The kind of excitement you get robbing museums?" I asked, taking my chance.

Gideon smiled broadly and wagged his finger at me. "I always liked you. So direct. Pretty too."

"I know. You don't have to butter me up."

"Confident too. Sassy. Well, to answer your question, yes, my father did like robbing museums amongst other places. As you've probably guessed, he was very good at it too."

"Until someone shot him."

There it was. The bullseye.

"No need to rub it in," said Gideon, his face falling.

For a moment I felt guilty. "Sorry."

Gideon stepped closer and I retreated, finding my back against the wall, my escape blocked. "I need your help," he said, brushing back a lock of hair that slipped over my shoulder. A waft of expensive aftershave, fresh and masculine, reached me. It should be against the law for criminals to smell this good.

"Have you tried the police?" I thumbed over my shoulder to the very building we were adjacent to.

"I don't think they will help me. I need *your* help, Lexi."

"Stop by the office in the morning. We'll listen to your case." Probably with the police listening next door, but I didn't tell him that. "There will be paperwork. Bring your checkbook."

"I'm here now. I need you to get something for me."

"Like what?"

"The police have something of mine. I want it back."

"You want the jewels found with your father." Not a question. A statement.

"I do."

"They're not yours."

"I beg to differ."

"They belong to Rachenstein." Another calculated guess.

Gideon's jaw stiffened. "They *belong* to me."

"We could be here all day doing this." I was tempted to check my watch sarcastically but sudden moves seemed a bad idea. Gideon had me trapped against the wall and no one knew where I was. *Damn it!* Surprise at seeing him had overtaken me. I should have called Solomon before I followed Gideon around the corner but I'd been so desperate not to lose him. I couldn't do that. Not after the embarrassment of insisting I'd seen Maddox's thief.

"I don't have all day. I need you to go inside and get my jewels. I need you to go now. I'm not the only person who wants them. All the vultures will be here soon. Did you leak it to the press?"

"No! Did you?"

"No."

"Did you kill your father?" I asked.

Gideon recoiled. "No!" Then he softened. "I'm not a killer. I'm a thief. Not the same thing."

"Do you know who did?"

"No."

"Do you want to know?"

"I want the jewels. You can tell me the rest later." Gideon leaned closer again, his body inches from mine. "Do you know who killed my dad?" he asked softly.

"I've got a good idea."

"Who?"

"Did you bug my car?" I asked, switching topics. If I could keep him talking long enough, Solomon would come looking for me.

"What's with all the questions?"

"Did you?" I pressed.

"Maybe."

"Why?"

"I think you're stalling for time. I've told you what I need you to do. I want you to go inside here," he said, tapping the building, his arm trapping me, "and get the jewels and bring them out to me. As soon as I have them, I'll be gone and you'll never see me again. Unless you want to." He smiled and tickled my cheek.

I drew up my hand and wiggled my ring finger. "I'm spoken for."

"I heard you were married. That doesn't bother me." He winked.

"How did you hear anything?"

"I have plenty of ears that listen. Now go inside and get my jewels." He mimed walking away with his fingers.

"I can't. They're in the evidence locker."

"Which is exactly why you're going to get them for me." Something jabbed at my ribs. I looked down, expecting to see his finger but instead, I saw the muzzle of a gun, just peeking from under his shirt. I forced a breath, forcing a calmness I didn't feel.

"I'm not a police officer."

"I've done my research on you, Lexi Graves, PI. You're related to half of them. Find someone to help you. Doesn't matter who or what crazy story you make up, just get in there, get the jewels and bring them here. I'm sure you can figure it out. You have thirty minutes."

"But..."

Gideon pressed the gun into my ribs. "Twenty."

I gulped. "No."

"I thought you'd say that so I made a backup plan. Your friend is Lily, isn't she? Such nice, blond hair. Lovely family. Really picture perfect. I bet you'd miss her."

Fear chilled me. "Lily? There's no way you could get to Lily." But even as I said it, I wasn't sure. I'd posted her outside the Dugans' house. Gideon could have seen her.

"You think I meant Lily? No, the 'her' I meant is Poppy. Cute, little thing."

I paled. My head swam as nausea filled me. "What?" I whispered, the word choking in my throat.

"I have someone watching her as we speak. If you're not back with the jewels in twenty minutes, poor, little Poppy is going to disappear. Poof!" His breath was warm against my cheek.

"But I…"

"No ifs, no buts, just get in there and… ooof!" Gideon's eyes swiveled then rolled upwards. He lurched against me but before I could push him off, he sank to his knees and keeled to the ground, hitting the pavement like a dead weight.

I looked up into a woman's eyes. The same eyes I'd seen only a short time ago. The face I thought I'd mistaken.

"I knew it!" I said and punched the air.

"You're welcome." The woman's lips slid into a half smile. She nudged Gideon with the toe of her sneaker. Slumped on the ground, he didn't make a sound.

"Who are you?" I asked. Her visage was the same. Same high cheekbones, set into a sweetheart face. Yet she looked completely different from the woman in uniform. The blues were gone and the pointed cap and sunglasses. Hair longer now, and blonde, falling around her shoulders. She wore fitted jeans and a frilly, peach blouse with neat, pointed pumps that I recognized from my wish list. Her jewelry was understated and elegant, just a couple of gold chains around her neck and studs in her ears.

Was this the real her? Or another version, another disguise? I wasn't sure I'd ever know.

I wasn't even sure why she was in front of me right now.

"A better question is what am I doing," she said, pointing to Gideon's crumpled body. In her hands, she held a light, retractable, baton. "Saving you, of course."

I grimaced at the weapon, another one far too close to me, but she didn't make any move to use the baton further. "Did you kill him?" I asked, stooping to check his pulse at his wrist. The beat was strong but when I peeled back his eyelids, there was no cognition. Gideon was out cold. I removed his fingers from the gun he still held and kicked it along the wall behind me where neither of them could reach it.

"No, I didn't hit him nearly hard enough for that. He's just going to have a snooze on the ground and then a nice, big headache. I heard what he said. Who's Poppy?"

"My niece."

"I doubt she's in any danger. Gid's not dangerous. Well, not usually. Definitely not to kids. He probably wouldn't have shot you either."

"Probably?"

"I doubt it's loaded. He's really not a guns man."

"You seem to know a lot about him."

She pulled a face. "Unfortunately."

"I'm going to call Poppy's mom all the same." I pulled out my phone and paused. I wanted to know something else first. "I know it was you in the police uniform, coming out of the station."

"No idea what you're talking about," she said but she couldn't stop the small upwards curve of her lips.

"If you know him, you probably knew he put a tracker on our car," I said.

"That doesn't surprise me. I put a tracker on his motorcycle. Gideon always thinks he's the predator but I'm top of the food chain here." Again, that flicker of a smile.

"I was interrogating him!"

"Oh, that's what you were doing." She tapped her forehead, mocking me. "My bad. Perhaps I shouldn't have stepped in."

"Why did he deflate our tires? Why did he want us out of the way?" I asked, stealing the opportunity to fill in the blanks.

"He did? I'm sure you can guess why." She inclined her head towards the police station.

"The tires blew! We drove off the road." I stopped, thinking.

She looked me over from head to foot. "You seem okay."

"No thanks to Gideon." We stared at him. He looked pathetic, crumpled on the ground, but I could only imagine his temper when he awoke. I didn't want to be around for that. Gideon liked to win and he'd just lost. Not only that, but he'd lost badly. "He wanted us out of the way because he had a plan to steal the…."

"Jewels," filled in the woman. "I'm sure every thief from here to Mars will sniff around while this police department has possession of them."

"Well, if he wanted us out of the way, then his Plan A went wrong. Apparently, I was Plan B."

"Sounds like Gideon. Always wanting women to do his dirty work." She shook her head in mock exasperation like she'd heard this before. Or been a victim of it. Yet she didn't act like she had been one of Gideon's marks. She was too self-assured and too... amused.

"Well, it was a waste of time for both of you. He'll never get them now. If you were after the jewels, you never got them either. I saw them not fifteen minutes ago. They're all accounted for."

"Isn't that good news?" she said, expressionless, like she didn't care one bit. "I'll get going. Let's not run into each other again, Lexi."

"How do you know my name?" I asked, frowning. How did she know me at all? I glanced towards the street at the front of the building. Had Gideon said something to her? Or Maddox? How well did they know each other? Or was it something she'd figured out by herself?

"So many questions, so little time. It was nice meeting you but I have to go."

"Hey..."

"Another time perhaps," she said, stepping away.

"Why did you hang around anyway?" I asked, both curious and stalling for time.

"I didn't plan to. I saw this idiot loitering near the station and figured he was up to no good. Then I saw you make a beeline for him and figured I better watch over you. Of course, he was after the jewels. Typical Gid."

"And his father."

"Imagine that. Like father, like son. Seems like Gideon will get a better end than his father did," she said, with a shrug. "And a lot of time to contemplate his misdeeds. Do encourage your police friends to lock him up, won't you?"

"It sounds like you know him."

"We've come across each other before. I guess you can take it from here?" She nudged him and for a moment, I wondered if she were contemplating kicking the man while he was down.

"What about you? Where are you going to go?"

"That would be telling," she said and tapped her nose.

"Is there a way to contact you?" I asked. "If I need help with anything questionable in the future?"

"Probably not, but I appreciate the asking. We'd be quite the team in another life." She glanced up and stilled. I followed her gaze and found myself looking at Maddox, standing at the end of the road beyond the police station. Too far to hear us, but close enough to recognize her. The look they gave each other was long and loaded.

"Why did you watch over me?" I asked, turning back to her, but she was already gone, leaving my question hanging in the air.

Maddox launched into a run towards us. Instead of bypassing me in pursuit of my mysterious rescuer, he skidded to a stop. "What happened here?" he asked wrenching his attention from down the street to looking from me to Gideon, then to the gun.

"Remember Ben Rafferty? Or Gideon Black as we now know him. He was after the jewels. He threatened me. He threatened Poppy!" Fear turned to anger inside me.

On the ground, Gideon groaned. His hand flapped to his head but his eyes didn't open.

"Why was Cass Temple here?" asked Maddox. He knelt beside Gideon, checking his pulse like I had done.

"I was going to ask you that," I said, noting her

name. *Cass Temple.*

He'd asked me if I'd heard the name Temple!

Who was she? Why had she come to my aid? What was I to her?

"What did she tell you?" asked Maddox.

"Nothing!"

"You were talking."

"About this!" I waved my hand at Gideon.

Maddox ran a hand over his hair, turning away briefly. "It was a good thing we spotted you both. Sadiq called Garrett. They'll all be here in a moment."

"She was inside the police station less than an hour ago. She was wearing a police uniform. She must have been after the jewels but she didn't get them. Neither did Gideon," I told him.

"Are you sure of that? Are you sure she didn't steal anything?"

"Garrett and I saw the jewels, if that's what you mean. The sergeant in the evidence locker unsealed the box in front of us and counted them out. We saw them!"

"And you just happened to run into her?"

"She said she waited around and saw Gideon. She followed him. She helped me."

"She's going to disappear." Maddox looked skyward, his fists clenching and unclenching.

Then Garrett arrived, calling to us, several police officers in tow, their weapons drawn as they circled Gideon. Someone tugged me back while another officer scooped up Gideon's gun. Another officer checked over Gideon as he groaned some more, then two pulled him into a seated position against the wall. I waited as he was handcuffed, and an ambulance called for.

"Hi, Garrett," I said when my brother took me by the shoulders, running an eye over me and giving a satisfied nod.

"You don't seem hurt," said Garrett, a deep frown marring his forehead.

"I'm not. But I need you to do something."

"Name it."

"First find out where Poppy is and make sure she's safe."

Garrett glanced at Gideon, his face darkening. "Why wouldn't she be safe?" he asked, his voice a low growl.

"I'm sure she is. I think it was just an idle threat but we need to be sure. Gideon said someone's watching her and Lily's with Mom."

"I'll call Jord now and tell him to get over to wherever she is."

"There's one more thing," I said, the missing pieces beginning to click into place. Cass Temple hadn't stolen the jewels... except... what if she had? What if we'd all been hoodwinked? Was it even possible?

"Go on."

"I told you I saw her but when we checked the jewels and found nothing missing, I figured I had to be wrong. But what if I weren't? What if I really did see her walking out of the building?"

"Her?"

"The woman! She was..." I looked around. "She was here. Maddox saw her!"

Garrett regarded me skeptically. "We saw the jewels," he reminded me.

"I know. Maybe she was casing the station or... or... I don't know but she was here! Everyone saw her!"

Garrett nodded. "Outside, not inside MPD. You can explain more about this thief later," he said, looking over my shoulder. "Or Maddox can."

My shoulders slumped. He was right, of course, the only witnesses to Cass Temple's appearance saw her outside. And the jewels were there. Plus, she had been tracking Gideon... hadn't she?

Finally, when I turned away, I looked directly into Solomon's eyes.

"What the hell happened here?" he asked.

"I'll explain on the way home," I said and reached for his hand.

CHAPTER TWENTY-THREE

"Hmmm." Mr. Lavelle, the small, stern man that had arrived with Rachenstein's entourage, made the noise again and breathed deeply through his nose. His lips were tight, his forehead wrinkled, and one eye was partially closed while the other was entirely obscured by a small, black lens. He turned the stone over, repeating, "Hmmmm!"

At the back of the conference room, deep within MPD, I hardly dared breathe. I'd waited several tense days for this. Garrett glanced over his shoulder, catching my eye, and raised his eyebrows.

We'd been in a tense wait for confirmation these past several minutes after Rachenstein's representatives filed in with an entourage made up of their jewel expert, a representative from the royal family, and four armed bodyguards. More security personnel waited downstairs with the limousine that had brought them. Much to my disappointment, there wasn't one titled member of the royal family.

Finally, Mr. Lavelle set down the ruby, then his

lens, and looked up. "Madame Rousseau?" he called, beckoning to the representative. She stepped closer, her glossy, black hair swinging around her chin, stooping to listen as he whispered into her ear, her expression not changing at all.

When he finished, Madame Rousseau said something I couldn't hear and motioned to his equipment. He packed away his items into a small, leather bag and scraped back his chair, standing.

"Mr. Lavelle says this is not the Queen's Ruby," she said, her words precise and hinting of a slight English accent.

"Our experts say otherwise," said Chief Davis, a tall, broad man in uniform boasting several stripes. Garrett's chief rarely made an appearance but apparently, priceless jewels and royalty dragged him out from his spacious office. Or not, as it now seemed.

Stunned silence filled the room.

"I'm afraid our expert is most clear. This is *not* the Queen's Ruby. It is a very good imitation but it is without value. However, all is not lost," said Madame Rousseau, holding her hands up to halt the sudden eruption of confused voices. "We are quite sure the emeralds and sapphires are from our collection. You may, of course, double check but we are quite certain and we have brought with us the necessary documents to have the jewels repatriated to Rachenstein immediately."

"And the diamonds?" asked Garrett.

"They are mostly real but they are not ours," she said. "We will not claim them."

"Mostly?" choked Garrett in bewilderment.

"Come through to my office," said Chief Davis.

"We can talk more in there." He flashed an angry look at Garrett.

"First, Rachenstein would like to express thanks to the officer who recovered the items. Lieutenant Graves, we understand you were in charge?" Madame Rousseau's gaze swept over the small assembly, searching for my brother.

Garrett stood. "I was. It was a team effort involving several officers, members of the public, and our consultant, Lexi Graves-Solomon." He gestured to me and her gaze roamed over me. I popped my hand up in a half wave and wondered if I should curtsy out of politeness. Or for the sheer fun of it. When would I ever get another chance to curtsy to a royalty-adjacent person again?!

"Then I should like to thank you both for your efforts in recovering the jewels so precious to Rachenstein. They have great importance to our country's heritage and you have partially solved what had been a great mystery." She smiled, at last, seeming to break some of the tension in the room. "Furthermore, the king and queen have instructed me to issue a commendation and thanks. We will arrange for a personal letter to be sent to both of you, and those also involved. I am sure you are aware that the full reward cannot be paid out under these circumstances but a partial one is in order. Please be assured how grateful we are to you both, Lieutenant Graves and Ms. Graves-Solomon."

"Let's refine those details in my office," said Chief Davis. Another officer had already opened the door, and the chief indicated for Madame Rousseau and her entourage to proceed from the room. "We'll need to return the jewels to the evidence locker."

"We will take possession of the emeralds and sapphires," said Madame Rousseau, indicating with a nod of her head to Mr. Lavelle. He selected each jewel with a gloved hand, adding each to its own small, velvet pouch.

"That won't be…"

"Rachenstein's diplomatic envoy and the state senator are on their way," she added warningly.

The chief nodded. "Understood," he said. "Let's work out those finer details."

Instead of leaving the room directly, she moved across to Garrett, said something briefly, and shook his hand, then crossed the room to me, shaking mine too. "Good work," said Madame Rousseau. "Rachenstein is grateful." Then she was gone, Mr. Lavelle, the bodyguards, and rank and file following close behind her.

"Wow," I said when the room was empty of everyone except Garrett and me. Outside the door remained a duo of uniforms, our entourage for the unclaimed stones. "I didn't see that coming."

"The fake ruby or the grateful thanks of an entire European nation?"

"Both. I'm not sure which I'm most stunned by."

"Me neither. Let's get Laura Reynolds in here," he said, scratching his head. "I want to know what the hell just happened. She said the ruby and all the diamonds were real."

"She's waiting downstairs. She's been so excited about it and I'm sure she wouldn't get something like this wrong," I said, thinking about the ruby.

"That's what I can't figure out." Garrett picked up the phone on the table at the side of the room. "Lieutenant Graves," he announced, "can someone bring Laura Reynolds to Conference Room B? Yes, right away. Thanks."

When Laura arrived within minutes, Garrett waved me to silence, instead instructing she should sit in the seat Mr. Lavelle had just vacated. "Can you look over the remaining jewels?" he asked.

"Of course! I see the emeralds and sapphires have been removed. Did Rachenstein take them?" she asked. "Gosh, I can hardly contain my excitement!"

"Yes," I said, "but we'd like you to take another look at the remaining ones."

"Of course! I assume there's some question of their ownership from their own experts. I'm not sure what else I can add but I'll do whatever I can. I'm surprised they didn't take the ruby. I've been researching it and I'm convinced it's the Queen's Ruby too. Why didn't they take it?" she asked as she pulled out her own magnifying lens and plucked the ruby. She looked at it, turning it over in her hand and frowned. "I don't understand." She glanced up. "What is this?"

"What do you mean?" I asked, playing innocent.

"This isn't the ruby you brought to me."

"What do you mean?" I repeated.

"Well, just that. It's… it's not a ruby. It looks like one but it's not." Laura glanced around. "Is this a joke? Are you playing a trick on me? Is there a camera in here?"

"Tell us what you see," said Garrett.

"It's a fake," she said, peering at the ruby again, turning it this way and that before putting it down. "Yes, I'm sure of it. It's fake. Take a look for yourself."

I picked it up, turning it over in my palm but I

couldn't see a thing different from the ruby I'd handled before. It was beautiful but was it lighter? I couldn't be sure. I passed the gem to Garrett and he did the same.

"Paste?" said Garrett as he tossed the jewel onto the depleted stack with a sigh.

"Not quite. Lab grown. It's one of the best lab-grown jewels I've ever seen," said Laura. "Expensive."

"Not Queen's Ruby expensive," I said.

"No, definitely not that. A fraction of that."

"How am I supposed to explain this to Rachenstein's representatives? And Chief Davis? I told them it was a ruby and handed them a fake." Garrett ran a hand over his hair and covered his mouth with his fist.

"I can't tell you that," said Laura. "All I know is the first ruby I examined was real. I will swear to it. There is no way I could make a mistake like that. And you said they took the other stones? It was easy to match them to Rachenstein's collection once I knew where to look."

"And the diamonds? Apparently, they're mostly real but they didn't claim them. They said they weren't theirs," I added.

"Decent of them. I got a call on my way here. The diamonds were stolen from a merchant that went out of business a long time ago. Insurance paid out on the theft so I imagine the insurers will want to collect them now they've surfaced. Wait a second... You said mostly?" Laura pushed the diamonds with her finger, then examined them one after another, pushing some out of line with her fingertip. When she finished, six gems were out of line. "These six are fakes. I know every one of them was real when you called me in." She looked up. "How could this have happened?"

"Dammit!" snapped Garrett. "I'm going to chew the evidence sergeant out for this!"

"Did I get someone into trouble?" Laura asked.

I shook my head. "No. Trouble just walked in and helped itself," I said, thinking back to a few days ago when Cass Temple walked out of the police station and feigned innocence.

Laura stood. "I can't say I know what that means but I hope you get to the bottom of it. I've sent you an email about the diamonds and I'm happy to add that I authenticated the ruby and that it's not the one you showed me today," she continued. "I hope we can work together again, although under better circumstances."

"I appreciate that. I'll get someone to walk you out," said Garrett. "Then I need to work out exactly what happened."

"I think I know," I said. "I have a theory I still need to iron out but you're not going to like it."

"And an arrest to make," he added, "but I'll like that."

"Sounds like a busy day," said Laura.

When Laura had gone, I explained my theory to Garrett and he took it a heck of a lot better than I thought he would before instructing me to remain in his office while he went to prove if I were right.

By the time he returned more than an hour later, I'd made several calls, thought in great detail about lunch, purchased a dress online, and aced the next level of my current phone game obsession.

"Let's go," he said, appearing in the doorway. "I'll tell you everything on the way."

"I'm all ears."

Garrett didn't talk again until we were turning out of the police lot in a black sedan with a peppermint scent tree hanging from the rearview mirror, not quite masking the lingering stale odor. "You were right about the stolen police uniform you saw our lady thief wearing," he said. "No one would own up to theirs going missing so I hauled in every officer who went into the evidence locker that day and had the desk sergeant identify them. He has quite the eye for faces. He didn't recognize one of them. A rookie named Walsh. Yet there was a log-in with her badge, depositing evidence. Walsh confessed to her uniform going missing from her locker. She found it in a trash can around the corner from here the same day so she figured it was some kind of weird hazing she was going to get in trouble for."

"She must be the female police officer I overheard saying her uniform had disappeared. I didn't think anything of it at the time. Walsh didn't report it so no one knew there was a uniform floating around, unaccounted for. Cass Temple must have stolen it to use to gain access to the evidence locker. I knew it!" My voice rose with excitement. Then the image of another woman flashed into my head. A uniformed woman I'd seen inside the police station and thought I'd recognized. Had that been her too? Or was my mind playing tricks on me? I wasn't sure I'd ever know.

"I should have done this when you insisted you saw her exit the station. Man, I screwed up! I saw the sealed box and the sergeant counted out the jewels."

"We saw what she wanted us to see," I said. "She must have grabbed tape from somewhere, unsealed the box, and resealed it."

"Damn," said Garrett, shaking his head.

"What happens to Officer Walsh now?" I asked.

"An official reprimand and six months of traffic duty. She won't make a mistake like that again."

"I feel sorry for her."

"Don't. She should have reported it the minute she realized her uniform was gone."

"What I can't fathom is how Cass Temple got into the building to even get the uniform. I know I saw her wearing it. I'm sure of it."

"I checked the cameras. A pregnant lady came in that afternoon. Big, floppy sun hat, tote bag, and begged to use the restroom. No pregnant lady ever came out so I figure she ditched that disguise in the trash and just strolled around until she could access the women's locker rooms. She probably caught the door as it was closing and picked the lock on lockers until she found a uniform her size. She probably put it on and walked out."

"Unbelievable." But even as I said it, I knew it was believable. I'd talked my way into buildings, and broken into them when necessary. I'd even gone undercover as a plush pony to access areas crucial to my investigation. If I had limits, I wasn't sure what they were.

"I'll say. Ballsy."

I monitored Garrett for a few seconds, wondering if he were impressed but I couldn't quite tell. "So Cass Temple dresses in the uniform and goes to access the evidence locker but she didn't want to set off any alerts from accessing that box since its contents were already attracting attention, so she requested access to deposit an item in a different one," I said, guessing now.

"Yeah, that's how it went down. The fake Officer Walsh requested to log in a pair of gloves and a crowbar purportedly used in a home robbery. I've sent them to be fingerprinted but I already know we won't find anything. She was on her own for long enough that she located our box, slit open the seal, swapped the rubies, stole the diamonds, and resealed it. I noticed a roll of tape under the shelving unit so you're probably right about that. As far as anyone knew, no one ever accessed our box. We wouldn't have known until we attempted to repatriate it to Rachenstein."

"By then, Cass Temple would be long gone, leaving us looking like fools. It's her bad luck you'd already called Rachenstein's reps and made arrangements to show them the jewels."

"Cass Temple *is* long gone and we *do* look like fools," pointed out Garrett. "I'm lucky I'm going to get to keep my job over this. Rachenstein's commendation saved my butt there. Annoying as it was, Gideon Black did us a favor deflating the tires to keep us out of the way. Since I was out of town when the evidence locker was accessed, it's officially not my fault that the jewels were stolen. Temple really pulled the wool over everyone's eyes. If I weren't so damn pissed at her, I would be impressed!"

"With the tracker you found, and the one Solomon found on my car, I figure Gideon had another plan to get the jewels that involved keeping us out of the way," I said. "Whatever it was, it tanked, which is why he came after me."

"Yeah, I guess we'll never know."

"At least we have him. Although I'm not sure

where MPD falls in the queue to prosecute. Plenty of other states must want their turn."

"Ah." Garrett winced.

"Garrett? We *do* have Gideon Black, don't we?" As I asked, Garrett winced more. I groaned, repressing the urge to scream. What else could possibly go wrong today?!

"I got the call minutes before we had the meeting with Rachenstein. Black escaped the hospital sometime in the early hours of the morning. There's no telling where he is now, except I'll bet it's hundreds of miles away by tonight. If not thousands."

"He escaped his guards?" I asked, amazed, yet somehow not. Of course he escaped. There was no way Gideon Black was going to wait around to see what his future had in store under the auspices of MPD.

"Guards, handcuffs, and a particularly flappy hospital gown."

"Unbelievable," I huffed. That guy was a one-man nightmare, not to mention more slippery than a snake. I'd hazard a guess he probably charmed at least one nurse or doctor in his short stay at Montgomery General. Even if he hadn't. Picking handcuffs was nothing to a thief like him.

"At least we'll make one arrest out of this," said Garrett, pulling over. We'd fallen into silence, each of us contemplating the case as the miles flew past.

We stepped out of the car, waiting on the side of the road near Barnham Correctional Facility. Behind us, arrived Jord in a squad car with two officers. I was surprised Lily and my parents hadn't turned up too since this kind of overwatch appeared to be turning into a family affair.

"Nice day for it," said Jord, grinning. "Thanks for having me along for the ride. Now I get to say I was part of this case."

"It comes with bragging rights," I said.

"I'll say." Jord grinned.

We didn't have long to wait for Kelvin Huff to take the long walk from the prison walls, past the last checkpoint, and through the tall wire tunnel, to reach the sidewalk. When he stepped outside, with barely a few words from the guard who closed the gates behind him, he stopped, put his hands on his civilian-clothed hips and smiled up at the sky. I could only imagine he thought he was going to have a great day. He looked around, searching for his ride and spotted us.

"Let's get this over with," said Garrett.

"After you," I said, and followed him, two of the officers only a few steps behind us.

"Hello, Lieutenant," said Kelvin, his eyebrows rising. "And Investigator. I suppose you have a few more questions for me, although I'm sure I've told you everything I know. You'll have to excuse me. My ride should be here any minute."

"She's not coming," I said bluntly. "Amybeth doesn't want anything to do with you. She's made that very clear."

Huff started to open his mouth to protest but Garrett cut in.

"I do have some more questions for you as it happens, and you're definitely going to answer them, but first I'm going to read you your rights. I'm arresting you for the murder of Charles Black," said Garrett before reeling off Huff's rights. "Cuff him."

"What the heck?" Kelvin gasped as one of the

officers moved to shackle him. "I don't even know who that is."

"Sure you do," I said. "You knew exactly what your buddy Timothy Wright was up to, and his alias as Joe Smithson. You knew he stole the jewels from the museum you both helped renovate and you followed him here to get your cut. He double-crossed you nearly two decades ago and you've been waiting for this day a long time. The day you get to collect your jewels. Only we got there first." I didn't add *and someone got there right after us*. Kelvin didn't need to know that. "We know everything," I told him.

Huff paled. "You'll never make this stick."

"I'm confident we will," said Garrett. "Take him to the station."

The officers walked Huff to their squad car and put him in the back, slamming the door shut on his loud protests.

"Is this the fastest arrest after release from jail or what?" asked Jord.

"I'm fairly proud of it," replied Garrett.

"Heard you lost Gideon Black."

"Don't rub it in," I said.

"Should we be worried?" asked Jord. "I couldn't find any sign of anyone watching Poppy but a heads-up on any more intel would be good."

"I doubt Gideon actually had anyone watching Poppy," I said, "I think he just said that to scare me into doing what he wanted. He gambled and lost."

"Good to know. Shotgun," called Jord as he headed to our car and the squad car pulled out, making a U-turn and heading back the way we'd come. On the backseat, Huff turned his head, looking forlornly through the window behind him.

"He won't have time to miss his cell," said Garrett. "He'll be back in it soon."

"I have a feeling if he ends up back here, he'll request a transfer as fast as he can," I said.

Garrett huffed, amused. "Let's head back. Where should I drop you?"

"How about the FBI field office?"

"Maddox?"

"Maddox," I confirmed.

CHAPTER TWENTY-FOUR

Maddox wasn't at the FBI field office. I declined to leave a message, instead enjoying the stroll back to the agency where I'd left my car earlier in the day. I finished up the paperwork for the Dugans, including the information that the reward money was now in doubt payable and only partially so. More likely to be dispersed across a small number of people. Then I updated Claudius Bridge about the jewels, knowing he would find the outcome fascinating, and sent off my report to my salon client, Marie. I also fielded calls from a journalist from *The Gazette,* who was reporting on Rachenstein's official visit.

Mom had insisted everyone arrive as early as possible for dinner so I texted Solomon to let him know I'd meet him there. That gave me enough time to dash home and change into a pretty red summer dress, perfect for an evening outside, before heading to my parents' house.

Before I'd even reached the front door, I could hear my nieces and nephews tearing around the backyard and the sound of my dad chasing them. I let myself in, aiming for the kitchen, where I found my Mom.

And Maddox.

"So this is where you've been hiding," I said.

"Hiding? Who? Me?" Maddox pointed to himself with a look of innocence.

"I tried to find you at your office and I called you and texted. Repeatedly. No one wants to double text!"

"He brought tarts from that deli you like," said Mom, reaching for a box to waft under my nose. It was hard to resist the sweet sugary scent but I was tough, I could do it. I could eat it later.

"You tore off out of there like you were on fire," I said.

"Out of where?" asked Mom.

"Not even an explanation," I continued. "Who is she?"

"Who is whom?" asked Mom.

Maddox shrugged. "I have no idea what your daughter is talking about."

"Don't *your daughter* me," I said.

"I didn't. I *your daughtered* your mom."

"I'm confused," said Mom.

"You know exactly whom I mean," I said.

"I don't," said Mom.

"Not you, Mom! Maddox!"

"Adam, dear?" asked Mom.

Maddox remained blank.

"Cass Temple."

"Who?" asked Maddox.

"Do you have a girlfriend?" asked Mom, her eyes lighting up. "Why didn't you bring her?"

"I do not," said Maddox.

"You can *never* bring her here," I said.

"Lexi, that's not a nice way to behave towards Adam's lady friend. You have a nice husband. Adam deserves a nice girlfriend."

"That's not the point, Mom!"

Mom sighed. "Would anyone like a drink?" she asked.

"Spill."

"I pour carefully," said Mom.

I narrowed my eyes at Maddox.

"Oh! *Cass Temple*!" Maddox leaned in. "Is that a little bit of steam coming out of your ears?"

"Who is Cass Temple?" asked Mom. "Is she your girlfriend?"

"That's what I would like to know."

"Me too," said Mom, waiting.

"That's a really good question," replied Maddox. "Who is Cass Temple? I'd love a beer, Mrs. G."

"I'll get…" started Mom.

"No beers for you," I cut in, grabbing Maddox by the elbow and steering him out of the kitchen and into the empty living room. I shut the door behind me, despite my mother's protestations. "I want to know what's going on that you aren't telling me about. You've asked a bunch of weird questions about this case and you know Cass Temple. I saw the way you two looked at each other. She's not just a suspect. You know each other."

"Cass Temple is one of the world's worst thieves," he said.

"She's bad at it?" I frowned. I thought she was excellent at it. She'd gotten in and out of a police station's secure evidence locker without even a whiff of suspicion. She'd run rings around us before we even knew who she was.

"No." Maddox cracked a smile. "No, she's very, *very* good at it. I've been on her tail a long time and I can't catch her. She's like a sneeze that disappears into vapor and gets carried off by the wind."

"That's the weirdest metaphor I've ever heard."

"It's a simile."

"Whatever." I crossed my arms, entirely unsure who was correct.

"Regardless, she's a thorn in my side and I was *this close* to catching her," he said, holding his thumb and forefinger up.

"How did you even know she was here?"

"I didn't. I had a feeling she might surface, given the Queen's Ruby discovery, but not so fast. It's just the kind of thing she likes."

"Priceless jewels?"

"I don't think she has anything against them but it's the story that would have attracted her. She's made a life out of repatriating questionable goods."

"What do you mean?"

"The Queen's Ruby has a dubious history. They've tried to wash it out of history, and I'll bet they've paid good money to cleanse all mention of its provenance from the internet, but there're still rumors of how they came to own it. It all boils down to colonialism, empire, and theft."

"Go on."

"I'm sure you know the official version. The ruby was a gift to the nation from a country in the Far East."

"I read that."

"But the real story behind it was that Rachenstein was an occupying power. They plundered the resources that were valuable at the time. Silks, spices, precious metals, textiles, but there were also beautiful temples rich with jewels and antiquities. The ruby was one of them. It was the centerpiece of a large statue in an important temple. Rachenstein insisted on having it. Maybe it was through threats or promises, who knows? But the ruby was removed and given to Rachenstein. Numerous diplomatic missions have made attempts to recover it. Both countries insisted it's rightly theirs and then it disappeared. Rachenstein thought they might have stolen it. While the other side thought Rachenstein had intentionally made it disappear. That created a whole new diplomatic argument with each insisting the other didn't possess it."

"Wow." I paused, thinking. "And that's where Cass Temple comes in?"

"That's where Cass Temple comes in."

"You think she stole it to return to its country of origin."

"Return. Give. Tomato, *tomahto*."

"What about the diamonds that also disappeared from the evidence locker?"

Maddox laughed. "Why am I not surprised to hear that?" he asked. Sobering up, he asked, "A nice bonus to add to her commission. Or perhaps she took the bounty. What did she say to you anyway?"

"She seemed to know Ben. Gideon. She knew I'd seen her inside the police station. She denied taking the jewels but I guess she had them on her when she came to my rescue." There was something I was missing, but what was it? As soon as the thought came to me, another pinged like a lightbulb. "She knew my name. She knew who I was, or knew about me, but I can't think of why. I'm sure our paths have never crossed. She's never been a suspect in any of my cases."

"Did she say something to that effect beyond your name?"

"No, it was how she looked at me. I can't explain it. Like she was confirming something, or judging me but not harshly. Just… curiously, I guess."

"It's unlikely she'll come back."

"She said something like that."

"But if she does, I need you to tell me. Lexi, promise me?"

I nodded but said nothing. There was definitely something missing. What Cass Temple didn't say then. What Maddox wasn't saying now. Yet if I pressed, I knew I wasn't going to get anywhere. Maddox would clam up. The truth always unfolded somewhere along the line; it would come to me eventually, whether he liked it or not.

The living room door opened and Solomon stepped inside, holding onto the door like he didn't intend to stay. "Garrett and I just got here," he said. "Do you want an update on the case?"

"Kelvin Huff?" I asked, wondering if his story had tumbled out under interrogation.

"That's right. The Dugans just got here too. Apparently, your mom invited them."

"I'll be right there."

Solomon glanced over at Maddox, nodded, and withdrew, closing the door behind him.

"I don't know what's going on with your pursuit of Cass Temple but it seems like she isn't your regular thief," I said.

"She isn't."

"So why not leave her be? Isn't she performing a service? Operating in ways the justice system can't?"

"Many would argue that, but it's still theft. Don't romanticize what she's doing. She can't be judge, jury, and executioner. That's not how it works. Plus, whatever you think about the ruby, she still stole the diamonds. I'm assuming there's nothing dubious about their provenance."

"It looks like Charlie Black stole them from a jewel merchant around the same time as he stole Rachenstein's jewels. Our contact was able to track the serial numbers. Insurance paid out, the merchant later folded. The insurers will collect the diamonds we do have and there's no one to prosecute."

"The police won't pursue Cass Temple?"

"I don't think they have a clear shot of her on camera. There're no fingerprints. No evidence at all. I saw her but she was in disguise so I couldn't even give an accurate description that would stand up in court. Whom are they going to prosecute?"

"Typical Cass," snorted Maddox. He reached for the door handle, pulled the door open and indicated for me to go.

Garrett was waiting in the backyard, beer in hand, with Solomon. Serena was giving them an earful about not scaring the kids with talk of unearthed corpses and murderers running around the neighborhood.

Her daughter, Victoria, snuggled into Delgado's arms sleepily, looked up and smiled at him. "Dead. Body," she whispered and giggled as she tapped his nose. "Bash on the head. Bop. Bop. Roger!"

Lily passed me on the way to the kitchen, shooting me a look, mouthing "psychopath in the making" with a side glance to Victoria, and darted away to join Ruby who was chatting to Alice.

My mom was dashing around the yard, making sure everyone had drinks and snacks while my dad was busy grilling at the far end of the patio. He wore a "Kiss the Chef" apron and was enthralling the grandchildren with an over-exaggerated story from his police days.

I waved to the Dugans, wondering if they were relieved or disappointed at the outcome of the case. The disappointment of not receiving a fat check for the discovery of the jewels could only be offset by the vindication that they weren't involved in Black's death.

My nephew, Sam wandered over to me with a hotdog. I watched it hopefully as he said, "Did you really find a dead body called Roger, Aunt Lexi?"

"I didn't find him but I helped on the case, and he's not really called Roger."

"Was it gross?"

"The case?"

"The body."

"Not really." I'd hardly seen it in the morgue. I'd hit the deck too fast.

"Dad told Mom you puked. He said it was spectacular. Mom laughed."

"I would never," said Traci, Sam's mom, as she zoomed past in pursuit of her youngest child, Chloe. "Garrett didn't say a thing."

I sighed. Of course that story was going to make the rounds.

"Patrick said he plans to go to medical school and see dead bodies all the time," continued Sam.

"Okay," I said.

"Do you think he can bring one home?"

"Uh…" I grimaced.

"They must have spares," continued Sam. "It would be like having a cool pet."

"A dog would be nicer."

"Maybe we could get a dead dog. Grandpops wants to know if you want a hotdog? Hey, this hotdog is kind of a dead dog." Sam guffawed and chomped on the end. Ketchup squirted out the other end and he laughed some more.

"I'll get food soon, thanks." First, I wanted a lengthy lie-down in a dark room. Maybe some therapy.

"Okay," said Sam before he wandered off again.

"Tell me you have good news," I said to Garrett who was pretending not to have heard any of that.

"I do but I think we should tell the Dugans too," he said, calling for them to join us. When he had our family and friends' attention, he started. "Good news. Kelvin Huff sang like a canary. Huff had seen his buddy that he knew as Timothy Wright undertaking work that was not on their maintenance schedule and figured out what was going on. When the jewels disappeared, that clinched it. Yet Black hung around. It seems Huff was biding his time, trying to figure out what Black had done with the jewels and keeping an eye on him. When Black up and quit, Huff got lucky and figured out where he was going and followed him here. But the wait got too long; it was going to be too hard to keep tabs on Black so Huff got desperate and confronted him." Garrett paused to take a sip, his audience fully captivated.

"It seems Black taunted Huff where the jewels were hidden and how Huff couldn't possibly dispose of them. When Huff demanded money instead, Black mocked him that no one would believe him anyway so why would he pay him? They fought and the gun went off. According to Huff, Black died instantly. If Huff called for help at the time, he might have gotten a manslaughter charge or less but not reporting the death and hiding the body changed everything.

"Huff was convinced the jewels were hidden nearby and spent days searching for nothing. Despite Black trying to convince him the jewels were in a safe deposit box, Huff gradually came to the conclusion while he was inside that the jewels were still somewhere in the house and once he was released, he would be able to recover them. The unearthing of the body created a problem in his plans. The discovery of the jewels ruined it."

"So he'll go back to jail?" asked Carrie Dugan.

"Yes. There will be a trial but it's an open-and-shut case," said Garrett. "His ex will testify that he tried to rub a huge payday in her face. Plus, the woman he tried to hoodwink here remembered that he boasted about hiding a gun in a basement once. She called in the tip. With the Dugans' permission, we were able to locate a weapon that we matched to the bullet that killed Charlie Black."

"You never said any of this," said Solomon softly to my ear.

"It's news to me too," I said, enjoying Garrett's moment of glory.

"Well done," said Mom. "You're a brilliant detective!"

"This case was truly a team effort," said Garrett. "Without Lexi, Lily, and the tip from Ruby, we wouldn't have gotten anywhere close to the truth."

Lily and Ruby high fived.

"Good job," said Mom and gave me the thumbs up. Before I could reply, she hurried on, asking, "What about the ruby? I've been hearing all kinds of rumors."

"Us too," said Carrie Dugan excitedly. "We thought we found it, then turns out it disappeared again, and the thief was killed at our home! A TV producer called us just this morning about being in a documentary that details it all."

"We've had several calls from journalists too," added Pete Dugan. "There's going to be a big story in *The Post* about the mystery of the ruby. And we're eligible for some of the reward money."

"Me too," said Ruby. "I got a call from Rachenstein's reps just as I was getting into my car to come here. I don't know what I'm going to do with it. I've never had that kind of money before!"

"Maybe I shouldn't say this, but I'm enjoying being a part of the ruby's history. Imagine that it was in our yard all this time and that we were amongst the last people to see it before it disappeared again!" said Carrie.

"I was there too!" said Mom. "I should speak to someone at *The Gazette*! Are you going to be on TV, Garrett?"

"I hope not," said Garrett.

"Lexi?" Mom turned to me.

"I don't have anything to add," I said.

"You'd look so good saying nothing," said Lily. "Just stand there looking mysterious."

"I could do that," I agreed.

"I love this scarlet dress. You should wear it on TV. Sexy and mysterious," Lily added while waving a hand at my dress.

"Most definitely." I nodded along, warming to the idea.

When the conversation descended into a riotous mix of questions, theories, and more questions about the reward money, I slipped away. I got a burger from my dad and found a chair to drop into. Lily came to sit next to me, having offloaded Poppy onto Jord.

"I'm trying not to cling onto her," she said watching the two playfully bond. "That asshole, Gideon Black has a lot to answer for."

"I really don't think Poppy was ever in any danger."

"It doesn't matter. It's the thought of it. I'm glad this case is closed. I hope he's as far from Montgomery as he can get and never comes back."

"Do you want to make sure?"

"How?"

"His father's funeral is tomorrow. Do you want to come?"

"Duh. Of course I want to come. I have the cutest black dress."

"I'll pick you up at ten."

"Do you think Gideon will show?"

I'd thought a lot about that. "Only if he's crazy," I decided.

~

The Eternally Resting Hills cemetery was a sprawling, undulating lot filled with a whole trove of dead folk. A long, winding road cut the lot in half and the gravesites ranged from large stones with carved angels filled with long, loving, testaments to their occupants to small, simple crosses. I couldn't imagine this being my final resting place but I knew I had relatives here somewhere just waiting for my unearthly mayhem.

"I am not getting buried," said Lily. She smoothed the pencil skirt of her black dress and adjusted her black velvet headband. She looked like a Mafia doll but I didn't tell her in case she was too pleased.

"Why not?"

"I don't like the idea. Cook me up and spread my ashes somewhere pretty. Or!" She grinned excitedly. "You could keep me on the mantel and chat to me."

"Why are you dying first?"

"I don't want to see you die. Every time you get injured, I think you're going to die, and it sucks."

I gulped down my guilt. "Sorry."

"Plus, I want someone to watch over Poppy and who could I trust more than my best friend?"

"Your husband?"

"Like I said."

"Okay, cool. I love Poppy but I expect her to be super middle-aged by the point I actually have to watch over her. I don't expect to do a great deal. I'll make her dinner and tell her what I think of her partners and be her hype girl."

"Deal." Lily extended her hand and we shook. "I hope you give her cousins."

"Working on it," I said.

"Do you need tips?"

"No!"

"Suit yourself. So what happens now?"

I wiggled my toes in my ankle boots and looked around, tallying our location with the guide I'd been given. The burial plot overlooking the town had been dug and was draped with cloth. A simple coffin rested on the plinth. Two workers had retreated a discreet distance away. The minister had parked a golf cart on the edge of the road and was striding towards us, Bible in hand. "We stand here and look pretty," I said.

"Easily done. I can probably spring a tear if necessary," Lily added. "But I have to draw the line at throwing myself into the grave."

"You don't need to do either. Just look solemn. I didn't think the city would spring for something like this." I'd expected a pauper's grave in a quiet corner of the cemetery, although my only experience of what one of those would be like was from watching period movies. Something simple, at least, was what I'd assumed. Yet the coffin seemed good quality and it was draped with a beautiful bouquet of white lilies. I reached for the card peeking from under the foliage, surprised at the signature.

"We should have held the wake at my bar."

"No one would come. We're the only two people here."

"Three," said Lily.

"I forgot the minister."

"Oh, four then." Lily pointed. My mom was barreling towards us, clearly in a race with the minister. She passed him a few steps before he reached the graveside and stopped next to us, heaving a breath.

"What are you doing here?" I asked.

"I did know him," she said.

"You probably met him twice. Years ago."

Mom bristled. "It would be rude not to come. I'm sure he would have done the same for me."

"He would wait until your burial was underway and the house was clear, then rob you."

Mom gave me a dirty look and before she could

retort, I waved her quiet, as the minster began his short sermon.

Afterwards, as we thanked the minister and shook hands, my mother peppered him with questions. I turned away and caught movement from the corner of my eye. Just a blur of a shadow next to a tree.

"Keep her occupied," I said to Lily quietly.

I walked towards the treeline, watching for more movement, but there was no sign of anyone. When I reached the trees, I stopped and said clearly, "I saw you."

"I intended you to," said Gideon, emerging from behind a thick oak, just enough that I could see him while remaining obscured from the burial plot.

"It was a nice service for your father."

"Probably better than he deserved."

"Wouldn't you rather he was interred with your mother?" I wondered.

"She was cremated," he said.

"Did you choose this spot?"

"The city did after my representative paid." Gideon gazed past me, then redirected his attention to me, a sad smile on his face. "It's nice. Peaceful. I don't think my father had a very peaceful life," he said. "He reined in his tendencies while my mother was alive but once she was gone... well, he needed to fend for me. That's what I told myself anyway."

"There're plenty of ways to do that without getting involved in a life of crime."

"Guess he didn't get the memo." Gideon smiled now, but it didn't quite reach his eyes. "It was good of you to come," he said.

"I wanted to make sure he got a proper burial."

His eyes sparkled. "You wanted to see if *I* would

come."

"That too." We were silent and I was surprised he didn't hit the road at knowing I'd anticipated his presence. "The Dugans sent the flowers."

"Thoughtful of them."

I nodded, unsurprised that he knew their name or that they now lived in his father's brief home. "You took a risk coming here."

"I suppose I did. Are you going to arrest me? Oh! Silly me. You can't. You're not a police officer." He winked.

"No, I'm not."

Gideon smiled this time, all the charm returning to his face. "I heard the ruby disappeared. It wasn't me."

"I know."

"But I would've stolen it if I could."

"You certainly tried. You also tried to make sure we were out of the way so you could."

Gideon winced. "Sorry about that. I didn't want you foiling my plans. Turned out it wasn't you I should have been worried about."

"You threatened my niece," I hissed.

"A regrettable decision. I'm sure you know now that she wasn't in any danger."

"It doesn't matter. You should have never threatened her at all."

"Would an apology help?"

"No."

"I'm not sticking around, just so you know." Gideon thrust his hands into his chino pockets, looking relaxed as he leaned against the tree.

"I never thought you would. Too many rich women out there to swindle."

"They secretly enjoy it." Gideon grinned. "And I only take what they don't need when I need an occasional side hustle. If I'd gotten that ruby, I would have packed it all in."

"I doubt that."

"Well, it's a nice idea. Any idea where Cass Temple is?" He rubbed his head where she'd whacked him.

"None."

"You might want to ask your friend, Special Agent Adam Maddox."

"I know he's on her tail."

"Is it just that? Work?" Gideon smiled and I had the suspicious feeling he knew more than he was letting on. "He hasn't told you all his secrets, has he? His and Cass Temple's?"

"What do you want from me?" I asked, knowing he wasn't going to tell me anything anyway. Not when he thought he had the upper hand. He was simply going to taunt me. At least Maddox was cute with it, but Gideon? Gideon had an undercurrent of something I didn't like.

And Cass? Cass impressed me. Whatever secrets she had, they would come out eventually. I wasn't going to beg Gideon to reveal them.

"Just to say thank you," said Gideon. "Thanks for finding out what happened to my dad. Thank you for putting his killer away."

"Team effort. You're welcome."

"Until next time." He raised an imaginary hat, saluting me.

"Gideon?"

"Yes?"

"Don't come back."

"Take care, Lexi, and thanks for letting me go," he said as I turned away, ready to return to my family. And what was left of his.

I paused, glancing over my shoulder. "Who says I did?" I asked and laughed as Gideon's face turned to panic. A police siren sounded and I turned toward the road, momentarily startled. When I turned back, only seconds later, Gideon was gone. Of course he was. He would never have come here without an escape route meticulously planned in advance.

"Was that him?" asked Lily when I returned to her as a trio of squad cars sailed past along the road. She'd waited and watched. My mother was chasing after the minister as he retreated to his golf cart, anxiously checking behind him to see if she followed.

"Yes."

"Do you think they'll catch him?"

"No."

"Just a simple game of gem warfare then," said Lily, hooking her arm with mine. Ahead of us, my mother was climbing into the golf cart. I hoped she wasn't quizzing the poor minister on how to be ordained.

"I'm not sure who the winner is," I said. I wasn't sure if I should be mad at Gideon for evading prosecution once again, or relieved that he was gone. Probably both.

"You. You solved the cold case."

"And lost the jewel."

"You get to fight another day and look fabulous doing it."

"I do, don't I?" I smiled. Yes, I did. And unlike Gideon Black or Cass Temple, I wasn't going to spend every minute of my life looking over my shoulder.

They may not have played by the rules, and Cass may have won this match, but I'd definitely won the game.

Lexi Graves returns in *Operation: Sapphire* out now in paperback and ebook!

A stolen ring, a buried truth, and justice waiting to be uncovered.

When a costly vintage ring vanishes, Private Investigator Lexi Graves is on the case. But why steal just one item when a full heist was possible? The theft is caught on camera, yet the culprit is a chameleon, slipping through every lead.

As Lexi digs deeper, the ring's past reveals secrets more tangled than she expected. What seemed like a simple recovery mission turns into a moral dilemma…

Should she follow her client's wishes or expose a long-buried injustice?

With every step forward met by cunning deception, Lexi must outthink a criminal who's always one step ahead.

Love mysteries? Get *Deadlines*, a gripping, fast-paced Hollywood whodunit, out now in paperback and ebook!

Shayne Winter thought she had it all: a dream job at the *LA Chronicle*, a sleek new apartment, and a picture-perfect LA lifestyle. But day one is a disaster -- her apartment is a wreck with a roguishly handsome squatter, and her new job as chief reporter has been reduced to writing obituaries after her predecessor, Ben Kosina, waltzes back in.

When her first assignment -- the accidental death of washed-up child star Chucky Barnard -- takes a twist, Shayne sees her shot at redemption. Chucky's sister insists it was murder, and Shayne is determined to uncover the truth. But with a stubborn detective, a cutthroat Ben, and a killer watching her every move, she's in over her head. To save her career and her life, Shayne must crack the case—before the killer sets her final deadline.

Love mysteries? Get *Curated Murder*, a standalone cozy mystery, out now in paperback, ebook, and audiobook!

Tess Hernandez was sure she'd land the manager role at Calendar's Town Museum—until the board gave it to Lance, the spoiled brat who shamelessly stole her ideas. Determined to prove she's the better choice, Tess pushes forward despite the setback.

But when Lance is found dead on the opening night of her curated exhibit, all fingers point to Tess as the prime suspect. Then when charming architect Ethan Ray is arrested, Tess knows she must clear not only her name but Ethan's too.

As a single mom with everything to lose, Tess dives into the investigation, uncovering secrets Lance took to the grave—and learning she's not the only one who wanted him gone.

At Calendar's Town Museum, the exhibits aren't the only things hiding deadly secrets.

Made in the USA
Columbia, SC
30 May 2025